ANDREW HALL

THE **CRIMSON** THISTLE

ISBN: 978-1-4907-2611-3 (sc)
ISBN: 978-1-4907-2608-3 (e)

Trafford rev. 01/30/2014

 www.trafford.com
North America & international
toll-free: 1 888 232 4444 (USA & Canada)
fax: 812 355 4082

To LINDA AND LINDA
for your inspiration and patience and my good friend and
Business Manager
GERRIE ROOS
who made it happen

I would like to thank Zane Smith and Linda Moe my editors and all those countless people who were the source of many ideas and anecdotes, God's blessings and many lucid and sane moments.

'He travels fastest who travels alone'

CHAPTER ONE

W inter visited once in my formative years, dragging its desolation and despair behind, bringing pain and distress to the core of my family. What it lacked in attendance, it compensated for with ferocity. A batter needs one bad egg to spoil the recipe. The devil abhors happy families. His sole purpose is to sow chaos. His arsenal holds a multitude of weapons. He impinges, sometimes with miniscule and immediate effect and other times his intrusions are extensive and prolonged. Old Nick works his magic indefatigably. Some say he will triumph. I reserve judgment.

Recollections of my earlier years consist of never-ending temperate summer days frittered away on the Yorkshire Moors and Dales and other locales; hiking and picnicking, playing rounders, gathering brambles, playing roll-in-the-blanket—an innocent name for an innocent game.

A weekend a month, June through August, my father would rent a chalet outside Great Ayton—a village some ten miles away from the grimy industrial town of Middlesbrough on the River Tees. As far as my memory serves, there was a row of wooden huts in a field rented out to weekenders. This tiny chalet would provide accommodation for my parents, me and my three siblings. The sleeping arrangements elude me; I was obviously exhausted by the time I went to bed. I recall falling asleep to the sound of owls. I think most nights the owl was Dad behind the chalet, making hooting sounds for our amusement. Perhaps my siblings were amused, *I* wasn't. Owls frightened me. My Mom told me when Dad is driving and sees an owl sitting in the road . . . he hoots.

The cabins were surrounded by gently sloping hills. Roll-in-the-blanket was played as follows: We would race to the top of the hummock wrapped in a blanket and roll to the bottom. It's relevant to size and age I know, but we came down that slope at one hell of a speed. I don't ever remember anyone being injured, however I did lose my breakfast at times, which normally put an abrupt end to the proceedings. The winner was the one who was first to his feet at the bottom of the hill. This game kept us busy for hours on end. The reason for a blanket is patent; every morning the farmer would herd his cows through the pasture to the milking shed adjacent to the cabins.

My eldest brother Joseph used words like, 'cowsh' and 'bullsh'. Everyone thought this hilarious. At the time, I didn't understand what he was talking about. The blankets remained fairly unsoiled as my mother always insisted on a 'poo-parade' before the games could commence.

Those summers were undoubtedly the best of my entire childhood, possibly my whole life. They were innocent years. We were a happy family who had time for each other. In my experience, this is a lot less common today. Nowadays, as a rule, both parents are required to work due to financial constraints and the 'keeping up with the Joneses' disease. This in turn leaves them less time to spend nurturing their children. Children cry out for attention and thrive on discipline. The youth of today are sadly a product of the absence of solid childrearing. We have unwittingly created a generation of selfish and disrespectful young adults.

The sixties new world movement with its mantras of love and peace, conversely produced a generation of violent, narcissistic and immoral layabouts. Dr Spock has a lot to answer for. Thank God for those wise and committed parents aware of the importance of sound discipline and solid moral advice. Narcissism was mentioned in Greek fables. Unruly children received tough love in dollops; they certainly weren't dragged off to psychologists, who diagnosed them with attention deficit or bi-polar disorders. Those terms didn't exist in a layman's vocabulary. Nowadays, most children are cursed with either one or the other or God help us, both.

Parents of the post-war years toiled and sweltered away with an almost religious fervour waiting patiently for their hard-earned gold watch, which seemed like an eternity in coming. Einstein hit the nail on the head when he said time is relative; three months in the 1950s, was proportional to a year today. We tend to live out our days in fast forward mode, as if playing a role in a Charlie Chaplin movie of old, flitting from one scene to the next.

The morning of our 'Great Show' arrived and we were blessed with a beautiful sunny day. The show happened once a month or so. The name originated from a TV programme on circuses. I had watched a documentary about life under the big top, on our miniscule black and white set and had decided to name our act in honour of it. It was poorly planned, if any planning took place at all; we were seven years old at the time and hence should be excused for our lack of foresight.

We, a bunch of primary school friends, organised these days for the neighbourhood clutch of snotty brats. Everyone was welcome as long as he or she could afford the one penny entrance fee. The events included throwing mud balls at one another, (why, I wonder) hide and seek and the favourite, the tanner treasure hunt. The contestants paid an extra half-penny to enter each event. It appears I was on quite a good racket back then.

This particular show, we had put the word out regarding a very special attraction. Douglas Green—not the brightest fry among us—had agreed to ride his tricycle off the washhouse roof, a height of some eight foot and again, I have to wonder why. It was a feat that would put him in the annals of show history.

The stunt would start when all adults were out of sight—I could depend on my parents going shopping on Saturdays. The sole family member at home that day was Stephen, my older brother, who was inside playing Scalectrix with a friend. It turned out to be a winner; my pockets were bursting and jangling with the sound of copper on copper, possibly all of two shillings. I was the self-appointed treasurer you see. To add some sort of perspective, my pocket money at the time was a tanner or sixpence a week. As I stated, I was on a real winner.

The time came and using a length of rope, we hoisted Dougie's trike onto the roof. I remember him donning a Lone Ranger mask for dramatic effect. The air was tense and the crowd expectant as he pushed his bike to the far end of the concrete slab. He turned to face his destiny. Then, with a loud cry of Hey Ho Silver, he peddled insanely toward the precipice. In that short distance, he managed to pick up quite a head of steam.

Whatever were we thinking? Do children of that age consider consequences? Obviously we had not. From my vantage point, I watched as he whizzed off the edge of the roof, to the deafening silence of twenty or so incredulous onlookers. He met the concrete slab with a resounding thump. It happened quicker than anyone had anticipated. A round of applause burst forth from the dumbfounded spectators. This was the greatest trick ever. This act alone was worth the entrance fee.

Dougie lay dead still. 'If that was me' I remember thinking, 'I'd be standing up taking bows and enjoying the limelight' or similar thoughts capable of a seven-year-old. The clapping faded away and someone shouted, 'Ere, I think e's dead!' The audience disappeared in a blinding flash as the organisers were abandoned to deal with the 'cadaver'.

We put our heads together and came up with a scheme; we should drag the body into the hedgerow behind the house and cover it with leaves and branches and make it 'disappear'. We dragged the deceased performer into the pathway, while Tubby half pushed—half carried the buckled tricycle round the corner and abandoned it on the curb outside the Green's house. We incanted a short prayer of sorts for the late Douglas Green and scarpered home like little angels.

Dougie woke up five minutes after his succinct funeral and interment. He would tell us later he had awoken thinking he was blind. He pulled up his cowboy mask, blocking out the light and then the pain had kicked in. His head was 'very sore' he told us. I'm sure it was! He found an egg-sized bulge on his forehead. His knees and elbows were raw and bloodied. He could have snapped his neck, broken his back or killed himself! As it turned out, both he and we got off lightly.

I had no idea what he told his parents regarding his smashed bike or his severe injuries—he was to tell me some twenty plus years down the line. He became a hero and a legend in his own time. I can't remember ever having another show; we would never have topped that most brave and perilous act.

My older brothers had an overwhelming influence on my life. Stephen gifted me with a love of music. Joseph—eight years my senior—had the most insane sense of the ridiculous; a 'Goon Show' approach to everything. Life was a colossal joke, he found humour all around him. Joseph would impact on our lives in a way no-one anticipated.

My eldest brother forever banned my access to the school grounds whenever he and his mates decided to mess around with a rugby ball. I had been forlornly watching through the school railings as they contested who could kick the ball the highest. The wind was blustering, blowing the ball off its intended course. Joseph ran over to me and surreptitiously whispered in my ear, 'Benjy, I'm sorry but you can't join in; you're too small. If that ball comes down on the top of your head, the pointy bit will go straight through your skull into your brain.'

That was enough for me. I scuttled home with thoughts of a most ghastly death spurring on my little legs. I heard laughter in the distance shadowing my retreat. To this day, I have a healthy respect for rugby balls. When I watch a game on TV, I wince every time the up-and-under manoeuvre comes into play. I'm too astute to attend a live game, naturally. What would I do if the ball ended up over my head? God forbid! I shudder at the very thought of it. Stephen and his gift of music will be spoken of later.

Guy Fawkes or Bommie night, as it is generally called, happens each year on the 5th of November. It's an English celebration, when an effigy of Guy Fawkes is placed and torched on large fires throughout England. He was a 17th century revolutionist, whom along with a bunch of co-conspirators, attempted to blow up the Houses of Parliament. I unreservedly abhor politics and politicians with their elongated snouts, snorting and grunting into troughs stuffed to the brim with tax payers' luverly lucre. Great work if you can get it I would surmise. Politics have in one way or another negatively affected my whole life.

This account deals with the tragic consequences following the gathering and guarding of wood required to create our own bonfire. The whole neighbourhood typically boasted six or seven bommies on the night and dry wood was imperative to all would-be effigy burners. November in England is slap bang in the middle of the rainy season. Most people will argue that this is an excellent oxymoron; when *is* the dry season in England? I digress.

The washhouse roof served more purpose than 'killing' would-be circus performers as this is where the wood hoards were squirreled away, under a large dirty tarpaulin. Still, the chances of theft were good to inevitable. We went on Bommie raids, so why shouldn't our enemies?

October 1962 turned out to be a relatively dry month and the Mcpherson kids collected a not inconsiderable stack of dry logs, branches and kindling. My sister Margaret designed a cunning alarm system using string, wire, pulleys and alarm clocks. The mechanical ingenuity would have made Fort Knox security take a second squizz. If someone yanked on a branch, any branch, the plunger of at least one alarm clock would be raised and the ensuing racket would spur my brothers into action.

Stephen and Joseph were not renowned as trouble makers nevertheless they unquestionably had the reputation of peacemakers. I can vouch for this; I cannot recall one instance of being bullied by local toughies. I would never have called upon them to fight my battles nonetheless I never had to.

Not to short change Margaret, she could stand up to the best of them. Defending family honour, protecting her little brother or fending off raiders of our precious lode came naturally to her. She was no slouch when it came to the art of pugilism.

Joseph's body was located shortly after seven o'clock on the Saturday morning. The police discovered him after having received a frantic call from my father at one in the morning. Whenever my parents arrived home late at night, they were in the habit of checking on all of us. He was found lying face down in a foot of water, in a small beck running through the estate. The rivulet meandered murderously through a thicket barely two hundred yards from our house.

That Friday night Mom and Dad had been socialising on the far side of the estate. The alarm system must have alerted Joe that Bommie Raiders were plying their trade. He, apparently resolute on challenging them himself, rushed off to his death, leaving Stephen and Margaret in oblivious slumber.

As to what, why or how things actually happened that night, we will never know. I lost my big and wonderful brother in return for a bunch of stupid wood. The autopsy report listed drowning as the cause of death. As his lungs were filled with water, the coroner had concluded Joseph fell into the shallow beck in an unconscious state.

The investigating team concluded that he had probably slipped while running on the muddy verge, knocking himself out on a tree trunk and fallen face-down into the shallow waters. We would never know who he was pursuing that night and nobody was talking. The sitting room curtains remained drawn for a long, long time.

Things changed drastically in the months following the tragedy. I was eight yet I could clearly understand the reason for the screaming matches, the accusations and insinuations and ultimately, long strained silences. The child's mind is a fragile and delicate mechanism; the eyes and ears should be shielded, turned away from adult matters. I was exposed to emotional issues too complex for my vulnerable make-up to process.

I should mention before moving on that I couldn't cry, I didn't know how to. I watched as my family mourned and fell to pieces engulfed in grief, yet I couldn't connect, I couldn't empathise with the mourners. I wanted to feel what they were feeling; even at my young age, I instinctively knew I needed to experience their emotional devastation. I was destined to deal with the effects later in life.

CHAPTER TWO

Some important politician, somewhere in the world, was assassinated. I listened to talk of Russians, grassy knolls, film actresses, conspiracies and a 'book suppository' I called it, much to the amusement of all.

The Beatles crashed onto the scene with songs of love; 'She Loves You' 'I Want to Hold Your Hand' 'Love Me Do' and lots more. I was smitten, completely besotted! The world had never heard the like. 'A passing fad' my Dad said at the time. Steve and I floated away on a cloud of ringing guitars and heavenly harmonies. Margaret was indifferent, unmoved; she had not the slightest appreciation of music in any form, the poor girl. She loved to dance the twist as her party trick, egged on by Mom.

'Come on Margaret; show everyone how well you can twist.' Margaret would die of embarrassment.

The family started down the long and bumpy road to recovery. It had in its' collective wisdom, realised the uselessness of residing, almost wallowing in the misery of yesteryear. The gaping, festering abscess throbbing in the heart of the family unit had to be exorcised. It had threatened to destroy the family from the inside out. Thankfully, functionality and optimism unhurriedly returned.

In June of that year, my father made a life-changing decision for all. We were to depart the cold and damp of England for the faraway shores of sunny South Africa; deepest darkest Africa where lions and tigers roamed freely in the streets. Big strong men, with ebony bodies glistening in the fierce midday Sun, were commanded to transport big game 'mbwanas' on divans, fanned their charges with massive exotic palms.

My Dad would say years later, after a particularly horrid incident, 'I wonder why I agreed to move to this damn hell-hole while living under a conservative government? I should have known things couldn't have got worse.'

I have never been able to work out what it was he was trying to say. I think Macmillan was Prime Minister at the time or was that communist residing at No.10? Either way, my Dad was mistaken. He hadn't agreed to anything, on the contrary he had initiated the move. The way of the distraught appears to be to avert blame when the proverbial hits the fan.

The big day came after weeks of Mom crying a river or two. Friends and neighbours popped in to bid their farewells and wish us all the best. (Aunts, uncles, rogues and vagabonds all lived on the other side of Hadrian's Wall). They warned us of dangerous wild animals, marauding bands of Zulus and so forth. Those were exciting times for a ten year old.

We emigrated through or by way of the Friends of the Springboks association. I have difficulty recalling the voyage; I remember sunny days and the swimming pool and loads of food, but no clear images. Apparently, Mom was laid up in her cabin most of the voyage suffering with seasickness. It is said on the first day of this malady you wish you could die and by the second day you wish you had.

We sailed out of Southampton via one of the Castle liners refuelling at Madeira and then on to Cape Town. Strangely enough, en route by train from Cape Town to Johannesburg, a two and a half day journey, I didn't spot a single lion or tiger! As for marauding gangs of assegai wielding Zulus, they were conspicuous in their absence. How disappointing for a ten year old expecting adventure in a big way. I had been vigilant too; perhaps I was asleep at the time.

A couple of days later, we arrived in Johannesburg, the financial hub of the Transvaal. A man from the association met us at the station by holding up a board with Mcpherson scribed on it. As I read our name chalked on it, I remember looking about wanting to brag to anyone there that I was a Mcpherson. I recall feelings of eminence for no reason I can explain. He drove us in a VW bus to Hillbrow, a somewhat scruffy suburb of Johannesburg, where this altruistic organisation had arranged a furnished flat until Dad could find a job. No school for a bit longer, I was ecstatic.

My Dad had been allocated two months grace, evidently 'more than enough time to find suitable employment' the man said. As it worked out, Dad was offered work in Durban, courtesy of a distant cousin. Within a week or two, we trekked to the South Coast by way of the South African Railways; not one sighting of aforementioned animals or war dancing Impi. Unbeknown to us, we had snaked and puffed our way through the heartland of the Zulu nation.

A quick change of vehicle and we were on our way to our final destination, Amanzimtoti, commonly referred to as Toti. At that time, Toti was a quaint little seaside village boasting four hotels, an amusement arcade and miles of white pristine beaches; a popular holiday resort frequented by up-country tourists. The south coast of Natal at that time was overwhelmingly English-speaking. There were pockets of Afrikaners, but generally, the language of choice was English.

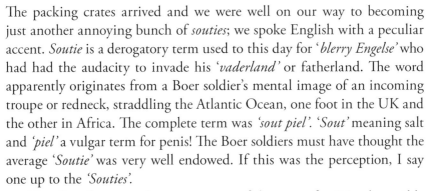

The packing crates arrived and we were well on our way to becoming just another annoying bunch of *souties*; we spoke English with a peculiar accent. *Soutie* is a derogatory term used to this day for '*blerry Engelse*' who had had the audacity to invade his '*vaderland*' or fatherland. The word apparently originates from a Boer soldier's mental image of an incoming troupe or redneck, straddling the Atlantic Ocean, one foot in the UK and the other in Africa. The complete term was '*sout piel*'. '*Sout*' meaning salt and '*piel*' a vulgar term for penis! The Boer soldiers must have thought the average '*Soutie*' was very well endowed. If this was the perception, I say one up to the '*Souties*'.

The first few months were uneventful except for Mom's terrible bouts of homesickness. She cried incessantly and suffered long periods of clinical depression. Time whizzed by, what with enrolling in a new school, making new friends and body-surfing in the forgiving temperatures of the Indian Ocean. Life was good for a ten year old.

The festive season was traumatic for Mom; eating Christmas dinner with sweat pouring down her brow was the last straw; she suffered a complete mental breakdown. Isn't it always the trivial things—trivial to others perhaps—that trigger big things? It wasn't to be her last however.

She became, as a result, a slave to 'that little yellow pill'. I'm not too sure whether my mother ever suffered her '19th Nervous Breakdown' but if not, it must have been close. I offer my sincere apologies to the Rolling Stones.

I blinked and it was 1965. I turned eleven in the summer and my brain and certain parts of my anatomy exploded forth with weird thoughts and deeds I never imagined possible. It seemed all I ever thought of was girls.

I wasn't totally naive, but at the same time, I had been protected and sheltered by Stephen and Margaret; the 'my little brother' syndrome. I'm quite sure being the youngest in the family carries both benefits and disadvantages. Losing their eldest brother had resulted in my siblings being unwittingly over-protective. Whether this was a benefit or a disadvantage, I have never decided.

It was the 6th of October, a Wednesday at about four in the afternoon. I had finished my homework and decided to take a walk along the beachfront to see if there were any friends down at the beach. The house was deathly quiet. Dad was at work, Steve was with school friends studying for matric exams and Madge was probably visiting one of her many boyfriends.

Mom had recently joined a local Bridge club and was playing a rubber or two at friends four blocks away from home. She had given me strict instructions not to leave the house.

She was still to overcome her deep fear of the unknown, the new and the dissimilar. In the early 50's, when we had moved from Scotland to Yorkshire, she had been dragged, figuratively speaking, kicking and screaming. My father, according to her, found relocating easy as he had 'a touch of the old gypsy' in him; a wanderer, a traveller. But I realised in later years, he was a man who endeavoured constantly to improve his lot in life. This in turn would 'benefit my family' he reasoned soundly.

'I'll only be around the corner my love' she said in that strong Scottish brogue. 'If you need me, you know where I am' she smiled. 'See you a bit later. I'll be home about half past five. Stay at home my Benjy. Love you.'

'Okay. Love you to Mom' I said.

Normally, I listened to my mother. Why had I disobeyed her that day? There are many times when the devil intervenes and changes lives forever. To paraphrase, 'when a butterfly flaps its' wings in Japan it can have an effect on the universe . . . etc.' I think it was Lyell Watson who put it so elegantly.

The esplanade was exceptionally quiet that afternoon. All of a sudden, a strong feeling of foreboding overwhelmed me, a premonition of evil waiting to swoop. I tried to shrug it off as feelings of loneliness or nostalgia commonly known as homesickness. Apparently it can linger for years.

My family were all in the company of others laughing and playing games, working or whatever and I was on my own, isolated, vulnerable and afraid. The southeaster whistled through the tall beach grasses. The clouds hid the Sun. All who know me are aware of my abhorrence, my utter loathing of strong winds. This hatred had manifested itself the year of Joseph's demise, my 'Winter of Death'. One afternoon, Mom handed me ten shillings and asked me to wait for Dimitri's greengrocer van and buy potatoes for the Shepherd's Pie she was planning for supper.

Always eager to please her, I ran down to the roadside and squatted on the curb. It was blowing up a gale. The van arrived and Dimitri walked to the back of his vehicle and rolled up the concertina door. He climbed in and lit the gas lamp. To this day I can 'smell' the melancholy aromas that would emanate from the interior of the Greek's van.

Neighbours were queuing, waiting patiently to do their bidding, when I noticed a pathetic emaciated runt crawl underneath Dimitri's van and wedge itself beneath the front wheel. I could 'read' the look on the dog's face as it eyed me. I saw desolation, wretchedness written about it. The dog was pleading with me to let it be; 'don't interfere, look away young human boy' it seemed to be saying. The wind gusted and chased loose bits of paper up and down the street, never quite catching any. The cur had me spellbound, mesmerized; I couldn't move, I was paralysed and had lost all sense of time.

I must shout a warning to the Grocer, I thought. 'Don't drive away! Don't move your van.' I broke the spell and turned my head to the rear and saw that the customers had gone, all served and satisfied. In the distance, I heard the motor turning over. Too late; Dimitri pulled away squishing the tiny mongrel. I had turned back to gaze upon the unfortunate creature, finding it impossible to avert my eyes. A voice inside commanded me to watch and learn from this ghastly experience! The dog's eyes popped out of their sockets, hanging off white strings. The innards burst out of its' ruptured gut and snaked across the tarmac. I squealed and bolted for the refuge that was my mother, indoors, safe from the crying wind and the macerated dog.

I believe to this day, the dog was consciously aware of what it was doing; it committed suicide. Whenever I have shared this dog of 'higher consciousness' experience, I am ridiculed and berated by many. I continue to tell the story nonetheless, as I know it to be true.

Why had I not turned for home and scarpered that day on the esplanade? I should have heeded my mood, my premonition *and* my mother! I had walked briskly for about five minutes along the path, when I noticed a movement in my peripheral vision. Something was there or was it someone, coming from the scrub on the beach, up and over the hand railings? I quickened my gait. It was someone and he was almost upon my tail. Black or white, I couldn't distinguish which. I sensed evil emanating from behind, like heat radiating off a pot-bellied stove.

I glanced back and caught a fleeting glimpse of a strange-looking man. He lunged at me and I watched helplessly as he raised his hand, armed with a baton of sorts, and brought it down hard, bludgeoning me on the top of my skull. He threw me to the ground and dragged me into the bushes separating the walkway from the road. I struggled aggressively and then another series of blows rained down on my shoulders and sides. The world around me started to fade away.

Two days later I awoke in hospital with my father at my bedside. He immediately pushed the call button which brought the doctor scurrying. The ache in my head was excruciating, as was the pain throughout my entire battered and bruised body.

I had been sexually abused and left for dead, beaten to within the proverbial inch of my life. My head was the size and texture of an over-ripe pumpkin. He had split my anus, torn my colon, broken three ribs and had cracked my skull. He or 'it' had gone to town on my entire body. I was found by an elderly couple taking their late afternoon stroll. They had spotted a strange little man jumping over the railings and running off carrying what they thought to be a torch or a short log.

I see the ball slowly spiralling down. The moist leather is shimmering in the late summer sunshine. I know instinctively the path of this falling missile has been programmed to perfection. Over there in the distance, my mother is standing outside a wrought iron gate waving her arms and screaming words I can't hear. Am I deaf or is my mother mute? Although the words are silent, I can read her lips and she is mouthing 'Run to me! 'Come home Benjy!

There is a raging torrent ensnaring me between the gate and the fields. My mother, my haven and sanctuary, is beckoning to me. She is so close almost within reach. My feet are leaden. My whole being is loaded down with something large and overwhelmingly heavy. The smell of dry rotting wood fills my nostrils. My feet are making sucking noises as they try in vain to pull free; to release me, liberate me. Is it quicksand, this thick oozing mud imprisoning me? I look skyward and see the ball hovering above my head. I realise what it is that I clutch so tightly in my arms, a white tarpaulin conceals a body made of rotting vegetation. It both repulses and fascinates me. I try in vain to heave it away but this fiendish cargo suddenly takes on a life of its' own; it moulds itself about my body. I scream and wake up as the ball penetrates my brain.

Sleep is supposedly a welcome release from both psychical pain and mental anguish. I wasn't to experience any relief. On the contrary, whenever I fell into light slumber those first weeks after 'my trouble', as it became known, Morpheus would turn his head and seemed to delight in my suffering. The nightmares were regular and intense. There were many variations on a theme, but they invariably included a rugby ball, things made of wood and water.

It was around this time I developed a morbid fascination with the number three. I became obsessive about objects and names; words that were divisible by three. For instance, I preferred Nestle or Beacon chocolate to Cadbury. I much preferred Rice Crispies to Cornflakes. I favoured reading The Hardy Boys as opposed to The Secret Seven. Do the maths. All of my favourite things are divisible by three. I have made important decisions based solely on whether the issue at hand can be divided by that irritating, cursed number. Much of my life has been lived by adhering to this maddening, controlling and irrational disorder.

I am conditioned to the point where I can glance fleetingly at sentences, book titles on a shelf, product names and distinguish their 'divisibility compliance.' I created silly phrases to go along with my condition; 'sixty-sixty compliance,' 'the three-factor' and 'the treble test', to name but a few. Note that the phrases I coined are not divisible by three. I know too well I had three operations following the sexual attack.

Yes I'm a trained psychoanalyst, yet even Freud no less admitted self-analysis was difficult, if not nigh impossible. And since I rarely have the proclivity to consult a colleague—only out of absolute necessity—regarding a multitude and varied array of psychological problems, I can but speculate as to the root cause of this morbid fascination with the number three. Incidentally, three is the third prime number. Associations with the number three that spring immediately to mind are the Holy Trinity, Three Wise Men, Three Blind Mice, The Three Bears, three's a crowd, the Three Musketeers and the Three Stooges. Three is the third number in our arbitrarily constructed base-ten numerical system. And I have viewed all of this with my third eye. The Introductory, the Penultimatum and the Conclusionarium are three stages of that influential fraternity. The triangle is their foundation. Every American President, with the exception of Millard Fillmore, has been scribed in their membership column. Fillmore should have been a member; do the maths.

The word three has *five* letters, is not divisible by three and *five* is the fourth prime number, all very frustrating if you happen to suffer with a similar syndrome.

My brother, sacrificing precious matriculation prep time, visited me twice daily. On my second day in hospital, he arrived before visiting hours. Being an immediate family member, he was allowed to walk straight through to my private ward. I looked like I had gone fifteen rounds with Henry Cooper. My face was varying shades of purple, blue and yellow. I peered at him through tiny slits. Steve stared silently at me for a few moments and then solemnly swore he would 'hunt down the low life scum' who'd dare 'fuck with the Mcphersons'. He was seventeen, a tall muscular young man, who was the star of his school's football team. I was impressed with his vocabulary. 'Fuck' was a word I had seldom heard but if my big brother used it, well that was so groovy, then so could I. Fuck that man who had hurt me. Fuck him . . . fuck him . . . FUCK HIM!!! I was angry and it felt good cursing my assailant; it inadvertently blocked out some of the mental anguish.

My father was rather perplexed when I paraphrased Steve's statement that night, 'fuck the scum who'd dare mess with the Mcphersons.' I watched as he turned away his head and I'd like to think he stifled a chuckle. He turned back to look at me. 'You're right son' he stated with quiet conviction. 'Fuck the bastard and the horse he rode in on!' We laughed and then for the first time in my life, he gently wrapped his arms around my aching body and held me in his loving embrace for a long time. We sobbed uncontrollably. I think my father cried for me, himself and the world in general in that order. I think I cried for my father.

I missed my mother; it was my third day in hospital and she was still to bless me with her presence. Had I become an 'untouchable', was I unclean? I asked after her and Dad said with detectable irritation in his voice.

'Mom's been a little poorly. She sends her love and asked me to tell you how much she loves you.'

The irritation, I realised was not aimed at me. I knew what type of poorly and for all intents and purposes, I was the cause of this latest attack of depression.

The barrage of tests complete and the swelling and pain receding, the doctor eventually agreed to release me after a week of pleading and nagging. I was ordered to a sickbed to convalesce for a couple of weeks. I was overjoyed to be discharged even though I was the nurses' favourite. I would always be served extra-large portions of pudding and seconds if I wanted. Nurse Mclaren took a real liking to me; she brought me chocolates and comics. Archie was my all-time favourite, Archie and Reggie my preferred characters. I wonder why? There is one thing that has worried me, on and off, my entire life—would things have been different if I had received trauma counselling? My Scottish father didn't believe in, 'so much psychological rubbish' he would tell me years later, his psychologist son.

'Those years' he added, 'there was a stigma attached to that sort of thing'. I assumed he was talking about the attack. Maybe he was talking about counselling. Maybe it was the thought of his wife *and* his son being under a shrink's treatment that deterred him from seeking professional help for me. One would have thought the doctor should have recommended it, and of course, there is always the possibility that he had.

The Mcpherson matriarch was ready to pack up and return to the UK. If it had been her unilateral decision, I would have been enrolled and attending school in Sterling in less than a jiffy. My mom had suffered another collapse the day following my trouble. Her psychologist had her admitted to a home to recover, hence explaining her absence from my hospital bed.

Whenever mom's state of mind or my dilemma was discussed, the acceptable terms used were 'my trouble' and 'Mom's trouble.' We shied away from talking openly about sensitive issues. Is that the Scottish way? Or was it the Mcpherson approach? I imagine it had been the earlier family tragedy which had resulted in a clamping down on emotional openness.

My mother was desperately unhappy. She pined away for the homeland, wanting things to return to what and how they used to be. Dad had struggled hard for years trying to make South Africa a happy place for us and to a large degree he had succeeded. Mom's health improved. It could have been a result of the pharmacological interventions, but I would like to think her eventual calmness and contentment were real; an acceptance of the new world around her with all its shortcomings and uncertainties.

I became aware of a hole inside me; a great yawning abyss. It was almost as if my attacker had stolen the 'me' in me, tossed it aside where it had been snatched up and wafted away by that malicious and malevolent wind. I had a wanting, a need to express something lying dormant way down in the very depths of my soul. I am, I suppose, my mother's son and always will be however, I recognised a yearning to be an individual, a persona all of my own and not a measly extension of anyone else, loved one or not. I now know that what I hankered after was to be anyone else other than myself. I wanted to be the unsullied one, the innocent eleven year old, pure and unsoiled. Perhaps this period in my life was the root of multiple personality disorder (MPD) which has plagued me all of my life. Be myself? What a joke. More like be me and me and me.

'Please refresh my memory Sir, to whom are you speaking?'

Two major events took place in the December of that year. First, a local journalist was rudely disrupted while assaulting a nine-year-old boy in the home of the youngster's single-parent. The boy's father returned from the corner cafe and walked in on a real-life Hieronymus Bosch canvas. He apparently wanted to remove the perpetrator's head with a carving knife. Fortunately for the offender, the neighbour apparently heard the raucous goings on next door and had intervened, thus preventing the beheading taking place. The police and ambulance services were summoned and the reporter was dragged off to jail. The attempted decapitation was possibly exaggerated, but it made for good pub talk. I don't know whatever became of the poor victim. All I pray is that he didn't endure what awaited me.

A while later the local rag stated that in addition to the standing charge, an animal called Pieter Gouws had confessed to sodomy and the grievous bodily harm of an eleven-year-old boy on the esplanade. His confession was hopefully beaten out of him.

Justice was swift those days in the old Republic. (My mom still referred to SA as 'the colonies') The end of February he was pronounced guilty on both counts and sentenced to life imprisonment in a maximum security facility. I wasn't informed; my father thought better of it, 'it may invoke unwarranted guilt' he told my Mom. My father thought he always knew better. I was to learn of his incarceration years later.

Second, Steve decided he was going to be the fifth member of The Beatles. Earlier that year, he had bought a very expensive acoustic guitar. He had saved for a long time and easily justified the extravagance, 'all great musicians need a great instrument Ben'.

December school holidays rolled around and Stephen had come to the realisation he was no budding George Harrison or BB King. Stephen was no budding musician full-stop. He did however go on to absolutely live for music in all its' glorious forms and styles, except for Boeremusiek, which is a simplistic style of Afrikaans country-come-folk music. He said to me once, 'Boeremusiek isn't dead, it just smells funny' and laughed easily at his own joke.

'Benjy, this is yours. I can't play a note! Learn to play it for me.' He presented me with a beautifully polished hunk of wood and steel.

Playing any instrument is well known for its therapeutic value. Saint Andrew must have had his ear to the ground. Those first years of playing the guitar and then obtaining a doctorate in music—majoring on cello—almost broke me free from the shackles of guilt. 'It can't have been entirely his fault?' I reasoned mistakenly; the imperceptible weighty baggage performing its black magic on my immature and impressionable mind. As we know, the unfathomable workings of the human brain are at the best of times mind-boggling. The guilt and mental anguish borne of sexual abuse is over-bearing; fact, which over the past few decades, has been well-documented.

Music is the only art that has the power to unite lovers and adversaries alike; it is the universal language of love. It has the power to propel warriors forth into battle, to lay down their lives for a religious precept or patriotic cause. Drums, bagpipes and the bugle are some instruments of war. The cello, pianoforte, violin, harp and the human voice are various instruments of romance and inspiration. Music is loved by great men, kings and queens, the common man and woman and the rich and the poor. It complements all our lives whether we are beggars or billionaires.

I hazard a guess, had it not been for Stephen's musical injection, in conjunction with the Scottish saint and a smidgen of divine intervention, I could have very well fallen off the tracks. The sexual abuse had affected me in ways beyond I was aware of, and more than anyone else could have predicted. I became preoccupied with the guitar to the detriment of my school work. I did, albeit reluctantly, invest enough of my precious time in the drudgery of homework, at least enough to keep the school-wolf from the door. Also, I paid rabid attention in class; I couldn't very well practice my scales during lessons.

My friends consisted of budding musicians; guitarists and piano players and one loco character called Michael Fourie. He loved to bang away on the skins. He had heaps of potential and in later years, using his God-given skills, carved out a very successful but short career.

In 1981, an Australian group toured South Africa. Their latest album 'Upside Down' had gone gold in Australia, here and throughout Europe. Their tour kicked off at Sun City, a luxurious gambling resort situated in the homeland of Bophuthatswana north of Johannesburg.

As luck would have it, the group's drummer died of an overdose of heroin—luckily for Michael that is. The band was in a pickle as it was less than a week before their first performance, followed by a tour of Europe The group's manager decided to hold auditions in Johannesburg and advertised in the national press. Michael auditioned and to coin a phrase, he 'shat in.' He drummed for the outfit while enjoying all the benefits of the professional muso; gorgeous groupies, travel, oodles of money and naturally all the shit he could stick up his nose or jam into his veins.

Mikey disappeared off the map after roughly four years of total debauchery. He ended up as so many ex band boys do; sound engineering, producing albums and laying down the occasional drum track or two. I was relieved he didn't go down the same road as the likes of Hendrix, Moon and the Joplins of the world.

That notorious little Japanese drummer was pilfering work from the percussion fraternity. Technology doesn't necessarily benefit the individual and in Michael's case was detrimental to his very livelihood. I'm a Luddite at heart. When a one-man-band can recreate the swells and dips and the fullness of a symphony orchestra, from a musician's perspective, science has gone a tad too far. How many potentially great musicians have been made redundant as a direct result of so-called progress?

Jocelyn played the guitar *and* the piano, a two-stringed bow. She also plucked at the strings of my heart, if you'll excuse the pun. She was from old-English stock. Her parents, the Borristers, were third generation sugar cane farmers. Joss, as she was known was an exceptional young lady. She played the piano as if she were ten years older and rode a horse like John Wayne.

I, as a twelve-year-old, interpreted these feelings of wonder as true love. It had to be! I didn't hold any other girl in such esteem. Gorgeous Joss, she was far too good for me.

Tuesdays and Thursdays couldn't arrive quickly enough. On those afternoons, the gang met up to make music at the local community hall. There was an old piano at the back of the stage and we would gather round it and work out the chord sequences to songs by The Beatles, The Stones, The Byrd's and other group's that happened to be 'groovy' at the time. And sometimes Mikey would drag his drum kit along and accompany us. He would always start out very subdued and grow progressively louder, building up to a roof-rattling crescendo, until we would all scream in unison, 'MIKEY!' Super guy old Mike; he was 'spaced out' even at that age. Jocelyn shared a truism with me; 'drummers are people who hang out with musicians'.

His timetable permitting, Stephen would arrive unannounced and egg us on, encouraging our rag tag ensemble to tackle more and even more intricate progressions. If I assumed I was deeply in love with Joss, I loved my brother at least as much.

Joss had completed an impressive number of musical grades by this time and she would lead us all as if she were Count Basie himself. She was a natural-born leader, both musically and in life. Besides my overwhelming feelings of puppy love, I had a deep-rooted sense of respect for Jocelyn and no more so than when she tickled the ivories. She of the orthodox beauty; the strong square white teeth, the auburn hair, the indigo eyes, sparkling with a hint of mischief and a cluster of feint freckles scattered over the bridge of her chiselled little nose. It was easy for me to imagine her taking her bows at the Royal Albert or Carnegie Hall.

On the 6th of September 1966, Prime Minister Hendrik Vervoerd was assassinated in parliament; stabbed by a Greek messenger, who was allowed to approach the South African Statesman under the pretext of delivering an important message to the portly man.

Joss was twelve when this occurred. I recall her words to this day, 'is it so tragic? I have been told he was the architect of apartheid.' Who was feeding her these ideas at such an impressionable age, factual or not? Did she have the capacity and was she that precocious to grasp the seriousness of the situation? I was overjoyed when the principal informed us—very emotionally, via the Tannoy sound-system—we were to go home and pray for our dear-departed and much adored leader. The way people carried on, one would have sworn *Jesus* had been murdered in parliament. He was a 'mere politician' who was probably 'looking for it' Joss said at the time. That was the sum of our most honoured head of state's demise; half a day off school and a few off the cuff remarks by my girlfriend.

CHAPTER THREE

S gt Pepper's Lonely Hearts Club Band was the eighth studio album by The Beatles released in June 1967 it included songs such as 'With a Little Help From My Friends, 'Lucy in the Sky With Diamonds' and my all-time favourite, 'A Day in the Life'. The album incorporated balladry, psychedelic, music hall, and symphonic influences. I found it to be inspiring and unlike anything I had ever heard. Producer George Martin's innovative approach included the use of an orchestra, much to our marvel and frustration, being a small group of struggling musicians.

Widely acclaimed and copied by many, the album cover—designed by English pop artists Peter Blake and Jann Haworth—was inspired by a sketch by Paul McCartney that showed the band standing in front of a collage of a number of their favourite celebrities. I gazed in awe at that cover hour upon hour, music blaring out while attempting to put names to faces.

I turned thirteen on the 5th of February; I was a fully-fledged teenager. Mom continued to cry a lot in spite of the copious amounts of Librium variety pick-me-up, calm-me-down medications she tossed down her throat. But overall, she was much improved. Dad was promoted to

Associate Something-or-Other, which took effect on 1ˢᵗ April. I remember how we had teased him relentlessly at the time about the promotion perhaps being some sort of cruel April-fool's prank. He morphed into a 'parent in absentia.' I hardly ever saw him. We became more affluent as a result of his career advancement, but at least both of our parents had 'been there' for us throughout the all-important early years of our development. The family relocated to a more affluent suburb—a four-bedroomed house with a pool. 'Why would there be a swimming pool?' I pondered, 'seems a bit over the top; the Indian Ocean is a hundred metres from our new home. Somewhat redundant' I thought.

Dad bought my mother a shiny new canary-yellow VW Beetle which fitted very easily in the double garage. Steve had been accepted to Natal University and was studying Sports Psychology; a relatively new field and one that suited him perfectly. Margaret was . . . well . . . just Margaret, the quiet content one. Her goals in life were straight forward; complete a teaching diploma and find a man her father would approve of, get married and somewhere along the line, punch a few kids out of her system. These ambitions included a little house with the proverbial white picket fence.

The Beatles continued to amaze Joss and me. We knew the chords to every song they had written to date and those we had not quite perfected, we improvised. Whenever Stephen made an appearance, he insisted we play two songs for him; 'Blackbird' and 'Michelle' which we did with faultless timing and chord perfection. (God knows, we had played them enough times) Joss and I had become extremely close; my parents recognising our mutual yearning and the way we fed off and grew in one another's presence, (well I certainly grew in her presence) approved of us spending weekends together on her parents' farm or at our home on Kingsway, Toti. The Borristers too encouraged our friendship as Jocelyn was an only child who spent a lot of time practicing scales and playing polo, being her sport of choice. Her father was concerned she may be a tad lonely and isolated. Joss had girlfriends, but she preferred my company and who was I to argue? My parents were extremely fond of her; she could charm the very birds out of the trees without a single faltering wing. The Borristers had a laissez-faire approach to life—I had thought at the time—which had definitely rubbed off on Joss. She was a nonchalant and easy-going girl. In addition, she was all her life haunted by a free-spirit, which often bordered on rebelliousness. To sum up, Joss was never an easy person to analyse or place in a box. When I think of her, even to this day the word 'maverick' springs to mind.

Half a mile west of the Borristers' Dutch-style homestead, is a river that meanders slowly through a rocky and infertile tract. Joss had planned to take me there and show me the waterfall and natural pool below. One Saturday morning she 'commandeered' her father's old four-wheel drive Jeep. Navigating at breakneck speeds, we careered along the service road adjacent to the sweet stalks of sugar extending skyward. The Jeep shuddered and juddered as Joss giggled mischievously. I bounced up and down and bucked from side to side, white-knuckled, clutching onto the door strap for dear life!

The setting was magnificent. The river cascaded approximately five metres into a pristine pool of chilly blue water. The banks were covered with immaculately maintained lawns. There was a circular slate picnic table and chairs situated underneath a thatched shelter. A colossal Weeping Willow dangled its extensive branches over the pond skimming the surface; an idyllic, tranquil setting.

She skidded to a halt, stopping the Jeep on the water's edge. Before I realised what she was up to, she climbed onto the bonnet and dived into the tarn, I followed. She climbed out and took a basket from the back seat of the Jeep. We sat at the table overlooking the waterfall discussing our future as if we were a newly-wed couple. We had an understanding between us which at that age was difficult to discern. We spoke of our dreams, our aspirations; what we would study later on in life, where we would live, how many children we would raise. There was something in her look that convinced me our futures would play out in tandem . . . together . . . as one.

Joss at the age of thirteen was unsophisticated, strong-willed and forceful. She was always in control and yet she could be tender and considerate. Always ready to be surprised and open to new experiences, she was the complete girl in my book. It would be five long years before we enjoyed the pleasures of lovemaking. In retrospect, I am of the opinion those five years were well worth enduring. Joss and I became inseparable. When anybody spoke of us, it was in the singular tense, we became one; a corny thing to say however, it is true.

CHAPTER FOUR

I n 1969, my Dad had been made a fully-fledged partner in the forensic accounting firm of Horwitz and Cohen. Five years to reach the pinnacle of his career; not too shabby for a Scotsman with the surname of Mcpherson. He was a content man and the family benefited accordingly. He had decided to take a leave of absence and take Mom 'home' for an extended holiday. Their itinerary was as follows: a flight to Cape Town, a two-week cruise on the Windsor Castle to Southampton, rent a car and drive up to Scotland via the scenic route. They planned to take a few weeks for the drive; stopping often and doing the tourist thing. I was sure this would be right up Dad's alley, being 'a bit of a gypsy' and all. The sabbatical was to last five months.

There was one downside to these happy plans; I was to attend boarding school. Not much of a sacrifice actually as Jocelyn had been a weekly boarder in Durban for almost a year, where she would complete standards eight through ten. In the January, I was to commence weekly boarding at DHS. Durban High School was then and remains today a prestigious institution, where the majority of students excelled both academically and on the sports fields.

My Mom had arranged that I spent my weekends with the Lloyds; a couple who had recently relocated from The Isle of Mann. The Lloyds were avid Bridge players who spent every alternate Wednesday night at our house playing the game. I was happy with this arrangement as first,

I liked the Lloyds and second, standard nine being the most challenging year in a scholar's entire curriculum, I could spend my weekends swatting, with the minimum of distractions.

Rodney and Jean, Jocelyn's parents, had offered to have me stay on weekends. Dad had declined gracefully explaining weakly, 'Ben needs to spend more time studying and this quiet time will allow him to do so.' I knew he was more concerned with what Joss and I might get up to. It wasn't a matter of trust, I knew he trusted both of us, but after all, he had once been my age. Being a pious man, he must have thought, 'why should I empower the devil?'

Joss had become a bit of a musical protégé, performing at important recital evenings, where as I had lost interest in the guitar and taken up on one of the hardest instruments to master, the cello. My over-generous father bought me a two thousand rand Italian instrument, slightly less than the cost of a family saloon at the time. It is said that to master almost anything in life, it takes about ten thousand hours of dedicated slog. I challenge anyone to truly master the cello given this timeframe. I estimate two life times would just about do it. Mind you, Ravi Shankar once said the same thing regarding the sitar. Jacqueline du Pré, I doff my hat to you. du Pré was a cellist, born in January 1945 in Oxford England. She died at the young age of 42 in October of 1987. She was my idol then and remains to this day, in my opinion, the most excellent and passionate cellist ever. I can only but dream as to the great heights she would have scaled had she lived on into old age. Mercurial is a word that comes to mind.

One Sunday morning, Joss and I had planned to meet at the Goodwill Hotel on Inyoni Rocks beachfront for Coke Floats—Coca Cola with a spoon of ice-cream floating on top—the thought of the combination repulses me today. Saturday had seen her attend a polo meet with her parents up country in the Natal Midlands. Polo was another activity Joss excelled at.

Nottingham Road is a small town situated in the foothills of the Drakensburg mountain range. It is supported by a well-to-do dairy farming community. Polo, a sport popular with the affluent—as would be expected—flourished in one of the last of the 'British Outposts.'

Incidentally, 'Notties' is the home of the prestigious Michael House, a school where well-heeled parents discharge their children from their latest model Mercedes or Range Rovers in the chilly, misty mornings, common to that part of the world. I was to learn later Joss' father had matriculated from there years earlier.

I had spent the Saturday deep in studying mode with two of my greatest friends; Michael the drummer and Ronnie, a guitarist who was part of our musical circle. Jocelyn's father arrived early and dropped her off in the parking area on the road side of the hotel. He arranged to fetch us both for Sunday lunch. I knew she had arrived early as I was there a good hour earlier than the pre-arranged time. I longed for her whenever we were apart, a psychical aching deep down in the pit of my belly.

We sat on the hotel balcony looking out to sea, catching up on the previous week's events. There was a fair amount of surfers smoothly gliding on the waves, as if the cumbersome length of wood beneath their feet was a fixed appendage. These agile, bronzed wave riders paraded their stuff on the north side of the swimming pool, carved out of the 'Inyoni' rocks.

Suddenly, people where running in all directions, screaming and gesticulating wildly. They ran into the surf and then out of the sea. They were like ants; stopping to communicate with one another, touching their antennae together, and then scuttling off in an abrupt and business-like manner. A young woman ran up the beach, in an obvious state of panic, screaming to no-one in particular, 'shark attack!', 'shark attack! Someone's been attacked!' I grabbed Jocelyn's hand and steered her protectively towards the interior of the hotel's dining room; averted eyes are happy eyes.

A bather had been dragged from the surf by two lifesavers. His head and torso were all that remained. He had been taken by a great white. The young man, as it turned out, was a local surfer, who had ridden the waves of Inyoni for the past twelve years. Two of the quickly expanding crowd tried in vain to keep him alive until the Medics arrived. He died within minutes, on the blood-soaked sands of Amanzimtoti, one of the most favoured holiday resorts on the South Coast of Natal.

The ambulance arrived for the sole purpose of placing the body in a big bag, or what was left of him, removing it out of sight of curious and morbid onlookers. They took it to wherever corpses are stored. Where do they take cadavers, the morgue, a hospital perhaps, or the local police station?

I had called Joss' father from the hotel. He jumped in his car and arrived in a matter of minutes. Her folks spent precious little time on any of their sugar estates which pleased me no end as it made travelling to and fro more convenient. Joss had once informed me her mother wasn't too keen on being a farmer's wife. She never felt entirely safe 'sleeping in the bush' as she called it, hence the amount of time they spent at their Amanzimtoti residence. I found it strange as I was under the impression Jean had lived all her life on sugar-cane farms. Jocelyn explained that her mother, although being a Hallett, had been a border all her life; from grade one through to her matriculation. Jocelyn's father was seriously considering selling up and retiring somewhere in the Midlands to rear polo ponies. They would, he promised his wife, buy a house in a town within daily commuting distance to his stud farm.

We were both in mild shock as we sat on the patio drinking sugary tea. Where had they taken Joseph's body that cold and miserable November morning all those years ago? Stop it Ben. Let it be. Blank, blank, blank it all out Alan. Alan? Death, abuse and pain, loss and yearning, longing and nostalgia, a gaping hole in my heart, in my soul, were the disparaging thoughts filling my damaged mind. Why had the death of a total stranger devastated me so? Ben blank out all those horrid memories. Think happy thoughts. Go to a happy place. Think Joss. She was there. She was with me, I could sense her presence. She and I are one. I can overcome. We can overcome by the grace of St. Andrew and a touch of divine intervention. Blank, blank, blank it out Alan. You dumb bastard, who the hell is Alan?

'Ben . . . . Ben. What's wrong?'

'What?' I asked returning from another place, a thick syrupy-like place.

'You were miles away!' Joss stated in a worried tone.

'I'm sorry' I replied. 'I was thinking about tomorrow's school work' I lied. The first lie is a betrayal. After that, being economical with the truth becomes progressively undemanding.

Jocelyn gave me a look that I had never seen her express before. Disbelief, doubt at the very least. Should I have told her the truth? Should I have shared with her that I was of the opinion I was gradually losing my mind? Should I have told her that sometimes I disappeared into myself, I almost became an extension of myself, another person; me, but not me, does that make any sense? There weren't words to explain my distress, not at seventeen anyway.

On occasion, I 'travelled' being the only way my brain could vocalise the experience. When I 'returned,' I suffered a sense of loss, almost a rupture in the time continuum. I would 'wake up' with an ephemeral sensation of real danger, loss of control. I would imagine I had been to another place, another dimension conceivably. A name returned with me and a sickly-sweet sugary-like taste in my mouth, the remnants of my 'out of body' incidents. Alan returned, like the residue, the vestige of my journey. Who was Alan and what did he have to do with me? These 'out of body' experiences left me drained, exhausted. I knew these episodes would not dwindle away or even diminish. On the contrary, they would become more aggressive, more frequent and these thoughts terrified me.

Should I seek Mom's counsel on their return from their sojourn? She may understand my 'condition'. Would the family eventually talk about 'my condition' and 'my trouble?' Was I destined to become known, not as Ben, but as the one formally known as 'my problem' now known as 'my condition'? I decided to let my ailment remain a secret between me and Alan, whoever he was.

They returned in the late May with hundreds upon hundreds of photographs, which Dad promptly had transferred onto slides. They came 'bearing gifts from afar,' dozens of presents for everybody. Jocelyn was bestowed a magnificent pendant with a cluster of small diamonds set in white gold, dangling on a gold chain. She hugged and kissed my parents and told them how much she loved them. From that day forward, I don't think she ever took it off her long and slender neck. I was given a compendium of Beatles lyrics along with the musical notation for all of their compositions to date. To this day, my dog-eared anthology remains one of my most prized possessions.

CHAPTER FIVE

Margaret announced that she had 'found the right man for me' Dad agreed. Mom seemed happy enough with her choice and within the month, Danie and my sister were engaged and wedding plans finalised.

They were married in the August and I was convinced I was shortly to become an uncle, I was correct. Marge had been heavily pregnant at the altar. Mom feigned ignorance and explained to everyone who would listen, that her Margaret had given birth to a very premature daughter. The 'premature daughter' just happened to weigh in slightly north of nine pounds. She was christened Anne Katarina Schoeman.

Danie was a recently qualified architect who worked in the city. I liked him from the word go. He giggled consistently, just like a big kid, yet he was six foot four and built like the proverbial brick shithouse; a gentle giant who towered twelve inches above Marge.

The Mcphersons had become truly 'Serf Efrican'. The reception went down a treat. Mom danced with each and every male member of Danie's expansive family. The males got smashed and Dad learnt how to dance the sakkie, a wild, spinning Afrikaner dance along the lines of the polka. Stephen was accompanied by a stunning lady called Louise, a marine biologist. I was suitably impressed and read the writing on the wall.

Things were going along exceptionally well for the Mcphersons; my parents seemed happy enough, father was excelling at his profession,

Mom had calmed down to a blur; a rub off of her trip home. Steve had decided to stay on at university and complete his honours. Margaret had her little white picket fence with the 'right man' and baby made three. I had my precious Joss, my cello and . . . . Alan!

What was I to do with him? Throughout the last year, he had become a frequent visitor. I had not been formally introduced to him, for when he lurked I was absent and of course vice versa. I knew instinctively that I detested him, plus he spelled big trouble, I could sense it.

Jocelyn mentioned more than once she thought I had become somewhat moody, as if I had a split personality or something. My God, how did she know? I explained it away by saying what with matriculation exams heading my way, cello grades becoming trickier and maybe my hormones weren't in check—implying of course that the hormone bit might be rectified by a certain person's loss of virginity. She didn't fall for it though, well not that day anyway.

Lies, all of it, God damn lies, except for the virginity bit. I had no fear of matric exams; in fact in fear of sounding conceited, I found school all too easy. The cello was exposing its secrets to me, empowering and urging me on to stroke its slender lustrous neck with absolute aplomb.

It was Alan. Who did I become when he was in the driving seat? Was he bowing my cello? Was it he who was caressing Joss when he decided it was his turn at the controls? Damn it, I had to get rid of this evil intruder. This malevolent and wicked apparition had to be inveigled, wheedled into the light and banished to his underworld for eternity.

I had become obsessed with my other half. He would not defeat me. I decided he could reside within me as long as I was in control; a pact or perhaps a treaty? Alan admonished me and decided to 'create' Alex. Oh no, had *I* fashioned this latest ghoul? Was this Alex character another extension of me? Was he a third me? Had I become a trinity; Alan Alex and the holy Benjamin?

Lucidity became my ambition. I needed always to read the road ahead. 'I am driving so buckle up and if you don't like it, get the hell off my bus.'

Throughout my last year of school, for some unknown reason, Alan and Alex stayed hidden. I shouldn't have fretted over Alex, for when he occupied my space, I inevitably 'returned' feeling good about life; confident and positive. How did I know when it was Alex? I didn't, I assumed. I think they were and to this day mentally slower than me and just a little bit wary. After all is said and done, I am the reason for their existence. So they had better be vigilant, as I was determined to oust them. Throughout my life, I have been prone to invite other personalities into the inviolability of my mind, but never one as portentous and sadistic as Alan.

I sailed through the final exams picking up four distinctions along the way and securing my place at the University of Natal. I would enrol for a BA in music and then what? As long as Joss was studying beside me, I could have enrolled to read Hamburgerology. She had chosen to read political science. I knew she had a social conscience even though we rarely if ever discussed the skewed political structures of the day. I pondered whether a degree in her chosen field could prove detrimental to our relationship. Earlier that year, Joss and I had decided on UN because frankly, it wasn't a bad university, not quite Ivy League, but its' location was ideal. There was a campus in Durban and Pietersmaritzburg, roughly forty or so miles north of the city.

One Saturday morning in the early spring, Joss had driven us to the waterfall. We had celebrated Joss' eighteenth birthday the previous night; I am just more than a month her elder. We found solace there as the natural aesthetics were stunning and always brought on a special equanimity. The gentle sound of running water, the exquisite setting, the added remoteness awarded it an almost spiritual quality; our own basilica in the bush. I sat reading while Jocelyn swam naked. I looked down at her, 'you are becoming a little cock teaser' I said light-heartedly. She tittered and replied with something along the lines of 'not for long' and laughed again. I went back to my book and vaguely heard her climbing out of the water. We had become totally comfortable with one another's nudity. Nonetheless, my manhood was always on the lookout and never failed to rise to the occasion, comfort factor notwithstanding.

'Benjy make love to me' she said in a husky voice saturated with lusty wanting.

Joss lay beneath the umbrella, her thighs arranged provocatively, allowing me to observe the ultimate reward; that special piece of womanhood man had lusted after and killed for since time immemorial. Today, I refer to a woman's anatomy as a weapon of mass destruction.

We consummated our relationship that day in the fields, next to a waterfall, on her father's farm. Jocelyn's squeals of pleasure echoed off the rocks and the water. We were gentle but strident, unrushed, yet there was a sense of urgency in our need to attain a climax, which when arrived, engrossed us in perfect unison. We rendered our virginity to one another, a solid basis on which to forge a life-long relationship. Before the tumultuous act of love-making had begun, she had awkwardly, yet softly, rolled a condom into place. I was forced to ask her to pause a few times as the deed itself had me in such a state of anticipation and delight, it became touch and go whether she would share in the action. A while later with Jocelyn nestling in my arms, I remember thinking with some trepidation, I could and would willingly die for this young woman. Was I throwing myself too deeply into this pool of dependence, with unqualified faith and trust, devoid of any life-saving apparatus, no lifeline of any sort? Only time would tell.

A month prior, on my birthday, I had become an extremely fortunate and most grateful recipient of one bottle green MGB GT of 1969 vintage. My old man had outdone himself this time. Mom was overjoyed; 'no more taking and fetching' she told me with relief.

I was eighteen and enjoying life. I was madly in love. The two bursaries combined allowed us to cohabitate in a tiny students digs within walking distance of the main campus; we could actually see the Memorial Tower Building from our window. Our parents had given their blessing to this rather liberal arrangement of the times. Life was good and we were filled with much hope and optimism. What could possibly go wrong?

⚓

Approximately four hundred miles north-west of Durban, Pieter Gouws awoke in Pretoria Central to another day of drudgery and mind-numbing routine. He put on his scratchy and unbecoming prison garb and waited for the guard to unlock the cell doors. He sauntered along the common walkway en route to the eating hall, softly humming some tuneless song.

Breakfast consisted of porridge, brown bread and tea six mornings of the week and then on Sunday's prisoners were spoilt with cold rubbery fried eggs and a spoonful of poor quality baked beans. A length of even poorer quality sausage finished it off with the ever available porridge and brown bread. Gouws was excited but was able to warily conceal his taut emotions. He must not act any differently, as he knew from experience the 'Screws' could sense the slightest change in their charges, causing them to be even more vigilant. The last thing he wanted was an over-attentive guard. That could trash years of planning.

Pieter Gouws had been incarcerated as a guest of The Prison Service for ten long years, 'a most cruel and unusual punishment' he remembered reading somewhere. He had done nothing wrong other than have sex with a 'willing and forgiving partner' he deduced. And now he was compelled to daily face his dragged out and slow demise until he eventually wished for it, craved it. Throughout his incarceration, Gouws had maintained a flicker of hope and one dominant objective; escape. The first few years he had resigned himself to his fate. He had to slog it out until he learned the system and could then begin planning his escape.

His first year in Pretoria Central had him thirsting for death. The average Joe Soap inmate is behind bars because he doesn't want to or finds it difficult to comply with societal norms and standards. Gouws believed societal norms and standards did not apply to him at all. He was diagnosed psychopathic schizophrenic or so he had been told on numerous occasions. 'What a bunch of arseholes!' he declared tenaciously.

The everyday garden-type detainees; murderers, rapists and armed robbers, all have one thing in common, an abhorrence of child molesters in any shape or form. It was no different in a maximum security prison like Pretoria Central. The word spread, 'Gouws likes to fuck young boys' and the game was on. The first two years of his incarceration, he endured numerous savage rapes and beatings. He was 'encouraged' to perform fellatio on at least forty inmates with a home-made blade held to his throat. There had been nobody to turn to. In desperation, after one particularly nasty gang rape, he'd 'gassed' to one of the wardens. The 'screws' have been known to turn a blind eye in cases involving the abuse of sexual abusers.

He had been informed bluntly, 'scumbag, you can dish it out, but you can't handle it yourself hey? Take it like a man Gouws! The next time it happens, I hope someone slits your scrawny throat.'

The server slopped a dollop of grey congealed porridge into Pieter's Dixie. He picked up a few slices of stale brown bread and a cup of stewed tea and sauntered across to an open stainless steel bench—he had never felt comfortable sitting with his tormentors—and the feelings were mutual. He had been shunned for ten years and as far as he was concerned, enough was enough.

'Christ,' he could hardly contain himself! 'Calm down Boet, (brother) calm down. This could work' he deliberated, 'no,' he thought determinedly, 'this will work, it *must* work! Within a week, I'm going to pig out on a big, fucking juicy T-bone and chips, as God is my witness! And then maybe a bit of boy action if I'm lucky,'

His loins stirred at the very thought of a sweet young boy splaying his legs. He finished the swill and returned to his cell to brood and fine-tune his 'flight plans' ten long years in the making.

❦

Jocelyn and I had a semi-permanent gig with a group called The Never New. I played lead guitar and Jocelyn tinkled the ivories and occasionally played some mean lead riffs. Brian the rhythm guitarist and Lofty, a brilliant bass player from Pietermaritzburg, were classified as coloureds; an outrageous and cruel classification for a race of South Africans, classified neither black nor white but of mixed heritage.

This particular night we had been booked to play at a nightclub up on the Berea, a suburb which overlooked the city below and the Durban marina and harbour slightly to the south. It offered a sweeping panorama for which Durbanite house-hunters were willing to pay a premium.

We had jammed a few times previously at the Crazy Dolphin. The club had a decent reputation as a place catering for a primarily well-behaved crowd. There was rarely any fighting or over-the-top raucous behaviour. Drugs were basically unheard of, just a crowd of well-heeled young people, out to have a good time and listen to some good music. We were fortunate to have Mikey on drums that night and were all very keen to see if he would fit in with the group as our regular drummer had left for greener pastures. What happened later in the evening, I believe eventually pushed Jocelyn over the edge.

In the middle of our second set, a squadron of policemen burst in uninvited, goose-stepped through the front doors and approached the bandstand. We were in the middle of our, may I add, excellent rendition of 'Under the Boardwalk'.

One by one, we stopped playing. People on the dance floor ceased their convulsive jerks and slowed to a standstill, staring open-mouthed in total disbelief.

Hitler's chief storm trooper, loaded down by a plethora of brass on his sagging shoulders, jumped up onto the stage and dashed to the switch board and flicked the main breaker. The silence was thunderous.

The head hog turned to face the rhythm and bass guitarists, 'The two of you must pack up and get out! Get out you half-caste bastards!

There was loud and instantaneous jeering from the dance floor. The pig on the stage shouted at the crowd, 'quiet man, you aren't involved. It's not your business.' The rest of the storm troopers positioned themselves, ready for action, paralysed with uncertainty, waiting on word from their portentous and arrogant superior. Jocelyn was the first to speak.

'Just what the hell are you playing at?' she said furiously. 'Just who do you think you are you pig?'

'Quiet lady' the cop replied menacingly. 'Just stay out of it if you know what's good for you.'

'Hey, I told you two to pack up. Move, move, move!

I sidled over to the piano where Joss was standing and whispered to her to keep her head together. I had never witnessed her 'angry eyes' before, almost black, unstable and hostile. There was a tempest brewing and I knew I had to remove Joss from this precarious situation before the storm broke and she ended up spending a night or more in the police cells or worse. 'You useless fucks' she screamed. I eventually convinced her to hold her tongue. With immense restraint, she checked herself and we walked out of the club and sat smoking in a side street waiting for the pricks to leave. We returned later and packed up our equipment. Brian and Lofty, who were quite inured to being considered a sub species, collected their instruments and left the club, not before the owner summoned them to his office and gifted them a double payment. Mr Abrahams pleaded guilty and was given a stern warning for allowing 'non-whites' to perform in his club. Can you believe it? That should have been that. Unfortunately, the whole ugly incident turned out to be more significant, to Jocelyn anyway.

CHAPTER SIX

I was staying alone for the weekend in our new digs in the Berea. Joss had gone on a polo tour to the Cape and I had an important paper to research as part of my finals. I wasn't eating too well as I didn't do the bachelor thing too well. This particular night, I had decided to call Roddy, a very dear friend, to see if he would like to join me for a meal at the Beach Hotel; a middle-of-the-road three-star establishment situated on the Marine Parade. Not that money was an issue as my father was still bankrolling me which I wasn't completely at ease with. With the money I earned from gigging and my hard-earned bursary, I was quite comfortable thank you very much. I could have, if I so desired, dined at the five-star Edward Hotel next door to the Beach.

Roddy jumped at my offer as he was subsisting on a pittance. He was a struggling student who had failed his first year at varsity and as a result, his parents had pulled the plug on his remittance. Fortunately for him, his older and well-off sister slipped him the odd hundred rand on occasion. He was a real friend and I enjoyed his company. He was a genuine person who could hold an intelligent conversation and on top of it had a hell of a sense of humour. He had a few months to go to until graduation and he assured me he would be awarded his post-degree in applied mathematics. Anyway, back to the point at hand.

I met Roddy in the Cockney Pride pub in the Beach Hotel, where some sorry sod with delusions of grandeur, was murdering Billy Joel's

'Piano Man'. We had a quick pint of Lion Ale and ascended the stairs to the veranda on the opposite side of the multi-storey building. I ordered a hot curry with all the trimmings and Roddy requested a rump steak. 'Walk it through a warm kitchen and don't hang around.' Over the years, he had confused more than one waiter with his standard request.

The Beach Hotel's veranda is a fine place to dine. One can eat good fare and at the same time watch the world pass by, particularly in holiday seasons. Thousands of pedestrians carouse on the frontage and it can be highly entertaining. Drunks and con men, pickpockets and gorgeous young fillies looking for holiday romance—their skirts a tad too short—and Zulu maidens selling beads and all sorts of trinkets, produced for five cents and marketed for a hundred times their intrinsic value. Prostitutes, young wanton and impious and their older and not quite as attractive colleagues, both male and female, jaded and struggling to scrape together next week's rent money.

Add to the mix, loads of innocent naive and fat-walleted holiday-makers in the throes of indecision; should we throw in the towel up north and move down here to this virtual Garden of Eden? Mommy, we can swim in the sea every day! Imagine that Daddy! What do you think kids? We'd be on holiday all year long! Naivety can be such a burden.

It is similar to the story of a man who sits at the gate of a hamlet in order to evaluate newcomers. A weary traveller approaches him from afar. The gatekeeper asks of him from whence he cometh, the man replies, 'from a place beyond the peaks and vales, where the townspeople are both cruel and most unkind.' The gatekeeper says to the traveller, 'better you journey on to the next village, as all our townsfolk are both pitiless and hostile.' The traveller moves on and not long thereafter, a second wanderer approaches the guardian of the gate. He poses the same question to him and the migrant replies, 'I come from a parish beyond the hills and valleys, where the citizens are most kind and generous' to which the keeper says with a broad smile, 'come and rest your weary head my friend, for the people you speak of are in abundance in my hamlet also.'

Roddy was telling me a joke of a Jew a Catholic and a Muslim who walk into a pub. The barman asks, 'what's this, some sort of joke?' I was distracted by the appearance of a strange little man strolling toward me. I knew him. Something about the look of him unnerved me. He appeared somewhat smaller than I had imagined. He had a phizog nobody could forget; even a brief glimpse would suffice. 'My God' I cursed to nobody in particular as the man strode farther down the Golden Mile.

'What's it? Did the penny drop?' Rod laughed.

'Damn Rodders. I've just seen the bastard who raped me!'

'Who . . . ? He's history Ben. Wasn't he locked away for life years ago?'

'I'm telling you Rod, it was him. I'll never forget that face. Not in a million years! Roddy, that *was* him' I said as I twisted my neck watching him disappearing into the throng of revellers. I jumped up and threw down two ten rand notes.

'Pay for the food Roddy, I'm going to follow him' I said standing and striding out in pursuit of the bastard who had left me for dead after rearranging my innards. I could hear Roddy's shouts receding in the distance behind me. 'Ben, it can't be him. BEN! BEN!' I scampered along in pursuit of my noxious prey.

Gouws was strolling down West Street as if he didn't have a care in the world. 'Shit, this is the life, I did it!'

To escape the high security prison in Pretoria, a detainee has to pass through ten security doors and gates. Without inside assistance, it is virtually impossible. In early 1969, Gouws had become chummy with one of the wardens. Pelser, a naive young man, was a loyal and ambitious worker who had lofty ambitions of one day being in charge of his own prison. He encouraged Gouws' friendship along with others, as it would award him an insight into the workings of the criminal mind. Pelser struggled with an Intelligence Quotient rather south of the standard one hundred. On the contrary Gouws possessed a very healthy IQ and was adept at manipulating anyone inane and gullible enough to fall under his almost hypnotic influence. Along with all his defects, Pieter had about him an old-world charm, which he was capable of turning on and off in an instant.

Some of the most agreeable and charismatic people in the world are psychopathic. They blend in with the general population, masquerading as doctors and politicians, managers and morticians and every-day Joe Soaps. It is a disorder that affects an estimated four to five per cent of all individuals. This percentage may be badly skewed, as the average psychopath will never admit to having anything wrong with him and hence will not submit himself to analysis or diagnosis; the 'I'm not mad but everyone else is' syndrome weighing heavily.

Within a matter of weeks, Pelser was divulging information with regard to prison security and other titbits he deemed harmless to discuss. Gouws worked in the metalwork shop and he had devised a cunning plan to smuggle out pieces of metal in his flask fashioned into shapes comparable to the chunky and badly-honed keys of the guards. In conjunction with the info garnered from Pelser, he had been able to formulate a timetable regarding shift changes and inherent weaknesses in the system along with what key opened what door. The most demanding aspect of his scheme was to get his hands on a warden's uniform. During one session, Gouws had manoeuvred the conversation to talk of laundry requirements of inmates and staff. Two years later in 1975, Gouws absconded from Pretoria Central Correctional Services high security facility.

Gouws laid low at a pre-arranged pad for two nights and with a little assistance from his helper, was kitted out with civvies, a few bucks and a .22 pistol to be used only in emergencies. He informed his 'helper' he was 'making a duck for Durbs.'

Pieter's helper was one of an underground nationwide gang of ex-convicts. For the right price, they would assist escapees with temporary digs, basics such as clothing, contact names and pin money. Gouws had once said to his cell-mate in passing, 'Even if it is possible to escape this dump then what, where would I go to from here without any support or assistance?' He had been pleasantly surprised by his cell-mates answer.

'You don't want to forget the two hundred rand you owe. Two months max okay?' He handed Gouws a piece of paper containing a first name and a telephone number garbled within a line of random integers.

'Sure' Pieter answered 'two months, I know' he replied, glanced at the name and stuck the note in his back pocket.

'You can stay around here if you want. There's lots of action in Pretoria you know. This is the queer capital of South Africa.'

'No thanks china, too close to home for my liking. And I'm not a queer, let's get that straight Boet. I'm hitting the road tomorrow, back to my neck of the woods. I think I'll be safer there'

And here he was, breezing down the main drag of Durban with not a care in the world. 'Well okay' he mused, 'I need a job or any temp work I can get, I'll take it.'

His helper had dropped Pieter off south of Johannesburg. Gouws donned a cheap wig tucked under a Yankees baseball cap which was augmented by a pair of new Levi denims, a blue and white striped shirt and Galaxy running shoes. This disguise substantially changed his appearance. Within the hour, he was offered a lift by a salesman driving a flashy Chevy Impala going all the way to Durban. The man asked him of his plans when they reached Durban. Gouws replied, 'I'm going to enjoy a fucking juicy T-bone steak and chips, my third in as many days.' The driver examined this ugly little man cautiously. To avoid any further attempt at small-talk, Gouws affected sleep for most of the journey which suited his nervous travelling companion just fine.

The rapist was oblivious to the fact that I was tracking him. I had turned the tables; I was the huntsman and Gouws the quarry, how ironic. He picked up his key at the reception of a flea-bag one-star hotel and disappeared up the stairway with its' threadbare runner and aroma of two-day-old cabbage.

'What a cocky prick' I remember thinking at the time. 'He *must* be a bloody fugitive for God's sake; ten years doesn't equate to life and he's strutting around as if he's cock o' the hoop.' I doubted a lifer would be granted probation after serving ten years. I was ninety-nine per cent sure it was him; Pieter Gouws, the junior reporter, the rapist, the violent abuser who exploited innocent young boys to satisfy his perverse desires. I had him in my crosshairs.

The following day, Gouws went scouting for work using his one and only hundred per cent safe contact in Durban. The ex-convict and all-round scumbag, was aware and readily accepting of Piet's predicament. He had received a call from his associate in the Transvaal. 'Ten years in Pretoria Central . . . . shit he definitely deserves all the help he can get, at a price of course.'

At around four in the afternoon, nothing doing work wise, Pieter returned to his hotel. While retrieving his room key, the receptionist handed him an envelope. He rushed back to his hovel and hands all atremble tore it open. He anxiously removed a single foolscap sheet and with incredulity, read the typed words on the page.

'I KNOW WHO YOU ARE. YOU ARE TRASH OF THE
WORST KIND EVER.'

The bolded letters were not lost on him: **IOU ONE**

'What the Hell?' he said out loud. He lit a Camel, splashed a treble brandy into his toothbrush glass, downed it, poured again and re-read the message. The following morning Gouws checked out of the hotel and relocated to an even seedier establishment four blocks to the south.

'What a dumb bastard!' I thought, as I watched him make his transfer while planning the wording of my next communique.

Someone else was making mental notes from deep cover. 'So this is the bastard, the fucker who nearly killed Ben my life giver! If we ever meet face-to-face my man, we are going to have a lovely time together, mark my thoughts!'

Roddy, after much persuasion believed me. He was nevertheless concerned for my safety. 'Call the cops Ben, don't stuff around.' I had explained how I was planning on tormenting the dickhead before handing him over to the authorities.

I made an anonymous phone call to the police to confirm Pieter Gouws was a wanted man. I told a constable at the Durban South Police Station that I knew the current whereabouts of Gouws, the escapee from Pretoria Central. I added that I would tell them of his exact location within the day.

When I made the second call I confirmed my suspicions; he was definitely on the run; a wanted man. I was immediately patched through to a Detective Sheppard. He asked for my name and number. The sense of urgency in his tone removed any doubt I may have initially harboured. I replaced the receiver quickly thus thwarting any attempt at tracing my call. Had I been watching too many crime movies?

The following afternoon, the receptionist handed Gouws a second envelope. He tore it open, read the message and began to sweat profusely.

'YOU **CAN'T** GET AWAY WITH IT **YOU** SHIT. YOU ARE GOING STRAIGHT **TO** HELL!"

'Who gave you this?' he asked brusquely.
'Some guy dropped it off just after you left this morning Sir.'
'What did he look like?'
'A tallish, nice looking young man Sir. He was wearing sunglasses, probably in his early twenties' he answered politely and feigned respect, as instructed by the Greek hotel owner.

Was I right to torment Gouws? Was I right to withhold his whereabouts from the police? Yes and no respectively. I paid a young black boy one rand to deliver the third note. Gouws was still staying at the Sherwood Hotel. Either he was incredibly stupid or incredibly brave, I couldn't quite discern which.

He tore open the third note:

GO TO GROUND, HIDE UNDER COVER. AWAY WITH
YOU SATAN, AWAY I SAY. THE LORD SHALL FIND AND
SMITE YOU DOWN. TWO TIMES HE WILL SMITE
YOU DOWN.

He decided it was time to relocate. He was baffled. Had he been spotted by someone from his former life he questioned, a reporter, a former acquaintance having fun at his expense perhaps? There was another remote possibility; a parent of one of his victims or perhaps a victim out to torment him. He must get away from Durban. He had to shake this bastard loose.

Gouws disappeared into thin air. He booked out of the fleabag hotel and simply vanished. The receptionist was of little help. Gouws had forfeited five day's advance payment. He added that he had read a message left for him at the front desk and immediately booked out. Damn and blast, I had chased him away and I hadn't been around to follow him.

Not long after the nightclub fiasco, Joss and I had a serious debate on the meaning of selfishness. It was one of the few times a discussion had developed into a heated argument. It had become so heated in fact that she had walked out on me for a few days.

I had read an Ayn Rand book called 'The Virtue of Selfishness'. I rather enjoyed Rand's books particularly 'Atlas Shrugged' as I could associate with many of her points of view. Joselyn had laid into me.

'How can you read this right-wing capitalist rubbish? We have to give and give again without questioning our motives' she said with verve. 'I'm no socialist, but we can't live guiltless lives. We are morally indebted, compelled to give to the needy, the poor, the, the, the . . . disadvantaged' she stammered, 'the downtrodden for Christ's sake!' she said angrily, unaware of the glaring contradiction.

'You know what Ben? I'm shocked at you, falling for that right-wing bullshit! Who the hell is this Ayn Rand idiot to say everyone is responsible for their own well-being? What of the millions world-wide who *cannot* take care of themselves?'

'Let me speak' I implored, 'all I said was I can relate to some of her beliefs. Jesus Jocelyn, won't you calm down? And by the way, you say you are no socialist, well you certainly talk like one.'

She stood, snatched up her cigarettes and matches and stormed out, slamming the door behind her. What the Hell? What had I said? Okay, I had challenged her political persuasions, but not too long ago, Joss would have laughed and told me to 'shut the fuck up' with a giggle and that would have been that. She had seemed different after the Berea incident. Something had changed, which I couldn't quite put my finger on. She had become introspective, distanced and I was doubtful as to her reasons. I couldn't imagine the incident at the nightclub was the sole cause. Whenever I tried to question her regarding her preoccupation, she would merely shrug and say I was imagining things.

She returned from the Cape and we decided to spend the Saturday night at the Drakensberg Gardens Hotel. I made a booking and we drove off in my little MGB. It was a scenic three-hour drive to a rather quaint place in the foothills of the most majestic mountain range in Africa. We booked in, showered and walked the short distance from our room to the hotel bar to enjoy a pre-dinner drink or two.

The Drakensberg is the highest mountain range in Southern Africa, rising to 3,482 metres in height. Its geological history lends it a distinctive character amongst the mountain ranges of the world. Geologically the range resembles the Simien Mountains of Ethiopia. The range spans the Eastern Cape, Natal, Lesotho, Swaziland, the Eastern Transvaal and ending in Tzaneen in the far north of the country and is a most magnificent natural geological disturbance.

Joss started knocking back the wine like nobody's business. By the time we decided to go through to the dining room, she was slightly worse for wear. The hotel was oddly busy for that time of year and it seemed as if all the guests had decided to dine in concert.

Jocelyn ordered a bottle of Reisling from the waiter. As he decanted the wine, she looked at me and asked, 'what strikes you as unusual when you look around at all of these faces?'

'How do you mean?' I asked.

'They all have one thing in common' she replied. 'What is it?' she challenged me. 'I'm not following you' I said truthfully.

The waiter appeared at our table and requested our orders. Joss paused while we gave them to him and the waiter had left our table.

'Come on Ben. What do all these people share?'

The penny dropped. 'Is it a white face?' I asked carefully.

'Exactly, they are all white. Not one coloured, black or Indian face in sight.'

'Well the waiters are . . . . '

'Don't be glib Ben, not now.'

'I'm sorry' I immediately capitulated. 'Yes, I see what you mean.'

'Do you know why this is so? Because the Nats say so, that's why! These bloody idiots decide which little box people fit into; who lives where, who can work where and when. And now they've decided in what language children must be taught. They shot at kids, live rounds at school kids. Young people died because they objected to their language of tuition. I can see big changes coming. I just hope things don't spiral out of control and we end up in a civil war. The black man is angry Ben, and justifiably so.'

'Okay Joss, I agree with you. But it's not my fault. There's no need to raise your voice at me.'

'I'm sorry my lovely Benjy. It's just that the injustice of the whole system is getting to me. I had a row with Dad on Wednesday over the same thing.' She paused to take a sip of wine and her shoulders dropped slightly.

She continued, 'I won't say another word, I promise. Let's enjoy the rest of the weekend. And pour me some more wine shit-face. I love you.'

'I love you too my darling' I replied with concern.

On the Sunday morning, we found a secluded spot along the river where we swam and made fervent love, standing up in the chilly mountain stream. Joselyn screamed shamelessly as her orgasm shuddered through her. Her screams of delight made me climax in a spasm of ecstasy exacerbated by the image of the two of us being furtively observed as we expressed our unadulterated love for one another.

Jocelyn seemed so much more relaxed on the drive back and placed her hand firmly on my upper thigh the entire journey home as if to say 'I am yours and you are mine'. We stopped at a farm stall outside the small village of Underberg and bought dried fruit, biltong and homemade jams.

We arrived home, dropped our luggage on the floor and proceeded to make love with a fierce passion alien to us; rough and completed within minutes. In retrospect, I think it was our way of exclaiming a parting of the ways. We had mutually envisaged the future and we were destined to live it separately. I'm known to be occasionally mistaken, thank the good Lord above.

CHAPTER SEVEN

J oss and I registered to do honours in our chosen fields and Margaret gave birth to twins on Dingaan's Day, the 16th of December. Danie and my sister named the boys Benjamin and Joseph. This caused more than a few quiet tears at the christening. My Dad however, wept openly and unabashed. Steve sobbed too. Mom looked embarrassed.

The family rarely mentioned Joseph's name as it always produced the same result. Well they would have to get over it wouldn't they. I was never that close to Joseph; although he had been a big factor in my formative years, the age gap had hindered that special bond that can form between brothers of a closer age. Stephen and Joseph, I've been told, were inseparable, yet Steve had been fortunate to do his mourning at the appropriate time.

Instead of spending another holiday abroad, my parents had decided to sponsor Uncle James and Aunt Margaret's holiday to South Africa. They would be 'chaperoned' around the country by my parents, from the Kruger Park to Cape Town and then along the garden route, up to the Berg and back home to Toti. Joss and I were somewhat envious and proposed doing the same one day in the near future, perhaps after completing our studies. Were we being too optimistic, considering the rift growing ever so wider between us?

Stephen had applied for a coaching position for a first division football team in the Transvaal. The Mcpherson family was rather disappointed to learn that any wedding plans were on hold. His fiancée Louise had been appointed as project manager on upgrade work to the South Beach aquarium and was consequently contractually tied for at least two years. She told us that it would add a lot of weight to her CV. I treasured family gatherings. So much love and caring and so much to learn!

❦

I 'awoke' with a sickly sweet taste in my mouth. It was as if I had sucked on a can of golden syrup. I was nauseous and exhausted. I had difficulty staying upright. My head was throbbing and I had the smell of stale alcohol about me. I could sense Alan's presence.

Something induced me to examine my hands. I turned them over and inspected them carefully in the glow of the street lamp. They were covered in what at first glance appeared to be a dull red paint of some kind. Definitely a matte red I decided and for a moment or two cackled uncontrollably like a maniac in a B grade horror movie. For some rhyme or reason, the idea of my hands coated with paint, there in the night, appealed to my sense of humour, or was it perhaps Alan's take on the situation? The circumstances were absurd, absolutely bizarre.

The dense treacly miasma in my brain began to dissolve. I gradually returned from the unknown. Then the panic and dread began to undulate through my veins in a hot rush of molten fear. I looked around. 'Come on let's pull ourselves together. Where are we?' Then I became conscious of the fact that my thoughts were processing in the plural tense. The sweat on my face turned ice-cold. Stop it Ben! I shook my head aggressively from side to side as if to shake him from my brain.

Think rationally Benjamin Mcpherson! Where am I? How did I get here, wherever 'here' is? What time is it? What's the last thing I remember? What had I been up to in 'Cloud Cuckoo Land'? I looked around uncertainly. 'This is Point Road!' I said out loud to nobody there. 'Can't be' I thought, 'it's deserted.' I glanced at my watch; the digital display flashed 03:10 in bright red numerals. 'What's going on?' I tried to reason, 'it's three in the morning and I'm alone in one of the most dangerous areas of Durban.' I was standing on the corner of Point Road and Rutherford Street. I re-examined my hands and realised the 'paint' was dried blood. I raised my hand to my nose and I recognised the odour; it was a salty, coppery mixture; the unmistakeable smell of blood. The front of my shirt was stained red. I noticed a bulge in my pocket. I stuck my hand in and retrieved a bloodied carpet trimmer. I returned it quickly to my pocket as I glanced around furtively.

Shit, what had Alan or Alex been up to in the dock area at this time of night? Blank, blank, blank it all out. Go to a happy place. Blank it out. My consciousness began to recede. I was drifting away. I made a concerted effort to remain cognisant and awake. Fight Ben, you can't acquiesce. I instinctively understood that if I allowed my conscience to be purloined, I may never retrieve it.

I drifted back and forth, coming and going. Had my arch-enemy declared outright war for domination of my temple, my holy shrine? I sensed my adversary gaining ground. I will not give in Alan. You are not as strong as I am, you conniving bastard.

'Are you okay sir?' I assumed Alan had fled into the dark recesses of my mind, scurried by the voice of the taxi driver.

'Can you please take me home?' I asked, patting my pockets for signs of my wallet.

'Certainly sir' he replied. I surmised he had seen worse in this part of town.

The taxi dropped me off at the main entrance. I looked up at our apartment on the third floor, lights ablaze, definitely not good news. I climbed the fire escape reluctantly. I knew that Joss would demand the truth the whole truth and then some and I was worn-out, I felt thoroughly drained. I would not be able to supply her with any plausible account of tonight's events, not tonight Joss, maybe in the morning . . . maybe.

I am lying in a foetal position on a church pew. It is as cold as death itself. Sitting to my right is an old couple. A peculiar looking man is wading up the aisle, almost engulfed by the dark torrent. He clutches a sword in his deformed, talon-shaped hand. There are channels of red sludge flowing down arched walls. I can see all of this without turning my head.

A young man is standing at the pulpit, staring at me with a look of scepticism as if to ask 'Why are you here? What is your business in the House of the Lord?' I try to answer but I am struck mute. I am speechless. In a flash, the young man disappears from the podium and re-appears hanging from a Crucifix that weighs heavily around my neck.

The man to my right transforms into a tree with branches for arms and knots for eyes. He looks at me sadly. He begins to juggle a ball and then smirks malevolently. The tree-man tosses his oval-shaped missile into the air as the old hag squatting next to him screams a caveat at me. I watch in abject terror as the projectile soars higher and higher, sailing through the trusses, surpassing the church steeple in altitude and out into the perfectly blue sky above. The elliptical weapon slows and begins to spiral downwards in its long agonising descent toward its intended target.

I awoke with a jolt, remnants of the nightmare spinning around inside my head. Memories of last night came rushing back like an incoming tsunami. Joss was sleeping at my side. I gave the wall clock a cursory glance; almost nine-thirty. I had tossed and turned for almost six hours.

I had entered the apartment to find Joss asleep on the sofa. She stirred and jumped to her feet. Before she was awarded the chance to start in on me, I said with finality, 'in the morning I'll tell all my love. I'll try to explain it in the morning. Right now I'm going to shower and then to bed.' She didn't say a word; the look on her face said enough.

We sat at the kitchen nook with a glass of orange-juice and a bowl of Pro Nutro in front of us.

'Joss, I have things to tell you, which I have hidden from you forever.' She scrutinised me as a scientist would examine a particularly repulsive germ under a microscope.

Please listen to what I have to say' I pleaded. 'It's not that I didn't *want* to tell you, I never knew how.'

'Go on' she said, with restrained fury.

'Two years ago, I was diagnosed with multiple personality disorder or MPD.'

'I know what MPD is Ben and it's a big deal!' she shot back impatiently. 'Why have you waited for two years to share this with me, with your soul-mate Ben? Damn it, that hurts.'

'Joss please listen, I had an episode last night that scares me to death! I 'disappeared' for I don't know how long. I don't know what I did, where I was and what I did when I was travelling. I woke up or regained consciousness or whatever in Point Road. Love, my hands were covered with blood; I had blood all down the front of my shirt. I know you noticed it when I walked in last night.'

'This morning' she corrected me.

'This morning' I assented. 'Plus I had this in my pocket.' I placed the bloody Stanley knife on the kitchen table.

'Oh shit!' she exclaimed. 'What are you telling me Ben?' she asked anxiously.

'I don't know Joss. I don't remember a damn thing. I'm scared love. It's like I have this evil alter-ego trying to take over my life!' I was beginning to get panicky.

'Okay my love, calm down.' Her mood had turned from anger to concern. 'Point Road you say? Maybe you just got into a fight or something.'

'Joss, you know I have never had a fight in my entire life. And where did the Stanley knife come from?' I asked. 'And by the way, he calls himself Alan' I added.

'Your alter-ego is called Alan?'

'Yep, he calls himself Alan' I replied.

'There has to be a rational explanation to all of this' Joss said hopefully.

'I was on pills for a while' I answered. 'They didn't work and I felt nauseous all the time. Do you remember a couple of years ago, when I was constantly bitching about queasiness? You said I should see a doctor.'

'Yes I do remember' she replied. 'And then all of a sudden the nausea disappeared. 'Okay, so you stopped medicating?' Jocelyn asked. I nodded in reply.

We determined that she had arrived home at five-fifteen. I wasn't here, so she left a note asking me to join her at her parent's townhouse for dinner. She'd called numerous times during the evening and had eventually returned to an empty apartment sometime after ten. Apparently, I hadn't been back to our apartment since playing squash with Roddy the previous afternoon. She sprang up and turned on the portable radio on the window ledge. The eleven o' clock news bulletin was about to start. There was nothing, no reports of killers on the prowl. It made me feel no less apprehensive. The following three days produced the same result.

The 'Pride of the Sea', a cargo vessel of some thirty thousand tons destined for Japan, set sail the following Friday minus one sailor. The junior crew member had already delayed the ship's departure by one day. The Captain was not a happy fellow. He would ensure this scoundrel never set foot on any ship under his command ever again. The authorities had been informed accordingly and the required documentation had been filled out in triplicate.

Three days after the Japanese vessel departed South African waters, the body of a badly decomposed young man of eastern origin was discovered by a stevedore on the fore shore. The corpse had been concealed behind a rusty row of long forgotten containers. He was naked, his penis and scrotum had been removed and were nowhere to be found.

After two weeks, the local CID closed the investigation and concluded that it had probably been as a result of one of two scenarios; a homosexual relationship turned sour and nasty, or a triad hit. 'After all' a detective reasoned, 'he's only a slant eye'. 'And anyway' another officer observed, 'Pyong Tong's ship has already sailed.' The docket was sent to central filing.

To add to my problems, I received a phone call from Jocelyn's professor. He informed me that she had been missing a lot of post-graduate classes. Before he chatted to her, he decided to call me to see whether I could shine some light on her tardiness. I had tons of respect for Professor Tattersall and if he had made the effort to call me, it must be rather serious. It seemed she had become immersed in campus politics joining all the student protests and generally neglecting her studies.

I was taken unawares. She'd not mentioned any participation in student marches or protests. Frankly, I considered her too old to be getting involved with this crap. She was an honours student, a post-grad for God's sake, not some second-year hothead attempting to change the world. The Prof asked whether he should talk to her and what did I think? I told him to let it be. I would have a chat with her and get back to him.

Shortly afterwards, before I had found it convenient to have a chat, Joss arrived home one afternoon with a dinner guest; some scruff who went by the handle of Red Rogers. When Joss introduced the two of us, the old shackles did their thing. I immediately labelled him as an arrogant, know-it-all bastard. He was a final-year student completing a general BA degree and president of the Students' Representative Council. Spot on!

What with my hatred of all things political, it was hard for me to comprehend how our relationship had survived the last couple of years. But we had decided after the incident up in the Berg to keep political discussions to the minimum and only when both sober and now this reprobate waltzes in! Joss was carrying a couple of bottles of white wine, which further pissed me off.

I informed her I would cook spaghetti bolognaise and disappeared into the kitchen. I hadn't wanted to be left alone to suffer small talk with Roy Rogers or whatever his name was. I could hear the two of them laughing and joking as I browned the onions. She had blatantly invited the enemy into our home and I was fuming!

Before we ate, I called Joss into the kitchen, under the pretence of not knowing where something or other was kept. I demanded of her to refrain from discussing politics at the table. She reluctantly agreed. She had seen fury in my eyes and probably decided she hadn't wanted a scene. The conversation that spewed out of his mouth was obtuse and immature. Red, my man, you are going to have a lot to answer for! And I had a gut feeling he would. It was almost as if I had a premonition, a forewarning of things to come.

CHAPTER EIGHT

L ife goes on, at least for some lucky souls. I had become a serial killer. No, that is not entirely accurate. The killing was taking place on my 'watch' and on a regular basis, but I was never in attendance, I was oblivious, I wasn't the perpetrator as such.

What was I to do? If I came clean, I would hang. Jocelyn and I had discussed every possible solution and it always boiled down to two scenarios; one, I handed myself over to the law and let justice take its course. Joselyn was averse to this because, 'the wrong man would be executed and I love that man' she reasoned. And she made a good point. The second alternative was untenable; don't do anything, sweep it under the proverbial carpet and pray that Alan stopped his murderous spree. There was however a third alternative; get treatment, which would be very risky.

I believed Alan was mentally sluggish, but most devious and I believed this to be an accurate judgment. Deviousness never is a true measure of intelligence as intelligence is never a guarantee of success. Alan was and remains the most cunning and conniving character I have ever had the misfortune with whom to share my body.

In mid-winter of 1978, Alan and Alex decided to take a vacation. The killing and mutilations of homosexual deviants in the greater Durban area came to an abrupt halt. Had I been let off the hook? Had Alan concluded his war of attrition against me? Had he conceded me as the victor?

I was receiving cognitive behavioural therapy or CBT for clinical depression by a psychotherapist, one Dr Shields. CBT is a psychotherapy based on modifying cognitions, assumptions, beliefs and behaviours with the aim of influencing disturbed emotions. At that time, it was a relatively new therapeutic technique. I hadn't mentioned any of Alan's escapades to her. I however shared my 'travelling experiences' and after a month of intensive analysis, she reaffirmed the initial diagnosis as MPD and commenced CBT. I understood the doctor patient privacy thing however, I remember reading somewhere that this became null and void if the patient had or could conceivably cause harm to others. Whether this was factual or not, I was not prepared to find out.

She suggested hypnotherapy. I vehemently refused, stating I abhorred all things supernatural. She found this rather amusing but didn't push the issue. What horror stories would Alan perhaps relay to the doctor behind my back? She then suggested a course of some new drug on the market in conjunction with the therapy and I was happy to give my consent.

Whether it was the medication or the treatment didn't concern me. I became my old self; optimistic and self-confident and my depression finally dissipated. Joss and I discussed our future and realised the only way to move forward with our lives was to pretend to forget. Blank, blank, blank it all out. We must not let ourselves fixate on the unfortunate victims. We were hanging on to the threads of our stormy relationship and my predicament was helping us to forget just how precarious it had become.

I was concerned about the possibility of Alan leaving clues or evidence at the scene that could point the investigating team in my direction. I was convinced Alan had committed at least three killings; the blood, the 'awakenings' in strange places, the sweet syrupy leftover taste and the powerful recollections of Alan succeeding these episodes. Plus, the carpet knives were piling up. Whenever a police van or ambulance passed by sirens blaring, my veins would flow hot as if they had been injected with boiling iodine.

In May and June uMkhonto we Sizwe sabotaged two strategic targets; SASOL 1 and 11. There were fortunately no fatalities. The timing of the attacks was apparently to coincide with Republic Day, celebrated on the 31st of May. I recall a comment Joss made after hearing the news, 'Not the first and definitely not the last. What do you think Ben?' 'I don't think it's the correct tactic to win over the enemy Joss. The result will be an even more determined and stubborn government. The consequence of an eye for an eye type conflict is a nation of blind people. I imagine you think I've been brain-washed, but I think dialogue is the way to go.' I was twenty six and politically naive but it made sense to me. Joss scoffed at me saying with a sneer, 'you know what Ben, you stick to your music and leave politics to me.' She had touched a raw nerve; she was well aware of my relative ignorance of the affairs of state.

'Jeezus alright Joss, hell's teeth keep your hat on!'

'There are times when I wish you would grow up Ben and smell the friggin' roses.'

Jocelyn was arrested on Friday 8th September. There had been a protest outside the Town Hall in West Street and approximately forty riot police had been deployed in armoured cars to disperse these 'blerry betogers' or bloody protestors, these 'tak hare' or long-haired louts.

She was at the vanguard of the protest, shouting obscenities and using impolite sign language. She stooped, picked up a loose brick and without any forethought hurled it at the centre of the swarming riot police. Joss, felled by a rubber bullet to the stomach, hit the tar and cried out in pain; 'you fucking pigs!' Shortly after, she was man-handled into the back of a police van. I sat on a bench in the charge office waiting for Joss to be bailed. Where was this all heading and when was it going to end?

I had to make some serious decisions in my life. I had recently been awarded a PhD in music and was lecturing at varsity. Rumour had it, I was to be offered a permanent position in the near future; tenure before thirty was extremely alluring. My mental tormentors had all but disappeared, Jocelyn, on the other hand, had quit varsity after scraping together an honours degree. She had flitted from one job to the other and was currently doing God knows what for the Black Sash. We were living two different lives and it was destroying me.

We were enjoying a lazy Sunday lunch on the Borristers' farm. Rodney had invited us to join them, as an old friend and his wife, who played cello for the Johannesburg Symphony Orchestra, were holidaying in Amanzimtoti. Jocelyn's Mom had prepared a sumptuous spread and in due course the talk turned to music.

'Music is pure indulgence. There are far more important issues to spend one's time on.' Jocelyn stated out of the blue and totally unprovoked.

'The world is full of inequality, famine and disease and people waste precious time on frivolities like music.'

This was *my* Jocelyn? I could hardly believe my ears. For her to embarrass her parents and their friends was totally out of character. I recognised right then and there that our relationship was coming to an end; we were drifting apart. The very thing that had originally brought us together was gnawing away at the fabric of our erstwhile relationship. A most awkward silence ensued.

Her father turned scarlet. Yet, his obvious wrath, under impeccable control said: 'Jocelyn my darling, first I expect you to apologise for that uncalled outburst.'

I watched Jocelyn as her father admonished her. It was her turn to redden.

'Second' he continued, 'please inform us who filled your head with such nonsense.'

'But I . . . '

'Please wait, I'm not quite finished' her father interrupted doggedly, yet with affection. 'Have you any idea how music down the ages has improved the lot of humanity, the rich and the poor?' he continued. 'It brings peace, joy and optimism to millions upon millions of the oppressed, the poor and the starving and diseased people of the world.'

'I didn't mean to be disrespectful. I was merely trying to explain how I feel about things.'

'There's a time and place for everything my love. This was neither the time nor the place to express politically motivated ideals on your badly misinformed musical philosophies' he chided her, 'especially when we are blessed with two fine musicians in our midst.'

'I apologise profusely to all present' Joss declared. 'My timing is poor but my tenets stand unwaveringly.'

Needless to say, Joss and I had not stayed for tea and cake. We made our apologies and proceeded back to Durban in silence, using our time to prepare for the inevitable row of all rows which would undoubtedly ensue.

Jocelyn asked for a 'trial separation' as if we were an old married couple. I readily agreed. I reasoned some time apart may lead to a rekindling of our respect and caring for one another. We were both well aware of our unwavering love; it was the political differences that had hammered into place a substantial wedge between us.

The fine details were negotiated and I vacated our 'matrimonial home'. I moved in with my parents until I could decide what was to become of me. Could I survive, deprived of the one person I truly loved? I acknowledge my love for Stephen and Margaret, I love my parents, and I love Roddy and Jocelyn's Mom and Dad along with the multitudes, all in my own unique way. My love for and devotion to Jocelyn scaled higher dominions. Years before, we had declared our undying love. It had been mystical; a devotion one reads about in cheap romance novels written by ladies clothed in pink.

My family was distraught. 'How has this tragedy come about?' 'Have one of you been unfaithful?' 'What on earth happened?' they asked. They needed answers as did I. Should I have fought harder? Should I have been more aware and supportive? Should I have compromised with greater sincerity and added gusto? There were so many questions and so few answers. I would, I knew, surely languish in her absence, of this I was certain.

I had one weapon in my emotional munitions store; work. I set out indomitably to be awarded the permanent post up for grabs at the university. To be offered tenure at my tender age was rare and highly venerated. I was putting in the extra hours and kissing the required backsides. The hard work and kowtowing paid dividends and I was appointed Head of Department. Not a well-paid position by any means, but nevertheless, a rewarding station, which fortunately occupied most of my time and thoughts.

⚓

Steve and Louise announced their marriage, which created immense euphoria within the family. I deliberated on hearing of their approaching betrothals; had Joss and I swapped marriage vows, would we have overcome the stumbling block of incompatible political sentiments?

The big day came. Everybody was suited up, clad and coiffed to perfection. The bride looked magnificent, flowing and beautiful. Steve came across as fetching, carrying with him an air of certainty and confidence. His look screamed sanguinity, as if to pronounce to all and sundry, 'I am me and she is me and we are all together!' 'And what are you going to do about it?' What magic, what a mystery, what a tour! When they kneeled at the altar I noticed that someone had stuck 'left' and 'right' signs on the soles of his shoes.

The reception was held at the highly exclusive Durban Club, situated on the Esplanade across from the Durban Yacht Club. The best man, Stewart Clough told a joke that day, which I have told many times. 'Two aerials meet on a roof and decide to marry. The wedding was fair, but the reception was outstanding.' Another thing he said which really tickled me; 'I have enough money to live comfortably for the rest of my life, as long as I die by next Tuesday.'

I had been seated at the 'odds and sods' table where the sad sacks are placed, those unfortunate souls devoid of the remotest possibility of attracting a partner until their late forties, if they are lucky. They eventually attract one another—commonality being the key—as surely as a burglar is drawn to an unlocked door. They settle down to a life of mundane, cataleptic drudgery, while clumsily turning out replica offspring. These freakish clones promulgate and disseminate their damaged viscous and scruffy and jaded genes and hence propagate the circle of 'odds and sods' life.

These were my thoughts as I sat in my 'odds and sods' chair, allocated to me on that most auspicious of occasions. I was feeling conspicuous, the proverbial sore thumb. I'd been hit on by a buck-toothed young lady with eyebrow-searing halitosis and decided to get very drunk. I summoned a waiter and ordered a large Scotch on the rocks. I gulped it down and immediately ordered a second. My psychotherapist had warned me off alcohol. 'It will negate the effects of your medication' she informed me. 'Fuck her' I decided angrily, as the first whisky hit the spot.

My interest in the rather gorgeous female who sat herself down opposite, had obviously been heightened by my copious, profuse intake of good quality Scotch.

Hi, I'm Benjamin' I slurred. 'Hi Benjamin, I'm Carol, Carol Moir' she replied soberly. 'Who are you in the zoo?' she solicited knowingly. 'I'm the groom's brother' I answered with difficulty. 'And where do you fit in?' 'Your new sister-in-law told me I would meet a handsome doctor if I attended her wedding. Have you seen him?' she asked.

I wasn't ready for a relationship but I was horny and pretty inebriated. It was all her fault I had been placed at this 'ship of fools' table and it irked me. I was angry with Jocelyn; she had declined the wedding invitation with no reason forthcoming. Stephen and Louise were astounded and I was shocked to the core. Louise had set me up with a blind date. She's a sneaky girl, our newly proclaimed Mrs Mcpherson. 'I must remember to thank her' I promised myself. I bought a gin and tonic for Carol and another double for me.

She worked at the aquarium with Louise. She had recently divorced an abusive husband and lived in Morningside on the north side of the city. 'Fortunately we didn't have kids' she informed me. Carol was roughly five foot ten, slender, capped with thick auburn hair. She was more handsome than pretty, however the whole package was very striking. Or was I merely checking her out, appraising her through rose-tinted 'whisky' glasses?

Stephen approached the table.

'I spoke to the band and asked them if they would mind if you sang 'Bridge over Troubled Waters' and they said no problem.'

'You rat!' I replied with a grin. Although I was a bit stewed, I knew the song backward. It was one of Stephen's all-time favourites. I must have sung it a thousand times. 'No problem, my big bruvver' I informed him. Louise's father had hired an exceptionally competent five piece that performed the song perfectly. It went down a treat and I received a standing ovation.

This must have impressed Carol; when I returned to my seat, she had rearranged the seating plan and when I took my place, she immediately laid her hand on my thigh.

'Not exactly up to Garfunkel's standards, was it?' I realised as soon as I spoke, I was looking for approval and praise from this fine specimen of womanhood, who was improving by the tot. She smiled at me and squeezed my leg provocatively.

The reception went the way of most receptions; children took over the dance floor, flailing their arms about madly and one or two male guests drunkenly stumbling around, kissing and hugging all the pretty young things. The bride tossed her garter, the cake was cut and Steve and Louise bid their farewells and vanished into the night. Mauritius was their choice of destination after spending their first night as man and wife in the Royal Hotel's honeymoon suite. I bid my farewells also;

I couldn't exactly ask Carol to accompany me 'home' for a nightcap or whatever. My 'home' consisted of a single bedroom in my parent's house. I contemplated asking her if I could perhaps follow her back to Morningside and then thought better of it. It was the booze and my libido talking. We swapped numbers and I arranged to give her a call the next day. I escorted her to where her car was parked. On our way, I sensed reluctance, unwillingness on her behalf to part ways.

The 8th Of December, 1980 on the other side of the world, a tragedy of epic proportions occurred; a disillusioned and damaged young man named Mark David Chapman, shot and killed John Winston Lennon outside The Dakota apartments in New York. This most tragic of deaths, was like losing a very dear friend. Stephen and I, along with millions all around the world, went into mourning. It had been a senseless and ridiculous slaying of a true genius, of a poet and composer that shocked and saddened his fans and a multitude of others to the core.

A man entered a well-known gay club on Smith Street. He paid the exorbitant entrance fee—inflated to deter would-be rabble-rousers and homophobes—and sauntered provocatively toward the bar situated in a dark recess beyond the dance floor of flashing cool-blue strobes. He was dressed in the latest fashion, including an expensive jacket of brown crushed leather, a dandy; a 'follower of fashion'. The lighting was subdued making the individual's facial features hard to discern, which suited the man. He found a stool at the corner of the bar and took a perfunctory glance around the room. It was after midnight, late-night prowlers continued to enter the club in dribs and drabs. He had caused a small wave of interest which rippled through the few scattered hunters yet to 'score'.

He ordered a glass of wine from, in his opinion, 'a screaming queen of a barman' and sipped it with an air of aloofness, the wine glass being a mere prop; occasionally slowly raised to his lips with effeminate flair, would sustain the pursuers' curiosity. His body language hollered: 'I am available 'girls'!'

He was approached by a tall gangly individual. His face, the man noticed, even under the flattering lighting, bared the deep potholed history of teenage acne. He had an elongated head, which reminded the man of a giraffe, albeit a spotty, pimply giraffe. Notwithstanding his, to say the least, mundane appearance, resided a confident and well-spoken young man.

'Peter' he said by way of introduction. 'And you are?' he asked. The man hesitated momentarily, as if deciding to reveal his name or not, whispered 'Alan.' He flashed Peter a dazzling 'come on' smile.

They shared another drink and Peter, totally infatuated and sexually aroused, eagerly agreed to accompany him back to Alan's hotel room. Mr Alan Smith unlocked the room and by way of inviting his lover inside said, 'I'm going to use the bathroom. I'll be with you in a jiffy. Why don't you get undressed so long?' Alan exited the bathroom naked to find Peter, prone on the bed, playing with his engorged giraffe-like appendage.

He dimmed the overhead lighting and lay down close to Peter. He reached over and began to fondle Peter's enlarged and stiffened member while sticking his tongue down the throat of this most willing lover. He slipped his free hand underneath the pillow and extracted a Stanley knife with its blade fully extended. In the semi-darkness, he calmly and with all the down-force he could muster, pulled the knife across his victim's throat, slicing through the oesophagus and ceratoid artery. Peter made a gurgling sound as large crimson bubbles rose and popped about the wound, as his limbs involuntarily flayed about like a shoddily choreographed marionette. The blood sprayed about the room and finally slowed to a leak; the mortal gash irretrievably offering up all it had. Alan lay partially over him, weighing him down, continuing to clasp the rapidly dying man's penis as it wilted and withered away; the engorging fluids changing course, as his blood pressure dropped to zero over zero.

Alan carefully and with much love and care, detached the flaccid and droopy organ from Peter's dead torso, as if he were a renowned surgeon, demonstrating the correct procedure to a bunch of interns in the viewing room above. As he operated on his ingenuous patient, his loins reacted and he became stiff with pleasure. 'This is for you my darling Ben' Alan said ingratiatingly.

After masturbating apathetically, 'it' being a burden as opposed to an act of preference, Alan Mcpherson flushed his short-lived meaty trophy and a pair of bloodied surgical gloves down the toilet bowl. 'You wanted to wallow in shit you sick bastard, now you can mosey in it for eternity you arschole sniffing bitch.' He showered, dressed, and wiped the room down thoroughly for any overlooked fingerprints, and via the fire escape, stole away unseen, into the night.

I was a honey badger; I was an ursine creature gorging on honey combs. The saccharine-treacly sensation had me gagging. I felt as if I had been stuffed with candyfloss and mounted; the dupe of an acutely deranged taxidermist.

Block, block, block it out. Think good thoughts. Blank, blank, blank it *all* out. Go to a happy place, go to Joss. No, I can't go *there*. My vision cleared and instinctively scrutinised my hands—clean, my clothes—clean. There was a small stain on the front of my shirt; whisky I surmised. The wedding and reception, ship of fools, an attractive female, Carol. After that I remembered zilch. I glanced at my watch, three ten. The scenario called for routine, check my clothes then the time and finally my whereabouts.

I looked about; I was standing beside my trustworthy MGB. The reflection of an overhead neon sign shone back at me off the highly-polished bodywork. I recognised my location in an instant, Smith Street outside a hotel, adjacent to a CNA book shop. Patting my trouser pockets, I discovered, to my relief, car keys in one and nothing in the other. My suit jacket gave up a half packet of Lucky Strike plain and a Ransom lighter. I must get away from here, urgently, as soon as I can navigate safely. I staggered to the rear of the car, exhausted and with hands atremble, inserted the boot key, without any reason or purpose, as if drawn there by a junk yard magnet. Inside, laid out neatly on the rug, was my tan leather half-coat with a Stanley carpet trimmer placed on top. My nemesis had returned.

I am galloping along on the inside of a Ferris wheel. My features are stretched, elongated. I realise why; I'm a horse, equus on the run. I see an exit ahead. I must hurry as it incessantly grows smaller. How can anything 'grow' smaller? I ponder this and gaze beyond, through the bars of the wheel and I see a grotesque caricature of myself glaring back, through a curtain of water, a misty saturated veil. My nails are painted bright red. My shirt and coat are cut from a bolt of green, a leafy green.

I sit at a dais, banging my wooden gavel with enormous force. The dais splits. 'Judge Mac presiding, you are sentenced to death and henceforth struck down from a blow through the brain for eternity.' 'Are you listening sickos?' The condemned throngs stagger threateningly towards me. They are dead. No, they are zombies, the living dead lurching, clutching swords and scales in their bony hands. The stench of them is offensive, sickening. A siren wails and I gallop off on a llama, mounted upon my own saddle.

On awakening, I struggled to capture the essence of this unusual and most remarkable dream. It hadn't frightened me as my earlier nightmares used to; this outing down the rabbit hole had been bizarre, inexplicable and irresolvable. I knew the origins of my nocturnal visions; Alan, the night-stalker, the maniacal avenger. We are, each and every last one of us, a product of our past, our conditioning and experiences and unfortunately or not our genetic make-up. I believe we are a concoction, a blend of both nurture and nature. The normal, sane human being, if there is such an animal, has obtained the right mental balance by fluke or old-fashioned good luck.

Roddy once said to me, 'you know what Ben? I am of the opinion that every last person in the world is mad, totally off their rockers, except for you and me. And if the truth be known, I'm not too sure about you.' He roared with laughter. Roddy was a lot closer to the truth than he could ever have imagined.

Sunday morning witnessed neither hide nor hair of me. I had dozed unfittingly on and off throughout the best part of the day. I awoke, post meridian; by my Mom's knocking, she entered tray in hand. 'Sorry Benjy, I was worried. We didn't hear you come in.' 'Thanks Mom' I replied, as she handed me the tray of tea and biscuits. 'I came in late' I added truthfully, relieved she hadn't asked of my whereabouts after the reception. At that stage, I could not have lied to my mother.

Mom said with a warm and loving smile, 'Sunday lunch is on the Salton; Yorkshire pudding, leg of lamb, tatties and the rest. Marge and Danie were here. Your 'Swaar' ate the lion's portion of the pudding' and laughed. 'But there's ample left darling.' 'Great, thanks Mom. I'll be through shortly.'

Shit! I had promised Carol Moir I would call her. I retrieved her number from my back pocket of my trousers and dialled. It rang unanswered for half a minute and I hung up. It's after three in the afternoon I cursed myself. As I replaced the hand-set, the phone rang, startling me. I answered, and this heartbroken voice said, 'Ben? Is that you?' It was Joss. 'Hello Joss' I said reticently.

'Benjy, my darling Benjy, I've missed you so badly.' There was a stony silence. 'Have you missed me Benjamin?'

'Of course I have.' There was another moment's silence.

'Ben, for some reason I woke up in the middle of the night and cried thinking about you and your dilemma. I've been plucking up the courage to call you all day long' Jocelyn sounded jittery, strung out. 'Did something happen to you last night? Has Alan been interfering again Ben?'

How uncanny! I thought 'It looks that way Joss' I replied solemnly.

She shot back, 'I knew it! My God Ben, are you alright? What happened? Can we meet somewhere and talk?'

'I would like that.'

And for the first time since that day in hospital back in 1965, my levee burst; I sobbed as a wet and hungry new born would, yearning after its' absent caregiver. Embarrassed, I asked 'call me tomorrow at the varsity?' through my sniffling and snivelling. How had she known? Where we truly 'one'? Had it required another 'attack' to reunite us? And of greater importance to me, was I heading for a nervous breakdown?

'Death in Room 505!' the headline yelled at me from the vendor's board. I had wasted the half-hour commute into town strategizing an approach to Joss; should I appear apathetic or enthusiastic, uncaring or fervent? To strike a balance would be difficult. I've always worn my heart on my sleeve. How ironic; I had, without a shadow of a doubt murdered an innocent man in Room 505 and here I was concerning myself on how to strike the correct balance with Jocelyn. Had I developed 'qua sera' insolence and had I adapted to and normalised these appalling set of circumstances?

There were a couple of novel twists however; first not a drop of blood, neither on my clothes nor on the murder weapon and second, he had been 'considerate' enough to 'drop me off' at my car. Was Alan looking after me, his life-giver? I was preoccupied with these new developments when my phone rang, it was Joss; 'I'm in the staff cafeteria.' I was shaken by the amount of weight she had shed. She appeared gaunt, emaciated. It undermined her natural beauty. Her cheeks were deep-set and her eyes were underscored with shadows of deep cobalt, her ribs strained to escape her tight chemise. She greeted me with a gorgeous smile and a lengthy embrace.

I first told her of the new expansions of Alan's modus operandi. We became more and more at ease in each other's company and within twenty minutes were comfortable and untroubled as if we had never been apart; holding hands across the table, like two love-sick puppies waiting on their single bowl of spaghetti. She had always been able to evoke a pathetic, succumbing part of my psyche. It had resurfaced and once again I was smitten. I was simultaneously aware that we had lost something, something elusive had fallen by the way side.

We read the sparse report together: 'Det. So-and-So stated,' 'body discovered,' 'not yet identified,' 'hotel whatever,' 'in room number such and such.' There was nothing of substance, the stock-in-trade report; change a few names and places and voila, a hot-off-the-press account of current happenings.

'What do you think brought this on Ben?' my undernourished Jocelyn asked.

'I cocked up' I replied. 'I got pissed at Steve's wedding.'

She lowered her head momentarily as if apologising for her absence.

'The psychologist warned me that alcohol would negate the effects of the medication. I'm an arsehole, a total dickhead. How bloody irresponsible! I get drunk and some poor sod has to die Joss.'

'Listen my darling; we've been down this road before. It's no use covering old ground. How do we get over this my love? How can I help you?' she asked in a tone set with conspiracy.

Her use of the personal pronoun gave me a warm feeling right down to my socks. 'We' she had said. God! I'm so vulnerable; such a sucker for punishment.

'I will have to shun alcohol in its entirety. I can never let him out of his cage again' I said cogently. 'I would have to continue with the medication as prescribed forever. I slipped up and I could slip up again. I can't get through this. I have to know who Alan killed and why. If he turns out to be some average Joe, I'll have to consider turning myself in.'

'You can't. We've done this Ben. Why should you be punished?'

'Because I'm guilty, I did the killing, not some invention. It's *me* who's doing the slashing and cutting, my hands and my body. I can't carry on blaming this monster inside of me. It's me; I'm the killer, the perpetrator, the fucking guilty party. Can you not realise that Jocelyn? I cannot be judge, jury and executioner any more. I just can't.' I took a drink of coffee, lit a smoke and continued. 'What I've just told you may sound banal or clichéd and defeatist, but I can't carry on living a life on the run.'

'You are *not* 'on the run' Benjy!' Joss interrupted.

'Joss, I spend every day listening for the sound of police sirens, expecting a loud banging on my door at any time of the day or night. Not on the run? Think again.'

We sat in silence for a few moments and then Jocelyn dropped a bombshell.

'I'm going to Russia for a while. I've been given a bursary to complete my studies under Professor Lebedeva at Moscow State.'

'What?' I yelled. People turned their heads. 'You're doing what?' I asked in a more subdued voice.

'I know this isn't the right time to spring this on you Ben, but I'm leaving for London on Friday.'

'I see you for the first time in months only to have you kick me in the balls. Jesus Jocelyn, thanks, thanks a fucking lot.'

'I'm so sorry Benjamin. But an organisation offered to pay and I jumped at it. Lebedeva is renowned throughout the world.'

It sounded as if she had rehearsed her little speech in an effort to soften the blow.

'What organisation?' I demanded.

'Please don't yell at me.'

'Okay, I won't, I'm sorry. Tell me.' I had a very good idea what she was going to say and it scared the be-Jesus out of me. I had been dreading something along these lines happening for some time. In a way it was inevitable; her political persuasions had finally got the better of her, had won her over.

'I joined the ANC six or seven months back. I was notified about two weeks ago that I'm under surveillance by state security and could be detained at any time. There, I've told you.'

Although I had suspected she had ties to this banned organisation, I never imagined state spooks on her tail, studies in the USSR and the like. Her timing is impeccable I thought mordantly. I felt the blood drain away from my face. My whole world was collapsing around me. 'Please tell me you're not involved with any terrorist activities, bombings or anything of that nature' I asked anxiously. 'You're not part of the MK or what's their name . . . . uMkhonto we Sizwe are you?' (Spear of the Nation)

'Not as such, no.' she answered dismissively. 'Ben, I have made a solemn commitment to the cause, the struggle. I cannot live under this regime any longer. I know you hate politics, but you would hate me even more if I wasn't open and honest with you.'

I had to agree with her last statement but remained non-committal.

'I *did* have a premonition on Saturday and I *do* want to support you. I should have told you a while back, but I've been procrastinating for obvious reasons. Ben I love you with all of my heart, but I have to do this. I could easily end up despising myself if I don't commit to my values, my beliefs. I know it sounds hackneyed, but I want to do my bit, I want to make a contribution. I have a conscience Ben, which I must appease. Please tell me you understand my darling.'

'I suppose a lot of what you say makes sense' I lied. I didn't understand in the least. As I have stated before I detest politics. I do however believe in egalitarianism, equal opportunities, non-racialism and the rest of those glorious philosophies. I am nonetheless, judicious enough to realise these beautiful sounding ideals will never materialise. Humanity will constantly strive to attain these righteous values, but given the nature of the beast we will forever fall short.

'Joss, however much I'm opposed to what you are doing, and I am, the least I can do is pray for your safety. You are messing with some bad-news boys. People have been known to disappear or wind up dead. Christ Joss, think again.'

'Sorry Benjamin, my mind's made up. I'm leaving on a journey of self-discovery, for better or worse.' she said histrionically.

CHAPTER NINE

E vander, a town in the Transvaal is situated 10 km north-west of Secunda. The town was founded in 1955 when the Union Corporation started its gold mining activities. The town is named after Evelyn Anderson, the wife of Peter Maltitz Anderson, one of the past directors of the corporation.

Pieter Gouws arose, showered and drove off to his place of employment some 12 km from his flat. After fleeing Durban in 1975, Gouws, fearing for his life, had gained employment on a fishing vessel out of Port Elizabeth and remained safely at sea for six years, earning a good wage for doing work comparable to hard-labour in a penal institute. At the end of the period, he decided it was high time and safe enough to become a landlubber; 'surely the heat has died down by now' he surmised.

In the early 1970's, the apartheid government gave the go-ahead for SASOL to construct additional oil from coal plants, following the 1974 oil crisis. Project management was awarded to Fluor, an American company. Construction started around 1975. In 1981, there was still an abundance of contract work on offer. Gouws managed to obtain well-paid work as a welder, a skill he had learned at sea.

On his return from the deep, he passed briefly through Durban for assistance. To his utter amazement, his criminal associate was still contactable. He had recommended the small mining town for two reasons; employment and anonymity. There was a wealth of transient workers passing through the area and it would be possible for him to meld in. His contact handed him an almost perfectly forged ID book, 'You owe me three hundred rand for this my man. Oh and I imagine you settled your PE debt as I never heard a thing. I wouldn't be helping you now if you hadn't paid up, cos you'd be dead' he added with a snigger. 'It's so nice to have real friends in the world' Gouws said derisively.

There was a mine club, a hotel ten kilometres away in Secunda and very little else. He declared Evander as 'not the arse-hole of the world, it is in fact the *haemorrhoid* on the arse-hole of the world. Evander is exactly one hundred and two miles from nowhere.' Gouws laughed at his inane humour. He was basically a loner, but occasionally he needed company. Pieter walked down the hill and presented himself at the Evander Club watering hole. He had good command of both English and Afrikaans; a result of his studies and journalist background. He could strike up a conversation and easily be mistaken as either. He introduced himself to the barman as Johnny; a name which could be construed as a moniker in either English or Afrikaans; neutral and easily forgettable. His newly counterfeited ID book read Jonathan Walters.

After a few beers, his tongue duly relaxed, Johnny partook in a few games of darts with a couple of blue-nosed locals. He bought a few drinks for the guys and steered the small-talk around to employment. One of the darts players happened to be a contract foreman on the SASOL project.

'Can you weld?' he asked.

'Sure can' Johnny replied confidently.

'I've got work for you then. One bird-shit joint and you're out okay?'

'Johnny' was subsequently employed at a fair hourly rate. At the end of his first three months, he was able to buy a Ford Anglia for two hundred down and a monthly instalment of fifty rand, without dipping into his rather substantial savings. He felt it would be unwise to pay cash; 'it could attract negative attention' he reckoned. Walters now had wheels which gave him license to go cruising. He felt a stirring in his loins as his mind filled with illicit recollections of a boy on the beachfront so long ago, too long ago. 'I need to go cruising' he slavered.

Jocelyn had been overseas for almost a year. It was a year of drastic change. After she disappeared from my life, certainly ever-present in my thoughts, I made a few major decisions. Work would no longer be my master. I began studying psychology, a field which had fascinated me all of my life. There were issues, I surmised, I would be able to tackle and possibly resolve—how naive I was. I had developed a caring yet cautious relationship with Carol who introduced me to scuba-diving. In addition, I was clocking up the hours to obtain a pilot's licence and to top it all, I was battling to break ninety at the Royal Golf Club. My life was hectic and I loved it.

Dad was undergoing chemotherapy for prostate cancer; the prognosis was nonetheless excellent as it had been detected at an early stage. Steve and Louise were the proud parents of Charles Teague Mcpherson and Margaret and Danie were planning to uproot and move to New Zealand. Mom was mortified; however Danie was having difficulty meeting the stringent requirements for entry that could quash their application. Mom mentioned to me, 'I don't think I would be able to handle losing them Benjy. It would kill me to be without the grand kids, never mind Margaret and Danie.' I told her not to fret over things that hadn't happened yet. This is the way of the female; worry prematurely with little foundation.

Alan was quite content to rumble around in a cluttered and chaotic mess others refer to as a brain. At least my busy schedule appeared to be restraining him, confining him under lock and key. By immersing myself in sports, especially golf had exposed me to the temptations of alcohol.

The nineteenth hole is infamous for its detrimental effect on otherwise stable relationships. After a particularly bad round—most of my rounds are atrocious—we were sitting in the nineteenth, discussing and dissecting our game.

'Doc, I notice you never have a drink with us. You're not a recovering alcoholic are you?' Martin asked, with no disrespect meant I'm sure.

'No, on the contrary' I replied, 'I very rarely drink. The last time I indulged was the night I met Carol and I made a bit of an arse of myself. I decided to give it a break as it doesn't agree with me.' No tall tales, no falsehoods, I have never been a good liar. I stick to the truth when I can. If you have to lie or even exaggerate, make sure you have a damn good memory.

Someone slipped me a Mickey Finn, I don't know who, but if I ever find out, I swear by all that's holy, I will put Alan on his tail. All it took to negate my medication was one drink. Some unscrupulous shithouse slipped a short or perhaps a double into my normally anodyne refreshment. Alan had taken the drink as an open invitation to have a bit of fun. Some idiot had sneaked him a key and he had snatched at it with murderous intent.

Carol and I had planned a barbeque for friends Stewart and his wife Susan and my brother and his wife. I was living with her at her home in Morningside. I was thinking of making an offer to purchase a fifty-fifty share but hadn't as yet discussed my intentions. And here I was on the beach homeward bound from 'my travels'. It was Sunday morning and the Sun was starting its daily trek, already peeping over the eastern horizon. Joggers were doing their daily exercises, men with baskets were fishing off the beach and people were walking their dogs on the firm wet sand between the water's edge and the high tide mark; so mundane so normal and so every day. I was drenched in blood, staggering around in a state of confusion outside The Cuban Hat Roadhouse. Just as well its doors had yet to open for the day's trading.

There was a cold water tap at the back of the building. I cleaned up as well as I could and became suddenly overcome with nausea. I heaved and hurled until my sides ached, bringing up a sweet-sugary bile-like substance. I found my keys in the back pocket of my golf trousers and stumbled off in search of my car, which I eventually located two blocks north. 'How do I handle this one? Oh God, Carol is oblivious of my condition.' I sat in my car contemplating, mulling over a plan of defence. It was easy when I returned home to Jocelyn; she knew and supported me. 'My God Joss, how much I need you now.' My mind kept wandering; I was mentally and physically exhausted. Had I been up all night long? And of much greater significance, what horrible act had Alan slash I committed this time?

I found a public phone and called home. I wanted to test the waters before diving in. It was answered on the first ring.

'Hello, Ben is that you?' Carol asked frenetically.

'Yes it's me love, I'm so sorry.' I still hadn't formulated any sort of plan. My thinking was to come clean, tell her the truth; that I was a 'traveller' with multiple personalities. But how could I explain all the blood? I'd been dreading this inevitability and had neglected to suitably prepare myself.

'Oh, thank God!' she said. 'What happened? Where have you been? Where are you?'

'I'll be home within fifteen minutes' I answered, ignoring her questions.

Carol sat mesmerised as I clumsily provided her with a watered-down account of my and Alan's history. My eyes were heavy with dark smudges underneath emphasizing the weariness behind them. She agreed I should shower, sleep and continue my horror story later in the day. She retired to the spare room. Her sleeping arrangement wasn't lost on me.

'Why haven't you shared this with Stephen? He would understand you know and possibly be able to help you.'

'It's not that easy Carol.' We sat on opposite sides of the lounge. She had made cups of steaming Milo for the two of us. It was a chilly afternoon. The wind was howling, blowing horizontal sheets of rain against the window panes. The skies had been clear that morning. 'Did you give my apologies to our guests?'

'I called Susan and Louise after you went to bed. I told them you had been mugged on the way to your car at the golf club and spent the night in Addington for observation. The nurse on duty apparently called a few times. I told them we must have been on the veranda and not heard the phone ringing. Please remember the story if anyone asks. Stephen is bound to ask.'

'Thanks Carol, but where do we go from here?' I asked. The cursed wind was driving me barmy. All I wanted was to return to my bed and sleep for days.

Her reply was expected.

'I need to get my head around this Ben. I need to be alone for a while. Whatever happens, you must be extra vigilant around alcohol.'

I packed a bag and left a tearful Carol to 'get her head around it'. I booked into the Four Seasons and went directly to bed. The wind had died down somewhat. Carol called at seven to inform me Steve had phoned asking after me. She told them I was asleep and she would ask me to give him a buzz tomorrow. I slept a dreamless sleep like the dead. I suppose under the circumstances, sleeping the sleep of the dead was apposite.

The next morning, I picked up a copy of the Natal Witness in the foyer. The story was covered on page two; 'Mutilated Body Found on Beachfront'. The report went on to state that the police were following up on a lead regarding a white male who had been acting suspiciously in the vicinity of the Cuban Hat early on Sunday morning.

'Oh well' I thought resignedly, 'you've had a good run Ben.' The biliousness hit me like a bullet train. I made the toilets with seconds to spare.

On Monday afternoon I visited the folks. Dad looked pale and gaunt but he was handling the chemotherapy with courage. He had always been a survivor and I was sure he would pull through with flying colours. There was a letter from Joss; the first correspondence in over a year. I almost ripped the envelope apart in my haste.

It had come via a friend in London. She was well, etc. etc. She had completed her studies, could converse in Russian and was soon leaving the USSR to work in the UK. She would be staying with Red Rogers in Birmingham until she could find digs in London, blah, blah. She promised to keep in touch, missed me, lots of love, etc. etc. Red Rogers; I had known he would return to haunt me. I was strangely unmoved by her letter, the mention of his name had put a damper on my initial excitement.

Whenever I thought of Jocelyn, I couldn't get a mental image out of my mind; Joss climbing through security fencing and affixing claymore mines to tanks of God knows what. I hoped, with waning optimism, that whatever her function was for the ANC, it was of a clerical nature.

The late edition of a national newspaper lay on the coffee table. I opened it and browsed. There was a follow-up report on the beachfront murder. The deceased had been identified, his name withheld until his next-of-kin were informed. He had been suspected of male prostitution, known for plying his trade along the Marine Parade. Detective Anderson, spokesman for the Durban Crime Squad, had released a statement regarding the imminent arrest of the perpetrator.

I phoned Carol at her work:

'Have you read today's papers?'

'I have Ben, and it's not looking too good is it?'

'No, it's not' I replied gloomily.

'I advise you to turn yourself in Ben. I know I must sound callous and uncaring, but what else is there to do?'

'I had a feeling you would say that' I threw back at her.

'Ben, listen to me, you're ill, you're mentally damaged. They wouldn't sentence a person who can't even recall killing any one would they? You'd be committed to a mental institute for a while until you got better.'

'One question Carol, how would I go about proving the killings were committed by this Alan character, my alter-ego, my personal Mr Hyde?'

'But the doctors could prove . . . . '

'Nothing, they can prove nothing Carol, not a bloody thing! They can't even keep him bottled up inside me. How could they prove to the court it wasn't me? The murder was committed by a figment of Mr Mcpherson's imagination your Honour' I said, my voice thick with angry derision. 'Think Carol, think.'

'Ben, I was up all night. There are still bloodied clothes in the linen basket. I could become an accessory to murder. I have to report you to the police.'

'Go ahead then. If you feel duty-bound, then do it. Why haven't you reported me already?' Jocelyn, with her abundance of empathy and understanding came crashing into my head. I would gladly put up with her politics and surreptitious ways if she were here with me right now, I realised.

'I wanted to give you the opportunity to do the right thing' she whispered.

'I can't Joss. Shit I'm sorry . . . . Carol, I mean Carol.'

The line went dead and I realised ironically, as dead as I was about to be. On the outside, I appeared composed, unruffled, as I told Mom and Dad I loved them, collected the rest of my post and said my farewells. Self-preservation is the most powerful instinct in nature. It is encoded into the genes of the simple amoeba and the mighty Blue Whale.

The amazing genome, passed down over literally billions of years, empowering species with an all-encompassing need to survive. Self-preservation is behaviour that ensures the survival of an organism. It is almost universal among all living creatures. Pain and fear are parts of this mechanism. Pain motivates the individual to withdraw from damaging situations, to protect a damaged body part while it heals and to avoid similar experiences in the future. Most pain resolves promptly once the painful stimulus is removed and the body has healed but sometimes pain persists despite removal of the stimulus and apparent healing of the body and sometimes pain arises in the absence of any detectable stimulus, damage or disease. Fear causes the organism to seek safety and may cause a release of adrenaline, which has the effect of increased strength and heightened senses such as hearing, smell, and sight. Self-preservation may also be interpreted figuratively; in regard to the coping mechanisms one needs to prevent emotional trauma from distorting the mind.

Even the most simple of living organisms, such as single-celled bacteria, are typically under intense selective pressure to evolve a response to avoid a damaging environment, if such an environment exists.

My self-preservation gene was functioning perfectly as I began planning my disappearance. I was evolving, surrounded by natural predators, who wanted my genes to come to an abrupt halt hanging by my neck from the gallows. If the police couldn't find me, Carol would surely assist by pointing them in the right direction. I had to get away; I had to find refuge. How had Carol turned from lover to collaborator in the whiff of a duck's fart? Perhaps she too had kicked into preservation mode. One consolation; I had not let on to Carol from where I was calling. This awarded me some precious time.

I returned to Carol's house, packed additional clothes, grabbed my passport and other vital documents and headed for Durban Airport. After abandoning my car in the parking lot, I managed to catch the red-eye flight to Johannesburg and on arrival booked into the Airport Hotel. In my panicky state I wondered if Benjamin Mcpherson was now officially a fugitive; a killer on the run.

The thought, however gave me a sense of both freedom and dread. I was alone in a big wide world. 'Ben, my survival is placed in your hands.' I was astounded; I had always been surrounded by supportive, loving people ever-present, swatting away potential danger and dicey decisions like the flies in summer. This supportive group consisting of family and friends were for now abandoned. I had forsaken them in the name of self-preservation or simple survival. I couldn't help but feel a sense of shame and cowardice as I lay in my hotel bed contemplating my next move.

Johnny Walters wasn't stupid; on the contrary he was an above-average intelligence psychopath; the owner of a cunning and calculating mind. He believed and abided by the rather crude axiom: 'Don't crap on your own doorstep.' He decided to do his game hunting away from Evander and Secunda; there was always a chance somebody may remember his face. He knew he wasn't exactly handsome; large flat nose, weak chin and black bushy eyebrows. 'I can't be too careful though.' he thought.

There were a few possibilities within a radius of fifty or so kilometres. He chose Bethal as his first stalking ground; a farming town 30 km to the east with lots of exits, albeit mostly badly-constructed sand roads. His ultimate ambition was to have his 'prize' in the comfort of a soft warm bed. He would have to get rid of the parents though. 'No big deal if I have to kill them first, so what? Then I can spend hours with my 'reward.'

Johnny Walters' surveillance had paid dividends; his focus was a family living on the outskirts of town, on a dark street, one son of about eleven and a scrawny-looking father.

'Just what the proctologist ordered!' Johnny cackled wildly.

He pulled his black Anglia to the curb a few blocks from his intended target's house and sat a few moments allowing his eyes to adjust to the dark. He removed a .22 pistol, equipped with a silencer, a length of rope and a balaclava from the cubby. He stuck the gun down the back of his trousers, pulled the balaclava around his neck and tied the rope around his waist as if to resemble a thick coarse belt. Although it was a short walk from his car to the house and it was late, 'I can't be too careful' he thought for the umpteenth time.

Johan van Niekerk awoke to the sound of breaking glass.

'Wat die Hel was dit?' (What the hell was that) he said turning to his stirring wife next to him. 'I'll have a quick look Marie.'

He picked up a sjambok off the floor next to his bed and exited his bedroom forever. Johnny saw him coming and shot him twice in the head; he collapsed in a heap, blood squirting from the holes in his face. Walters got his bearings and in an instant, darted into the master bedroom. He delivered three rounds into the wife's brain as she struggled to her feet. The van Niekerks hadn't known what hit them.

He stood dead-still listening for sounds of movement. The house was silent, except for the sound of a ticking clock in the kitchen. No yapping dogs, no screams from the boy's room; 'damn, I'm good' he thought arrogantly and grinned in anticipation of pleasures still to come as he removed his balaclava. He spent two hours in the unfortunate lad's company. He finished as the young man gasped his last breath.

'Can't be too careful' he thought as he flushed the used condom down the toilet.

He helped himself to slices of cold lamb roast spread with a thick coating of mint jelly, washed down with a Black Label and left the house of hell.

Walters took the long route home and sneaked into his flat allowing just enough time to shower, dress and drive to work looking smug and revived by his nocturnal activities. The foreman enquired on his demeanour.

'You look happy with the world Johnny. Did you win the Rhodesian sweepstake or something?'

He shrugged and replied with a grin, 'boss, life is good, that's all I can say.'

Fortunately I was the holder of a current British passport. I departed Jan Smuts with ease and entered the UK effortlessly. My main concern was medication; I had a week's supply left. I'd become dependent on a few tiny pills I took daily. Aripiprazole, Mellaril and Chlopromazine are some of the chemical compounds I have used over the years with which to poison my system and balance my spirits. I hoped my brand was available locally. Either way, I had to consult a psychiatrist as soon as possible. The cocktail Doctor Shields prescribed managed to keep Alan at bay, or should I say they prevented the 'switching' occurring. I had delved into the books and had become pretty knowledgeable on 'Dissociative Identity Disorder'. I discovered that besides a lack of medication, apprehension, trauma and alcohol were enough to 'trigger' an attack or an out of body experience.

I passed through customs with two pressing concerns utmost in my mind; what new developments if any, regarding the latest slaughter, and how was I to explain my sudden vanishing act? I briefly considered placing a call to Carol from Heathrow and then thought better of it; give it a day or two. I felt friendless and vulnerable which brought on brief thoughts of ending it under a London bus. 'Grow up Ben, snap out of it' I chastised. 'My God!' it suddenly struck me, 'I wonder if Gouws is still at large?' Imagine that! I was on the run wanted for murder, Gouws was on the run wanted for multiple rape and Jocelyn was in a sense 'on the run' from the South African government. How ludicrous! My life was becoming a three-ring circus. Was I the chief clown or the ring-master?

I caught a taxi to Trafalgar Square and entered South Africa House. Outside, a group of ever-present demonstrators loitered, holding placards displaying anti-apartheid slogans. I half-heartedly scanned the crowd for signs of Joss. Inside was a notice-board covered with scraps of paper. The majority offered accommodation; 'male wanted to share costs of flat-let in Bayswater' 'room to let within walking distance of Charing Cross' and the best, 'four brute Aussie males looking for fun female to share digs' fat chance fellas. I wrote down some of the information and caught a taxi to a musty smelling hotel at the top of Queen's Road. I paid for a week in advance.

To the north-west, Jocelyn made a late breakfast of sausage and eggs for herself and Red. Over their third cup of tea, Red discussed a protest march scheduled for Saturday. It was to start at Elephant and Castle and terminate at the SA Embassy. She showed scant interest which riled Red Rogers.

'What's up Joss? You've been elsewhere since the other night.'

'What other night?' she barked at him.

'Since, you know . . . . since we shared a bed and all that' he replied awkwardly.

'I made a mistake, a *big* mistake; I was drunk and you took advantage of me.'

'Don't start your crap Jocelyn! I put you up *and* feed you. I've tried to make you feel needy. I introduce you to the local branch members, sing your praises and convince our comrades of your commitment and what do I get in return? I made a big mistake.'

'The other night was the first time I have ever been unfaithful to Ben. And I hate myself for it, okay?' Tears came spewing forth, taking them both by surprise. 'And please don't start on about Ben. You know how I feel about him. Anyway, I'll be out of your hair soon.' Joss wiped her eyes dry with the back of her hand, sniffed and waited for the vitriol to erupt.

'Once you've played your part, you can fuck off to Abu Dhabi for all I care' Rogers said with menace. 'You promised to assist with this operation and you *will*. Do you hear me? Are you listening?'

'Yes I'm listening. I'll help and then I'm leaving Birmingham. I'm considering going home, I'll take my chances. I don't think I'm cut out for this.' Her tone was both reticent and ingratiating. She didn't want a screaming match.

Since her return from Russia, she'd had doubts about everything; the USSR was a joke, the inequality was as bad as anywhere in the world. The Brandenburg Gate and the Berlin Wall kept millions of its subjects in abject poverty, trapped in an existence of hopelessness and desolation. She had witnessed this and it was startling *and* unanticipated. 'Communism is not a viable alternative. There will always be the rich and powerful, as there will always be the poor and the disenfranchised somewhere in the world; it's the natural order of things, whoever heard of the lamb's share?'

'I am disillusioned, homesick and I miss Ben and my family' she realised. 'What am I doing six thousand miles from home?' She decided then and there to call Ben and tell him of her plans. 'Oh God, I hope he's not seriously involved with anyone.'

She made an excuse of having to pop out for smokes and walked down the street to a phone booth. She dialled Ben's mother as she reckoned his Mom would have his contact details.

***

I eventually got through to the varsity and spoke to the bursar. I explained to him I had suffered a bereavement in the family and would be absent for a week or two. That temporarily sorted, I called home and Mom answered.

'Mom it's me.'

'Benjy my love, you will never guess who just called. Jocelyn phoned from England and asked for your phone number. How are you my darling Benjamin?'

'I'm okay Mom, and you and Dad?' 'We are all fine my love. This is an awful line though. You sound like you are a million miles away.'

'Mom, I'm in London.' There was a prolonged silence. I could 'hear' her processing what I had just said.

'London? What are you doing in London love?'

'I'm on business, standing in for someone. It was all very sudden. I could be away for a few weeks' I lied blatantly. 'Did Jocelyn leave her contact details Mom?'

'She did love. Just a minute while I get my specks . . . . okay, here's her number.'

It was three thirty on Thursday SA time when I eventually plucked up the courage and called Carol.

'Hello Carol, Benjamin here' I said submissively.

'Ben, thank God you called. I tried to get hold of you at your office this morning. Your secretary said you haven't been in the whole week. Did you read today's papers? They've arrested somebody on suspicion, a beach bum or surfer or something. Thank God I didn't report you Ben. I'm so sorry.'

Carol was in denial; I had revealed Alan to her in overt detail the previous Sunday, which now seemed like a hundred years ago. Whoever the poor sod was who had been arrested was completely innocent, at least insofar as *this* crime was concerned.

'Will you please come home Ben? Can I expect you for dinner and I can make it up to you later on tonight?'

'I won't be able to make it' I answered. I heard her slight intake of breath. I laughed and explained the reason why I wouldn't be home for supper. I further explained I needed a bit of a break from work and would be staying abroad for a week or two.

It was not safe to return home, at least not just yet. Plus I had something to brazen out with Red Rogers, if I was given half a chance.

I dialled the number my Mom had given me. A man answered and I recognised his voice immediately. It had been a few years since I had last spoken to Red Rogers but his child-like nasal twang was unmistakable, whizzing down the line from Birmingham. Like a forlorn schoolboy I hung up and felt almost relieved she hadn't answered. I wanted to talk to her privately. If or when she picked up, I would rattle off my hotel's name along with the single word London. I waited ten minutes and redialled. Joss picked up and I conveyed the message. She listened silently and then I heard her say, 'Wrong number I'm afraid, that's no problem sir.' The line went dead. I waited for what seemed like ten hours but in fact was more like ten minutes.

The front desk patched the call through to my room.

'Ben!' she squealed with delight on hearing my voice. 'Ben, Ben, oh my God, I'm so happy to hear your voice! I can be in London in a few hours. Can I? Can I come and see you Benjy? I could hardly get a word in edgeways.

'Can I rather meet you somewhere in Birmingham tomorrow my love?' I asked.

I visited a bank, rented a car and drove at a leisurely pace along the M1. We met outside a coffee bar cum bistro on Corporation Street in the centre of the City. Jocelyn was as gorgeous as ever. She was back to her fighting weight, turning heads as we entered the restaurant. We took our seats and she flashed a dazzling smile which couldn't quite veil the sadness and weary resignation in her eyes. My mind flashed back to the last time I had seen her in the campus cafeteria. She had been filled with a youthful expectancy; defiant eyes ablaze with compelling political convictions. Now she seemed jaded, almost cynical.

We talked for hours; Joss telling me about her experiences in Russia, her initial stupefaction with Moscow and the political system, her studies under the 'brilliant 'Professor Lebedeva, the amazing resilience of the Russian people and her growing scepticism and eventual disillusionment. I spoke of my work and my relationship with Carol, my illness, my reasons for being in London. I paused at one stage and did a quick 'I, me, my count' and was shocked to realise I had discussed myself as would a devoted narcissist. I told her so and Joss laughed.

'It's riveting stuff except for the part about Carol. Are you in love with her Benjy?'

There was only one answer and that was an honest one.

'I do love her Joss but I'm *in* love with you. At one stage, I thought I had lost you and I compromised. You know I find it hard to live alone; almost impossible. I haven't lost you have I?' I asked optimistically.

'We are soul-mates Mr Macpherson, and you know that. The killing back home, was it Alan?'

'I think so, in fact I know so' I answered softly, glancing around the cafe suspiciously. I was becoming paranoid.

Jocelyn went on to inform me of work she must complete before thinking about returning to SA. I asked as to the nature of this 'work' and she sidestepped the issue saying it was insignificant and she didn't want to bore me.

She slipped out momentarily, returned and asked if she could return with me to London and could we stop at a Boots to buy a few personals. I readily agreed.

Rogers was really pissed off.

'She disobeyed me; I told her we were on standby, the bitch! That 'wrong number' crap was bullshit.' He slammed down the phone and left for his local where he proceeded to get very drunk.

Suffice is to say the night was pure magic and we promised one another things in the heat of passion which could prove difficult to keep. The next morning Joss refused to let me drive her up to Birmingham insisting on using British Rail. I dropped her off at Paddington. She promised to call me later in the day.

She arrived at Red's bungalow to find him in a foul frame of mind. He was hung over and started cursing and swearing the minute Jocelyn walked in the door.

'Christ I can smell you from here. You reek of sex' he screamed at her accusingly. 'Who did you screw last night you whore? Screwing two guys in one week is not too shabby!'

'What has it got to do with you? Maybe I was at an orgy; maybe I screwed ten guys for all you know.'

He ran at her and she instinctively ducked but not in time to dodge a haymaker which struck her on her cheekbone. Jocelyn collapsed to the floor. He straddled her unconscious body and planted a sadistic kick to her ribs.

'That'll teach you to fuck around with me, you slut.'

She stirred five minutes later, head pounding and a stabbing sensation in the ribs. She dragged herself to the sofa and with difficulty clambered onto it. The sound of Rogers mumbling in the bedroom drifted through and she sat quietly holding her aching face and side. She remained motionless until she heard loud snoring emanating from Rogers' room, as was his way when he was seriously hung over. She tiptoed to the kitchenette and removed a frying pan from its hook and crept to the bedroom. The first blow ensured he remained 'asleep' and she set about him with a controlled ferocity.

Red Rogers awoke, bloodied and bashed about the face and found a note on the bedside table:

*I MADE A COMMITMENT TO THE GROUP AND I WILL
HONOUR IT. IF YOU EVER LAY A FINGER ON ME AGAIN, I
WILL KILL YOU AND THAT'S NO IDLE THREAT!*

Later, Jocelyn arrived back at the bungalow to find a cooked meal waiting for her. Rogers was in his room feigning sleep.

Kenneth 'Red' Rogers, was an orphan who had passed through the system and been spat out the other side bitter and twisted. He was a victim of schoolboy bullying and relentless ridicule due to his ginger hair and knock knees. He was a lonely boy who overcame his unfortunate physical attributes by becoming an A plus scholar and was consequently awarded a bursary to Natal University. He was attracted to politics primarily because, on feeling the water was accepted as one of the clan. He thrived on the sense of 'belonging' when in their company, this clandestine brotherhood. He had never been a 'member' of anything or any group before and introduced himself as Red, thinking it would endear him to the left wing fraternity.

The minute he had set eyes on Ms Borrister, he had fallen madly in lust with her. She became his sexual fantasy, this unattainable goddess. The very notion that she was a member of the same political in-crowd he belonged to was enough to send him into ecstasy. There was a problem however, she was accounted for; some musician prick who thought he pissed eau de cologne and shat Mars Bars, often picked her up from campus accompanied with hugs and kisses.

He befriended Jocelyn and used to hang around her quoting Marx and Engels and doing her fetching and carrying. She treated him with kindness and respect; he misunderstood Jocelyn's inbred concern for attraction. And when she had invited him to her place for a meal, he thought he was 'In like Flint'. That was the first time he had come face to face with that pompous, know-all bore.

Rogers 'found' a slip of paper in Jocelyn's bag with the name of a hotel scribbled on it. He had no idea where the hotel was located, what town or city, but he did know one thing; people don't carry bits of paper around with hotel names written on them without cause. She had spent the night at a hotel with someone and he was going to get to the bottom of it. Now that he had 'had' her, she belonged to him; a woman who was 'owned' should never two-time her master. He hadn't particularly enjoyed striking her, but she had provoked him and he couldn't be blamed for that. But her reprisal had been unforgivable.

The call came on Sunday morning. Joss and Red sat scanning the papers in stony silence; she with a black swollen eye, he, his face a mass of bruises and cuts. The jingling phone startled them.

Red beat her to it; 'hello, Rogers speaking.' A long pause ensued and Rogers said, 'yes, I understand' and 'okay, yes.' He replaced the handset and said curtly to Jocelyn, 'it's on, Tuesday night.'

CHAPTER TEN

S ix weeks earlier, 'Andre du Plessis' arrived at Heathrow Airport and cleared immigration on an 'official' South African passport. He took a taxi into the city and registered at The Wesley Hotel in Camden; within walking distance of Euston Station and more importantly close to the Euston Square Hotel.

The South African Bureau for State Security (incorrectly given the abbreviation B.O.S.S. by journalists, was established in 1969 and replaced by the National Intelligence Service (NIS) in 1980. The Bureau's job was to monitor national security, which largely existed of attempting to neutralise the ANC's efforts through political propaganda and by detaining dissidents by the score, if they were lucky enough to learn how not to fly at John Vorster Police Station, thrown out of aircraft or disappearing down old mine shafts. It was headed by 'Lang' Hendrik van den Bergh.

The Bureau is perhaps most infamous for its involvement in the Information Scandal or Muldergate Scandal, when South African Government funds were used to establish a pro-party English newspaper, The Citizen. This scandal was the main reason for its replacement in 1980. Andre du Plessis, a former agent for B.O.S.S, had been tasked by NIS to 'deal with' a member of uMkhonto we Sizwe exiled in the UK. 'We want it done publicly and we want him to die painfully' his superior instructed him. The handler didn't mention who 'we' were. One of the 'we' was a man with the name of King, George 'Georgie Porgie' King.

Georgie Porgie was an exceptionally dangerous individual who had been under close scrutiny since his days in the National Defence Force. He had risen to the rank of captain during his twelve month national service, which at the time, was rarer than a Point Road virgin. King was a natural born killer and leader of men—with a well-disguised soft side—who had served time in Angola, fronting raw troupes into combat against battle-hardened Cubans under insurmountable odds.

By the closing stages of his extended stay of four years, he would be promoted to the rank of Major and awarded more medals for bravery than is good for anyone's ego. After finally being released from the defence force, he attended The University of the Witwatersrand where he completed a BSc in chemical engineering, sponsored by a clandestine government organisation.

In 1980, following the disintegration of B.O.S.S. the newly-formed NIS instigated a recruitment campaign and King was caught up in their lattice work. His recruitment officer was a man by the name of Rodney Borrister.

Sam Pillay was suspected of masterminding a bombing in the Free State and the Minister of Defence had declared, 'No stone will be left unturned. The perpetrators of this most appalling act of terrorism will be brought to book.' This statement could be interpreted as, 'Look out mother-fuckers we are coming to kill you.'

Pillay had, from afar, master-minded the bombing of a Dutch-reformed church in a small farming town in the middle of the ultra-conservative Orange Free State. Instructions were sent and received via a crude computing device which was capable of deciphering and ciphering code flowing back and forth between ANC agents stationed in the United Kingdom and their masters in South Africa.

Eight had perished in the blast; a fifty three year old minister along with seven children out of a group of ten, who had come to the front of the church to sing 'All Things Bright and Beautiful'. The seven children who were murdered had attended the local Afrikaans primary school. They were between the ages of eleven and thirteen. Another fifteen were seriously injured; the organist lost both her legs. The minister's wife was blinded and their sixteen year old daughter, who was seated next to her mother in the front pews, lost the use of an eye and was scarred beyond repair.

The avenger had the weekend to do some sightseeing and sup on a few local brews.

'Not a bad assignment' he thought, as a short-skirted filly passed by. 'Wanna get me one of those in Amsterdam' he said under his breath.

Sam Pillay downed his Rum and Coke and turned to the man sitting next to him. The Euston Square bar was well-adorned, up-market, plush and comfortable. It encouraged imbibers to overstay their welcome; Pillay didn't need much persuading at the best of times.

'So are you sure all arrangements are complete?' he asked knowingly for the tenth time. His Indian-accented words were slightly slurred. He had quaffed four doubles and it was starting to tell.

'Yes, everyone who was invited have sent confirmation, the key-note speaker has booked in and the hotel catering crew are prepared' he replied tolerantly. 'We're 'A' for away; cocktails at six, followed by the keynote address at seven.'

Koos Maaintjies was Pillay's second-in-command, a competent and likeable young man, who originated from the Cape Flats; a politically volatile area of Western Province.

'Thank you Koos' he said minimally. 'I'm going to rest for a while. See you just before six.' He considered ordering a last drink but thought better of it; 'It's a big occasion tonight' he reasoned thirstily.

Pillay was a nasty embittered little man who could peel an orange in his pocket wearing a boxing glove. His was not a righteous conviction; it was built on voracity.

'A gentleman in exile warrants a luxurious lifestyle. After all, this is a perilous vocation' he convinced himself.

His position was gained as a result of a wealthy father who owned a string of haberdasheries from Eshowe to Margate. He was a benefactor of the ANC who insisted on employment for his lazy son in return for large cash donations. Due to Sam's deep-rooted hatred of the white man and his zeal for the downfall of the apartheid system, his father had wangled him a position in uMkhonto we Sizwe. Killing and maiming innocent white women and children was a sport he excelled at.

Du Plessis sat in his room, double-checking his plans, his modus operandi. Quite simple really; execute Pillay in the foyer of the Euston Square Hotel and make his escape.

His check list consisted of an umbrella—check, gloves—check, hat—check, false moustache—check, hair piece—check, and contingency money—check.

He dressed accordingly, slid the invitation into his suit pocket, dropped off his flight bag at the station and walked three hundred yards to the hotel. He was cleared through security, which had been beefed-up for the conference, and walked nonchalantly to a closet on the left of the banquet hall. The down-lights at this end of the foyer were dimmed. He slipped unseen into the tiny space.

The waiting was the hardest part. The political bullshit he had endured for the last two hours was getting to him, doing his head in. He listened to crap about equal rights, water and lights and big corn bites; it was all the same to him.

He heard papers ruffling, chairs being moved around and the blether of voices. He removed the cap from the tip of the umbrella, exited the closet and mingled with the group filing out into the lobby. He spotted his target and approached him.

'Mr Pillay, it's so nice to see you again.'

Pillay looked surprised while thinking, 'who's this guy? I don't recognise . . . . '

The sharpened point of the umbrella penetrated his oesophagus. Du Plessis squeezed a trigger on the handle and a highly concentrated stream of aconite poison squirted into Pillay as he fought for control of the murder weapon. Du Plessis withdrew the umbrella and threw it to the ground contemptuously, as the man stumbled around bug-eyed raking at his neck as if to tear out his windpipe.

'Andre du Plessis' calmly walked out of the hotel removed his disguises and discarded them in the nearest waste bin. Pillay died the following morning, writhing in agony at about the same time the agent was boarding a flight to Schiphol Airport for a couple of days of R and

R. However, this time, the passport he used was issued in the name of Richard Crawley.

The fourth estate had a field day; front page headlines read, 'activist killed with umbrella,' 'apartheid slaying,' 'NIS assassin suspected.' One of the tabloids erroneously blamed the killing on B.O.S.S. The Guardian referred to it as 'The Brolly Affair'.

There were murmurs in parliament for the return of the death penalty for terrorist murder, which was rejected by Margaret Thatcher at the end of July.

'Did this constitute a terrorist murder and if the killer is apprehended and found guilty, should he hang?' was discussed at length on numerous talk shows. The brutality of the killing—in plain sight—exposed a nerve in the British public. According to the numbers, the majority of people polled, warmed to the idea of capital punishment in these instances.

Joss had called on Sunday evening and apologised for not calling sooner; there had been a new development, which she would tell me about on Wednesday.

'I'm leaving Birmingham Ben and I'm never coming back. Please get us booked into a double room, if that's okay with you? Ben, I love you and I want your babies. I never want us to be apart ever again.'

This was music to my ears. This was all I had ever wanted. It was clear by the tone in her voice, the old Jocelyn had returned.

'What about Carol?' she asked.

'Who's Carol?' I said. The way she had acted after the beachfront affair made me realise I couldn't be a part of her life and neither she of mine. 'And anyway, I have Joss back' I thought selfishly.

I had an appointment on Wednesday with Dr Manning, a psychologist just off Harley Street. I had called Dr Shields in South Africa who had arranged it within a matter of hours. She called back and said 'She will give you a prescription Ben. I know her personally; we studied together.' Things were looking up; Joss back, medication organised. Looking out the window, I noticed the weather was atrocious. I decided to brave it and go and see a movie and at the same time, buy a copy of George Harrison's album 'Gone Troppo' which had been released on Guy Fawkes Day.

When Jocelyn had originally been approached by MK she agreed; yes, things must be done to help 'our people', a balance must be attained, one man one vote, etc. However, she had been adamant, 'I will not hurt anyone. I will not be part of any violent activity.' Jocelyn had a conscience to mollify; she'd observed the labourers on her Dad's farm. Although they were comparatively well-paid in the farming community—the best of them lined up to work for 'Baas Borrister'—their 'lot in life' disturbed her. There was desolation about them. They portrayed a hopelessness that was tangible. Their entire existence revolved around work and drink. There was no real substance to their lives. What did they know of art appreciation—in any form—holidays abroad, holidays in South Africa for that matter, fine cars, fine clothes, a fine education, fine anything? However, there was more to it; the vast majority of South Africans were disenfranchised and suffered the degradation of racial segregation. How could a government in the twentieth century deny its' citizens the vote and chase and whip them—God forbid shoot them—if they dared express dissidence?

Jocelyn had realised she was hopelessly romantic; quixotically tilting at windmills and possibly ignorant to boot. Whenever she discussed politics with her father, he constantly shot her arguments out of the sky; never angrily or condescendingly, always calmly with sneaky logic. It would normally end up with Jocelyn typically storming away in utter frustration. He would speak of the complete failure of communism in the USSR, China, Cuba and other places throughout the world.

'Do you think citizens of these countries are any better off Jocelyn? Do you think *they* have a vote when they are under the rule of authoritarian despots?' These one-sided discussions had had the effect of strengthening her resolve; she had to see for herself.

Rogers explained the plan to her for the umpteenth time.

'Shit Red, you treat me like an idiot. It's straight forward. In fact an idiot could do it.'

'I know, maybe that's the reason they chose you' he added with a snigger. 'No seriously, MK wants a commitment from you, that's all. Christ Jocelyn, we've been over this before.'

'Alright already, don't get your knickers in a knot.'

Red continued calmly, 'We pick up the merchandise and drive it from Liverpool to Folkestone. If for any reason we are stopped, we're newly-weds on our way to a belated honeymoon in Margate.' We rendezvous with the boat at 02:00 transfer the goods and Bob's your uncle. And by the way as I said yesterday, we got these bruises in a car accident and that's why we're using this van. Our fight worked out well'

'Who honeymoons in Margate?'

'We do' he snarled. 'Now pack some clothes and let's hit the road.'

The drive from Birmingham to Liverpool was uneventful. They arrived at Canada Dock after five on Tuesday afternoon. They pulled up outside warehouse 57, a dilapidated building long in need of a few coats of whitewash. Rogers hooted twice and a ruddy-faced bearded man emerged, dressed in overalls and donkey jacket. He glanced around and then approached the panel van.

'You Rogers?' he asked in an unmistakeable southern-Irish lilt.

'Are you Conroy?' Red asked.

'What happened to you?' Conroy asked. 'You look like you were hit by a bus with no brakes.'

'I got into a bar fight, me against three Irishmen. You should see what they look like.' His feeble attempt at humour was ignored by Conroy.

'It looks like your missus was in the same brawl as you.' He looked at Rogers disapprovingly. 'Pull the van inside and let's get to it.'

The consignment of Claymore mines—packed in tens in wooden crates—was much heavier than Red anticipated. Each crate weighed roughly twenty kilograms. By the time Rogers and Conroy had completed loading the twenty cases, they were sweating profusely.

'Christ' you could have organised a fork-lift.'

'If you can take on three Paddies, surely you can load a few crates' Conroy said contemptuously.

The Claymore is a directional anti-personnel mine used by the U.S. military. Its inventor, Norman MacLeod, named the mine after a large Scottish medieval sword. Unlike a conventional land mine, the Claymore is command-detonated and directional, meaning it is fired by remote-control and shoots a pattern of metal balls into the kill zone like a shotgun.

A similar design is in use in many parts of the world for example: the former Soviet Union, Serbia, France and the Mini MS-803 produced in South Africa. Not a device the human race should be overly proud of.

MK preferred to use Claymores manufactured abroad; a subtle show of support from their overseas allies in their terror campaign against the South African government.

They drove in silence until they reached their destination; a well-concealed jetty on Hythe Road south of Folkestone. They were early and parked in a pre-arranged spot back from the road. Jocelyn had placated her disquiet with the contents of the cargo some weeks ago.

'As long as I'm not directly involved with the killing and maiming of anyone, I'll do it' she had said sanctimoniously, albeit mistakenly.

The shipment would be transferred at sea to a Greek cargo vessel registered out of Vladivostok. The Claymores would sail to Lorenzo Marques in Mozambique and finally by truck to a small village in eastern Zimbabwe bordering the Republic. Here they would be stashed until required.

They took turns catnapping until Rogers saw the intermittent flashing of a torch about a hundred metres out to sea. He started the Bedford and crossed Hythe Road in darkness. He rolled down to the waterfront and killed the engine. The fishing trawler inched its way to the side of a small pier and a large man climbed down a rope ladder and hopped onto the wooden jetty. Rogers left the warmth of the cab and walked toward the silhouette which seemed frozen to the spot. There was a flash of gunfire and Rogers collapsed in a heap. Jocelyn was literally scared stiff; she sat motionless, her white knuckles clutching the sides of her seat.

She heard someone calling her name.

'Jocelyn, it's going to be okay. I'm a friend of your Dad's. Jocelyn? I'm going to walk toward you slowly.'

The large man approached the van cautiously, unsure whether she was armed or not. Jocelyn whimpered as a combination of shock and terror engulfed her, her mind a total blank. Primeval instinct kicked in. She slid off her seat onto the floor of the cab and curled into a foetal position. She wailed.

'Please don't hurt me. Please don't hurt me.' Andre du Plessis opened the door and gently cradled her until the sobbing subsided.

CHAPTER ELEVEN

I kept my appointment with Dr Manning, thanked her for seeing me at such short notice and returned to my hotel feeling upbeat. Joss hadn't arrived yet, so I bought the Guardian and made myself comfortable in the lounge with coffee and cream scones. Lunch came and went. She had told me her work obligation wasn't far from London and she would be here mid-morning. I tried calling Rogers place with no success. I dialled repeatedly through the day with the same result. I retired to my room at ten after picking at spaghetti bolognaise. Made well, it is one of my favourite dishes. Mom called it 'Spag Bog'. 'Who's up for Spag Bog tonight?' she would ask. I tried Rogers' number again, no reply. I switched on the telly in time to catch the late-night news bulletin.

The space shuttle Columbia had completed its first operational flight, Lech Walesa had been released from prison and a professional boxer had died in the US after fighting Mancini or someone or other. Of greater significance to me, there were no reports of terrorist bombings or slayings. I was apprehensive when I had turned on the TV. Whatever Joss was involved in wasn't ten o' clock news worthy. I called again and let it ring for a full five minutes. I slept restlessly, tossing and turning, my head filled with thoughts of Joss and her wellbeing.

Friday morning I received a puzzling phone call from Rodney Borrister. The gist of the brief discussion was that Jocelyn was presently in Paris, she was safe and well. He had spoken with her and she had supplied my contact details. Jocelyn would be returning home over the weekend and she needed to see me as soon as possible. I tried unsuccessfully to get more information out of him but he cut me short.

'All will be explained on your return Ben.'

And so my succinct stay in London came to an end. What awaited me back home? Would I be arrested at Jan Smuts I wondered? Joss was worth risking it all for. She needed me and that was enough. Had I been subconsciously pursuing her? Had I decided to seek asylum in England because of her? Retrospectively I think so.

Andre carried her aboard the boat and placed her on a bunk. She fell immediately into a sound sleep brought on by a combination of fatigue and shock. He returned ashore and with assistance from a crew member, loaded the mines onto a pallet and winched them onto the vessel. They then tied a thick rope around Red Rogers' torso, secured him to the hook of the hoist and raised his body to the deck. Half-way between Folkestone and Calais, the Claymores were dumped into the North Sea. Red Rogers was tossed overboard as so much crab bait never to be heard of again. He would be searched for in vain by the British authorities. His missing person file remains open to this day. The Ford Transit was impounded and eventually sold as scrap three years later. Du Plessis was chuffed; 'another very successful operation. Mr Borrister will be pleased. I must buy 'Conroy' a bottle of the finest when I next see him' he grinned.

Andre had used the train journey to Paris to console Ms Borrister. She was still in slight shock and perplexed regarding the whole chain of events. He explained to her that the NIS had received information, via an Irish agent, concerning an up-and-coming deal involving the IRA and MK. Names were forthcoming and when her name was mentioned, her father intervened and set up the operation.

'My Father did this?' Jocelyn asked incredulously.

'I will leave that for him to explain Ms Borrister.'

'Please drop the Ms crap. My name is Jocelyn. You must be the only person to ever have addressed me as Ms' she said irritably. Du Plessis blushed.

'Jocelyn' he said with some discomfort. 'I work for your father . . . . indirectly' du Plessis corrected himself. 'I'm telling you this because Mr

Borrister said you may not co-operate if I didn't tell you what's going you. He said you may run off and that's the last thing he would want.'

'You killed Red' the moment of his demise lucid in her mind's eye. 'You shot him in cold blood.'

'Ms Borrister . . . . Jocelyn, I have to tell you a bit about that man. He was a cold-blooded killer, a wife-beater and a conman.'

'A wife-beater, you are sorely mistaken. He was never married . . . was he?'

'When you were in Moscow, Rogers married a Kenyan called Sylvia Obate. It lasted for five months. He beat her to a pulp, apparently after an argument in a pub. He was drunk and had taken exception to her talking to another man. He was eventually charged with common assault and found guilty. He paid a piffling fine of two hundred pounds. Obate deserted him and returned to Kenya short of sight in one eye and laid a charge of attempted murder from abroad. She was too terrified to go to the police in England; scared of the possible repercussions, we later learned from her sister. We kept a close watch on that rubbish Miss.'

'That didn't give you the right to kill the man. You can't go around killing people on a whim. Who made you judge, juror and executioner?' She thought immediately of Ben who had used the phrase in the varsity cafeteria. 'God, I wish he were here right now' she thought dejectedly.

'Your father did. It was his Op and after he was informed of the incident on Saturday, he made his intentions clear.'

'What incident?' Jocelyn asked 'We have it on audio tape; the argument and the sounds of Rogers hitting you, which are apparently an accurate account by the bruise on your face. Your father is a tolerant and reasonable man, but don't let anyone cross him.'

'You were bugging the bungalow?' Andre nodded, ending the conversation.

Rodney Borrister was third generation South African. He had matriculated from Michael House and gone on to read at Oxford, majoring in African politics. He was awarded his colours for rugby—an Oxford Blue no less—and lent his hand to rowing for the first team. On completion of his studies, he returned home and joined his father Joey and brothers in the family business growing sugar cane on the east coast of Natal.

In the early years, he had dabbled in right of centre politics and then he had met Jean, the daughter of a highly successful sugar cane dynasty that farmed in the Tongaat vicinity on the North Coast. Within a matter of months, he asked Jean for her hand in marriage. The families readily agreed to the union, resulting in a lavish wedding held at the homestead of the Hallett family. The first years of marriage were barren and then at thirty five, Jean announced her pregnancy. Both families were ecstatic and the result was a daughter christened Jocelyn Olivia Borrister or Job as she was initially known. Her father had told everyone it had been a hell of a 'job' creating her and yet it had been a labour of love.

He was approached by a well-known businessman who suggested Rodney would be the ideal candidate to run for mayor of Amanzimtoti. There were pressing issues needing attention in the Kingsburgh constituency and he consented somewhat reluctantly.

In his first year of mayoral service the problem of hundreds of defiant 'non-residents' being bussed in to the beaches on public holidays was remedied. In his second term, he endeared himself to the residents by embarking on a road-fixing campaign and an overhaul of council taxes. At the end of his second year, Rodney stepped down to concentrate on his ailing farming interests; much to the chagrin of the local electorate. His natural flair for things political caught the eye of men of higher power and muscle.

'Would you consider being a member of a brotherhood concerned with the preservation of the status quo?' It was an elegant proposal, which Borrister found difficult to discount.

The Broederbond is renowned for its Afrikaner exclusivity. It was and remains a powerful association of businessmen determined to keep South Africa an economy grounded in free enterprise and capitalism. This was a badly flawed philosophy as the national government of the day put into place, boards controlling everything from potatoes to milk to eggs.

Membership was largely secretive and contrary to popular belief it has within its order, a couple of English-speaking associates. Business acumen and sway are two of the necessary characteristics for acceptance into their midst. Rodney Borrister had an abundance of both and he rose quickly through their ranks. His ascendency was a natural progression; he was introduced to people who knew people and his name became known in ministerial circles. He was referred to as 'That Engelsman from Natal', never with disrespect or banter. It was inevitable that he be approached to serve as an advisor to the National Intelligence Service. Borrister had always held his cards close to his chest and the intelligence agency viewed this as a most admirable trait.

Jocelyn and I arrived at Jan Smuts within a few hours of one another, she from Charles de Gaulle and I from Heathrow. I approached passport control with dread, my heart pounding and hands clammy. As I was a permanent resident, I expected to pass through freely. I held my passport in hand. I was at least fifteenth in the queue when two muscular plain-clothes men strode up to me.

'Please come with us Sir.'

For a moment I considered fleeing, but to where I thought despairingly. I was tired after the long flight.

'What about my luggage?'

'It will be taken care of Mr Mcpherson, please just follow us.'

My legs were buckling as I was 'walked' to a small interviewing room off the side of the Arrivals Hall. The one in charge pointed to a plastic chair at a table.

'Please take a seat Sir, this won't take a minute. Security asked me to fast-track you through immigration and to ensure you are on the next available flight to Durban. I need you to complete this form and then I will get you across to the domestic terminal.'

What was this all about? 'Oh shit,' it dawned on me, 'the Durban Crime Squad has been tipped off of my departure from Heathrow.' My heart sank once again and my bowels turned to liquid.

There was no policeman waiting to arrest me. Jocelyn and her father were standing outside the security barrier. Rodney Borrister stood to one side as Joss and I hugged. Both appeared sombre, he shook my hand and said, 'welcome home Benjamin' with little affection.

'My car is parked over the road' I informed him.

'I'll have it picked up in the morning' he said abruptly as if questioning my authority.

I threw my bag on a trolley and we drove the short distance to the farm in virtual silence. I sat in the back of the Mercedes and observed the two of them. They had had words, that much was obvious. It was unusual to see her father in a state of irritation. He was the sort of man who had his say in a quiet authoritative style, but always remained in control of his emotions. I had never seen Mr Borrister lose his cool. The closest thing to it was the Sunday lunch when Joss had been rude to his guests from the Transvaal.

I was twenty nine years old and I had the impression I was about to be summoned to the Head Master's study for a bollocking.

Sean Johnson had been released; the police had nothing to hold him on. They had hit a dead end; 'back to square one' Detective Dave Anderson was thwarted. When they arrested Johnson two days after the 'Cuban Hat Case', he was convinced they had their man; he was carrying a knife, homeless, he was fair-haired, had previous convictions for grievous bodily harm and he 'hung out' at the Cuban Hat Roadhouse, also, he had no alibi for the time of the killing. However, it was all circumstantial; not a shred of concrete evidence.

'Johnson is just another product of drugs and bad choices' the detective determined. He decided to follow-up on the one and only lead they had, but had neglected to pursue when they mistakenly thought Johnson was their man. An early morning jogger had reported seeing a man in a red BMW travelling south, stop at a callbox and seemingly make a brief phone call. Plus he had stated he remembered the man's clothes were stained and was fair-haired. He passed the jogger some two hundred metres further along, heading in a northerly direction.

'I must interview that jogger again' Anderson realised.

Johan van Niekerk's sister-n-law walked the short distance to her sister's house. She hadn't heard from Marie regarding the church cake sale; 'It isn't like her.' Santa's husband was of the old-school; 'no TV, no telephone and no 'voertuig' (vehicle) for this Christian fundamentalist. The place of worship they devoted themselves to and attended three times weekly was a branch of the Pinkster Calvinistic Dutch-Reformed Church. His devoutness and not his church demanded his almost Amish way of life. His piousness occasionally annoyed her. However she loved Koos dearly, even though he had stopped making sexual advances towards her shortly after they were wed. He had called it the devil's work. Her greatest regret was not bearing a child she could love and who would alleviate the tedium she endured daily. Her church work helped to a certain degree, but she would have loved to have a son like her fortunate sister's little Brendan.

The blue uniform of 'crimpolene' dress and hat and dark stockings trapped the heat of the midday Sun and her face glowed with perspiration. The first alarm bell started ringing when she noticed the open gate at the front of the house. 'That's unusual.' She noticed the front door ajar. She knocked and then pushed it open. 'Marie is jy daar?' she enquired in a raised voice. She entered and got no further than the body of Johan lying in a pool of congealed blood. Then the stench of death and faeces invaded her nostrils and she turned and ran. She stumbled and fell headlong down the veranda steps into the front garden, with scant elegance. Santa clambered to her feet, retrieved her hat and raced down the road wild-eyed while producing a throaty whugh-whugh sound as she went.

A Crime Scene Investigation team was deployed from Ermelo, a town approximately forty kilometres to the east of Bethal. The bodies were left as they were found. Captain van der Merwe headed up the team and what he came across made this hardened veteran gasp in revulsion at the sight of the young boy. He was trussed like a wild boar; naked, legs spread apart. He had been garrotted with a length of thin nylon rope. Contusions covered his entire body. His eyes were open, staring sightlessly at the pressed ceiling above.

'Cappie', as he was affectionately known, had attended numerous murder scenes throughout his distinguished career. On ceremonial occasions, he wore his assortment of medals with pride. Cappie was just north of six feet, wiry haired, eyebrows of hoary grey and a flattened nose earned the hard way. Dries van der Merwe would never be considered MENSA material nevertheless his tenacity and methodical approach to criminal cases won him gongs and citations at an impressive rate.

'What we have here is a perpetrator who committed a crime in order to commit a crime. We have a paedophile capable of peripheral homicide. Are you following?' There was a nod and one brave 'yes Sir.'

'This crazed individual eliminated the boy's parents for one reason and that was to have his sick way with this little boy. This tells me a few things. What does it tell me Sergeant Botha?'

'Sir, I think he must be crazy.'

'We've already established that Botha. What else?'

'Sir, he's mentally deranged?' 'You've just said that Sergeant.' Cappie said patiently. 'He's done this before, he planned this meticulously and it's not a one-off. Gentlemen and lady, I am of the opinion we have not seen the last of this sick bastard. Let's get to work on this place, tear it apart. I want to know if the killer farted in this house. I want you to use the fifth degree on the neighbours, not the third. I want a list of everything, including any stolen or broken items. Did he eat anything, inside and outside footprints, photos of tyre tracks in the yard and on the road in front of the house, sightings of suspicious characters or unknown vehicles in the neighbourhood? You know what I'm talking about ladies. Let's get to it.'

His closing statement always raised a laugh or two. Botha occasionally replied in a falsetto voice, 'will do Cappie.'

My supposition of being summoned to the Principal's office was accurate. Mr Borrister asked Jocelyn if she minded joining her mother in the sitting room as he wanted to have a chat with me. She left the room with reluctance after flashing her father a stern look.

The first question asked was, 'are you a member of the ANC Ben?'

'No Sir I am not.'

'Have you ever had any relationship or dealings with uMkhonto we Sizwe?'

'No Sir I have never had any dealings with them' I replied honestly.

'Are you involved with any covert operations to undermine or damage the National Party?'

'No Mr Borrister, but I don't understand this badgering.'

'You will shortly' he replied tersely. 'Look Ben, I apologise for this but I have two last questions, so please bear with me. Where you aware that Jocelyn is a member of the MK?'

'No again. She informed me a year ago that she had joined the ANC, but not the MK, no Sir.'

What were you doing in the UK these last ten days?' This was a tricky one and I certainly didn't want to add him to my list of deceived family and friends.

'I needed to get away for a while' I replied in all honesty. 'I wanted to get away from everything that was getting me down, stressing me out.'

I wished someone was recording this conversation; I could never be accused of lying to Rodney Borrister!

'Ok, I believe you. I have a few things to tell you and if you ever repeat anything I say you know I will have to kill you' Borrister said threateningly. I smiled but I didn't notice him return my smile.

'Red Rogers was shot dead by an NIS agent on Wednesday morning in Folkestone in the UK.' I decided to keep my mouth shut rather than whoop with delight.

'He was caught in the process of helping to smuggle two hundred Claymore mines from the Irish Republic to Zimbabwe. Jocelyn was an accomplice.'

That explained her reluctance to share the nature of her 'work' with me when I quizzed her back in London.

'I was made aware of her role and consequently instructed our agent to bring her out. The MK Op was compromised. Fortunately I was involved from the outset and managed to persuade certain contacts to let me salvage what I could. I convinced the Director that her role was miniscule and she was clueless regarding the nature of the cargo.'

'Jesus Mr Borrister, the very idea that you are involved with Government agencies dumbfounds me.'

'Well it's not something I advertise Benjamin. Please address me as Rodney; God knows you're old enough.'

Rodney continued, 'Jocelyn is livid. I suppose I can't blame her, she told me earlier her entire life is a sham. How did she come to that conclusion? If anything, I'm the one living a lie' he stated introspectively and returned to the present. 'I need, no I demand your absolute silence Benjamin. I'm sorry to have to put you under pressure, but if this goes public, there could be grave repercussions.'

'You won't allow Joss to be charged with anything will you?' I wanted to tag 'Rodney' on the end of my question. I couldn't as I felt it would have seemed gauche somehow.

'Jocelyn is a very lucky girl. If she denounces the MK and keeps her nose clean, I may be able to protect her. Ben would you like to see her arrested and charged with treason or at the very least terrorism which is treason by another name?'

I shook my head imagining Joss banished to Robben Island.

'Well I *definitely* don't want anything happening to her as you know' Rodney said with conviction. 'Oh by the way, I ordered the hit on Rogers; he used his fists on Jocelyn. My position does have some hidden benefits.' He smiled for the first time since Jocelyn had left us alone.

His grin sent shivers up and down my spine. 'Well done Sir.' I said with mixed feelings of apprehension and grudging respect. It seemed as though I wasn't the only killer in the family.

Jean offered Joss and me a place to stay until we could make alternate arrangements, we both accepted, in fact we jumped at it. I had nowhere to go except Carol's place and that was a no-no. Joss informed me 'our' meagre furniture and other belongings were in storage in Claremont. I decided to take a couple of additional day's absence from work. I needed to discern where Joss and I were heading, my immediate future with regard to living arrangements and employment, Carol and an abundance of issues needing attention. My life was a mess. I was turning thirty in a couple of months. I had no place of my own and to top it all I was a wanted serial killer.

Jocelyn and her father buried the hatchet. Within a week of her return, she had revealed her political delusions and clarified her reasons for her fury. His empathy, logic and calm manner had won her over. At the end of the prolonged session Joss was once again madly in love with her father and eating out of his hand.

The following week I went 'travelling'. I had tendered my resignation without the slightest idea what I was to do. I had funds and had for some time considered opening a small practise on the North Coast, if Joss was amicable to this proposal. It would mean relocating to Umhlanga, an expensive chic spot north of Durban. Where there is money there are loads of bored housewives, dying to spend their husbands hard-earned cash on therapy; 'my poodle's constipated Doc, I'm so depressed', 'my husband's screwing my best friend, I'm so depressed', 'my husband's screwing my best friend's husband, I'm so depressed Doctor, I need something to help me through the day'. And the worst case scenario, something all therapists dread; 'Doctor I think I'm falling in love with you, I'm so depressed.'

Although Umhlanga is within commuting distance of Toti, Joss and I decided to spoil ourselves by spending two nights at the Beverley Hills Hotel; a five-star establishment, catering to high-flying businessmen and well-healed travellers. We would use the days to do some apartment-hunting in and around Umhlanga. It was high season and our accommodation was hellish expensive, but well worth every cent what with its Jacuzzis, luxurious rooms and magnificent restaurants.

We had spent the first day searching for something 'befitting a doctor and his deserving wife'—Joss teased with a chuckle—without much success. We ate a sumptuous meal and retired early to our suite on the tenth floor. We were pooped-out from all the walking and climbing up and down stairways.

I 'watched myself' as I left the bed, pulled on a pair of shorts and a shirt, walked to the door, unlocked it and pushed the call button on the elevator panel. I was floating somewhere above and to the side of myself. I watched as Alan climbed into the lift and I jumped in as the doors closed behind me. I noticed a man stand aside as 'we' entered. He looked at my bare feet with a look of mild surprise.

Alan smiled and said politely 'Good evening. Do you have the time?'

The man looked at his watch and replied, 'it's ten past eleven.' 'Thank you' Alan replied graciously.

'We' exited on ground floor and walked toward the main entrance. I 'floated' back into my body and regained control as the doorman walked over and asked, 'is everything alright Sir?'

I made some feeble excuse about wanting ice to which he replied, 'there's an ice dispenser on each floor Sir.' He eyed me up and down and enquired as to my room number. I gave it to him and turned and took the elevator to the tenth floor and luckily found the door unlocked. I undressed for the second time that night and climbed back into bed next to Joss who slept on soundlessly, undisturbed.

I slept fitfully for the rest of the night. At breakfast, I filled her in on my late-night quest for ice. Joss being Joss, commented mischievously, 'at least Alan had the decency to put on some clothes.' We laughed at the image of me entering the lobby of a five-star hotel buck-naked. That would have surprised the doorman! It cheered me up immensely. I had interfered with Alan's intentions. I had intervened and stopped him and this pleased me greatly. Perhaps I was wrestling back a degree of control over my nemesis.

I phoned Carol and arranged to meet up with her. She sounded standoffish, maybe *my* reserved manner had filtered down the line. We agreed to rendezvous at a Wimpy Bar near the aquarium. It went smoothly enough. I told her the truth about my uncertainties and my fear of living with somebody dear to me who didn't and probably never would understand my condition. Finally I told her I was still in love with Jocelyn and that we were living together. She cried and asked whether we could remain friends. She was my sister-in-law's best friend, how could I decline? It was inevitable we would occasionally see one another at the diving club, family functions and the like. The least we could do was be amiable with one another.

Rodney asked if I would accompany him to a family sugar cane farm up north. I had previously met his brothers and their wives at family gatherings and was delighted to accept the invitation. The brothers were the closest thing to peas in a pod I had ever witnessed, almost carbon copies of each other; the same hue of thick red-tinted hair, strong-jawed with straight broad noses, which if had been a single centimetre shorter would not have been in sync with the dimensions of their large and powerful heads. All three brother's work clothes consisted of khaki trousers and shirts, with veldskoene. Did I mention they were like peas in a pod?

The farm was situated west of Stanger, jokingly referred to as the capital of India. The descendants of the drive for a cheap Indian workforce some hundred and fifty years back had it seemed, all decided to make Stanger their home away from home. I remembered a story about two men in a bar discussing where to buy the best dish of curry in Natal. The one mentioned a hotel in Stanger. The other enquired as to the nationality of the chef. His mate replied that the chef was an Indian. To which the first asked in mock disbelief, 'What, an Indian . . . in Stanger?'

Following the emancipation of slaves in 1833 in the United Kingdom, many liberated Africans left their former masters. This created an economic chaos for British owners of sugar cane plantations. The hard work on hot, humid farms required a regular, docile and low-waged labour force. The British colonialists searched for cheap labour. This they found in China, Portugal and *especially* India.

The British crafted a new legal system of forced labour, which in many ways resembled enslavement. Instead of calling them slaves, they were called indentured labourers. Indians began to replace Africans previously bought as slaves, under this indentured labour scheme, to serve on sugarcane plantations across the British Empire which included South Africa.

We arrived early on the Saturday after a fairly quiet trip. Thomas and Robert insisted on showing us a piece of land that was up for sale. I had a suspicion Jocelyn and I were being set up for the farming life. I couldn't have been further from the truth. The reason for our little sojourn became abundantly clear as soon as we set off to view this 'piece of land for sale'. 'That was a ruse Ben' Rodney explained. 'We are going to a meeting of the clan, the brotherhood, better known as the Broederbond.' We drove for half an hour. A dirt road of some hundred yards, lined with Flamboyant trees on either side, led to a stately home, fashioned in American ranch style. I was about to be introduced to the local 'clan'.

The gathering of the brotherhood was held on a sprawling farm near the village of Mandeni; a small town which housed the employees of the pulp and paper factory situated on its doorstep. Besides the overwhelming stench emanating from the works when the wind turned cruel, it was also a breeding ground for politically right-wing whites. Whether this hamlet bred or attracted this particular type of person is immaterial, the point being, it was a breeding ground for nationalism and all that goes with it.

We were greeted by four serious-looking individuals, one of whom stuck a glass of brandy and coke into one hand and a plate of meat and porridge or pap in my other. I placed the brandy on the camping table and reluctantly chewed on a length of Boerewors; a coarse highly-spiced beef sausage eaten by the truckload throughout the land. I wondered about the numbers attending; four Afrikaners and four Englishmen, had it been planned or was it coincidental. I wished we had totalled six.

CHAPTER TWELVE

J ohnny Walters sat smugly listening to the guys in the pub talking about a maniac or maniacs who broke into a house in Bethal and slaughtered the whole family. 'It must have been a mad Kaffir' someone said to universal agreement. He wanted to correct them by saying 'a white maniac, not black maniacs, you racist idiots.' It was of utmost importance to play the game; look shocked and glum and throw 'Shit!' or 'What?' into the discussion when he deemed it appropriate.

'I could have been a famous Hollywood actor if I'd put my mind to it and then young schoolboys would *pay* me to screw them' he chortled.

Johnny had always fancied himself a bit of a wag, a comedian.

'Is there something funny Johnny?' asked one of the guys.

'Ag sorry man, I was thinking about what the cops are going to do to that mad black man when they nab him.'

'Damn it, I must keep my cool' he thought resolutely. 'You can't be too careful.' He was on his fifth beer and not to steady on his feet. He had considered going on the hunt that night but was waylaid when his buddies started discussing his handiwork and consequently imbibed a few too many. When a few drinks worse for wear, he loved an audience did Johnny.

Captain van der Merwe was at his wits end; his detectives had hit nothing but dead ends. A random slaying was the most complex of crimes. He knew the motive; it was a straight forward sex crime, a crime driven by perversity, committed by a seriously sick-minded individual. 'If I had to detain every sick-minded bastard on suspicion of murder, I'd be busy until doomsday' he concluded. 'There must be something we've missed, something we've overlooked, probably staring us in the face. If it takes me for forever and a day, I will track you down Bliksem and that is my solemn promise to Brendan.' Cappie should have been christened Andries 'Tenacity' van der Merwe instead of Andries Dewald Leon Stoffel after his father, his grandfather and great uncle respectively. He was known by family and friends from his teens as 'Ou Boet'. Somewhere down the line his descendants would burden his monikers onto their sons; who would be all their lives addressed as 'Ou Boet' or 'Blikkies'. It is the Afrikaner way.

Andries was born the first son to Andries and Sannie, third generation maize farmers in the Ermelo district. In previous years, the family had suffered through a few dry seasons and consequently Ou Boet and his five younger siblings had often been packed off to bed with a gnawing hunger in their bellies. Andries would philosophise later in life that as a result of his earlier hardships he was what he was; empathetic and concerned for people in general, so long as they stayed on the right side of the law. Andries senior had often said through the hard years, 'A Boer maak n plan'. (A farmer makes a plan)

The team had uncovered very little; a carving knife and an empty beer bottle found on the kitchen table tested negative for any unidentified fingerprints. According to the brother-in-law, there was nothing missing or out of place. But he couldn't be certain as he very rarely visited his in-laws. He started on about the evil ways of his late extended family and Sergeant Botha immediately listed him as his 'numero uno' suspect. He loved his command of Italian and tossed this term around whenever he was given the chance.

'It's normally the religious freaks Sir' he suggested to the Captain.

'Two things I can deduce, this 'freak' as you call him, is employed and probably has a criminal record too.'

'How did you work that out Boss?' Botha asked genuinely puzzled.

'He didn't take anything Sergeant, he didn't lift anything. He probably has quite a well-paid job and didn't feel it was necessary taking any risks. This is one careful freak Botha. As for the previous record, well, somebody as careful as this guy has learnt from his mistakes.'

'Jeez Cappie, that's good hey.'

'It's high time *this* Boer 'makes a plan' Cappie thought.

Their arguments were well thought out and presented with assurance and acumen. It had been a team effort and I was dizzy from the onslaught. These were men with a vision, a mission and a clear objective; maintain the status quo at any cost.

'Do you know what the outcome of capitulation would be ten years down the line?' asked Ferdinand—an extremely affluent businessman from Richards Bay—in fluent English. He didn't allow me to gather my thoughts before continuing.

'It would be another drastic failure as we have seen in most African countries. Mark my words Benjamin; keep your eye on Zimbabwe for example, it will become just another failed attempt at democracy; one man one vote *once*. It's plunging headlong to becoming a socialist dictatorship and the dictator has already taken his seat on his majestic despotic throne. Zimbabwe will collapse dramatically and drastically for the white population. The very people who developed the infrastructure and agriculture, introduced Christianity and capitalism, and one of the best educational systems on the whole continent will be discarded, forced out at best, if not butchered in their own beds.'

'The mines, banks and large business will be nationalised' Rodney added. 'We need you on our side' Rodney continued. 'We would like you to contemplate everything that's been put to you today.'

Ferdinand concluded the gathering, 'on behalf of our Chairman, Professor JP de Lange, the Broederbond would like to extend a hand of friendship to you to join our association.'

The Afrikaner Broederbond, meaning Afrikaner Brotherhood is a clandestine, exclusively male and Afrikaner Calvinist organisation dedicated to the advancement of Afrikaner interests. It was founded by H. J. Klopper, H. W. van der Merwe, D. H. C. du Plessis and Rev. Jozua Naudé in 1918 and was known as Jong Zuid Afrika or Young South Africa until 1920, when it became the Broederbond. Its large influence within South African political and social life—sometimes compared to that of Masons in Freemason conspiracy theories—came to a climax with the rise of apartheid, which was largely designed and implemented by Broederbond members. Between 1948 and 1994, many prominent figures of South African political life, including all leaders of the government, were members of the Afrikaner Broederbond. The requirements for admission—exclusively by invitation—are business shrewdness and influence, and a dedicated belief in a Calvinistic South African republic, governed by a predominantly Afrikaner cabinet.

'I will need some time to consider your offer if that's okay with you?' I looked at all seven in turn. 'I am honoured to be asked, yet I feel obliged to discuss it with my future bride.' Rodney gave me a broad smile.

Jocelyn and her mother drove through to Durban for lunch and a movie. Someone had recommended 'Terms of Endearment' and Jocelyn and her mother had cried throughout.

At lunch, Jean approached the subject of Jocelyn's future plans. 'Is Ben seriously considering opening a practise?'

'I think so Mommy, we've done some house-hunting and I know he wouldn't want to move to Umhlanga willy-nilly and frankly neither would I.'

'Jocelyn, you know Dad is well-connected with most government and quasi-governmental bodies don't you?' 'Uh huh' she replied, signalling ennui or indifference. Jean could not discern which of the two.

'Well don't be alarmed, but I have a hunch there is more to today's visit than meets the eye.'

'In what sense do you mean Mommy?' her interest tweaked.

'I think your father is trying to have Benjamin recruited into the Broederbond.'

'No way, Ben wouldn't join any political organisation; he's totally apolitical. I've never met anyone as anti-politics as he is!'

'They are very persuasive my love. They have a way of convincing level-headed individuals that they are knights in shining armour; the saviours of the white race and their way of life.'

'But I was under the impression they are a bunch of geriatric rubber-toothed dinosaurs. Do they have any real clout?'

'My darling, any fraternity having presidents and cabinet ministers past and present on its membership role is no paper tiger. It's time you knew that Dad *and* Uncle Thomas and Uncle Robert all belong to the Broederbond. We, as a family, have a combined wealth of millions and are very influential in the world of business. They need the likes of us on their side.'

'But why Benjamin, he certainly doesn't have anywhere near that sort of money?' she asked as she gently fondled the diamond penchant around her neck.

'Because your Dad told me he wants to take him under his wing, plus he believes one day soon he will look forward to being Ben's father-in-law.'

Rodney and I arrived at the farm in time for dinner. On the way back we had made small talk; Currie cup rugby, any developments on my planned practise, etc. Then he asked an odd question.

'I haven't seen you take a drink since Steve's wedding, is there a problem Ben?'

'I find it doesn't agree with me Rodney, so I avoid it.'

'Well you'll certainly have to have a few at your engagement' he chuckled.

The TV and radio stations were crammed with Christmas adverts and I found it hard to believe how quickly the year had hurtled by. Joss had agreed to my suggestion of spending Christmas Day with my family and Boxing Day with hers. I had bought an engagement ring and planned to pop the question on Christmas morning. Rodney was pushing me for an answer regarding the Broederbond invitation and to postpone my decision I had requested a little more time.

Holding the engagement at my Mom and Dad's was a clever ploy as Joss had bought sparkling grape juice for the festivities. I was certain the rest of my family would more than make up on the drinks front and quite frankly I took a dim view of killing on a Christmas Day. On Boxing Day it would be easier for me to shy off the drink feigning a hangover. Rodney's two brothers and Jocelyn's four cousins would all be in attendance on Boxing Day and as a result the Borristers would in all likelihood be 'babbelas' or hung-over. There wouldn't be much drinking going on.

My entire family was present to witness me going down on one knee. It was a happy day and Mom, Margaret and Louise outdid themselves, Dad made a large haggis—not for the faint of heart—and a big puffy Yorkshire pudding to go with the lavish spread of various meats, game and veggies. Christmas pudding was unfortunately off limits for me as Mom insisted on practically saturating it in brandy.

Steve had settled into a very rewarding job at Durban High, Louise was lecturing part-time, Danie was a partner with an architectural company in Westville and Margaret was . . . well . . . Margaret. Mom entertained the grandkids and looked happier than I had seen her in years; Danie and Margaret had decided to stay put and give the Land of the Long White Cloud a miss. Before we left for the Borrister farm, Dad made a toast to Joseph and there wasn't a dry eye in the house, even Danie, who had never known Joe, sobbed along with the best of us, bless him.

Hogmanay came and went. Jocelyn got a bit sloshed at a party held at Roddy's place and when I got her home, I took advantage of her and she screamed in ecstasy resembling a stuck pig. I wonder what the Borristers must have thought as our bedroom was right next to theirs.

We planned the wedding for July as this would award me sufficient time to get a counselling and therapy practise on the go. We were still in the market to buy a place of our own. As a combined wedding present, Rodney and Dad had decided to gift us the money needed to make an offer on the house of our choice.

I reluctantly agreed to join the Broederbond, oblivious as to the role I would play. I had, however, naively stipulated that some leeway be forthcoming as I was setting up a business, soon to be married and relocating. Unbeknown to me, a certain Detective Anderson of the Durban South CID was by degrees, as surely as a bear shits in the woods, tiptoeing up on me.

Johnny Walters decided to risk it and head to Sun City for the festive season. He was flush, what with his leave pay and Christmas bonus, could afford the exorbitant prices of a five-star hotel, for at least a week anyway.

He was lonely as his few workmates had gone home or on vacation for the festive season. Loneliness was an alien emotion to Walters; he put it down to his age, he would shortly be turning forty and for the first time in his whole life experienced a yearning for something he couldn't quite define. He felt . . . homesick; that was it, that same feeling he used to get when he begged his step-father to bring him home.

'Shit Pietie, you came home last month, be real man. I can't afford to fetch and take all the time. Maybe I can make a plan next month, if your mother can get off her lazy fat arse and make some money.'

When he was sixteen, Pieter developed previously latent fantasies of killing his family. He would take a knife to the fat bastard of a step-father; he would cut off his penis, the same member he'd had jammed up his butt all those years, the same penis the bastard had used on his little sister. He would daydream about sitting and watching him slowly bleed to death. Then he would cut his mother's throat. Okay, his Mom had realised what was going on and packed him and Hannelie off to separate state boarding schools, but why couldn't she have left the bastard or reported him to the authorities?

When he turned eighteen, he had managed to get work on a local rag as a junior reporter. Pieter had a natural flair for journalism and it wasn't long before the editor recognised his skills and had him enrolled on a journalist course. He passed with distinction and along with his promotion was able to rent a pokey flat. Things were going swimmingly and then the rumours started; 'Did you know Gouws likes the company of young boys?' 'I heard he had a youngster spend the night.' His colleagues started to shun him, until one day the editor called him aside and informed Pieter the director had demanded staff cuts. Since he was the newest member of staff, he was the one who had to go; the LIFO rule applied, last in, first out.

This embittered Pieter, as he was well aware he was one of the best the newspaper had to offer. Fuming at the world, he eventually found work at a bigger and better newspaper however, as a junior reporter on a lower pay scale. As a narcissistic psychopath, Gouws blamed all his woes on everybody around him rightly or otherwise. His childhood had been a Petri dish; a breeding ground for moulding characters of his ilk.

Sun City was busy, as it was high season. A porter carried his bag up to his room on the second floor. He had requested a room close to the ground floor, as it was easier to make a hasty retreat, he had neglected to add. 'You just can't be too careful' he thought to himself. Feeling like a million dollars, he unpacked, freshened up and headed to the bar on the side of the casino for a few brandies and cokes each with two pieces of ice, no less and no more.

The following morning, Johnny pulled on a snazzy pair of new shorts along with an equally new tank-top and swaggered off to the dining room. While enjoying breakfast—a great improvement on the pigswill on offer at the work cafeteria—he made a solemn promise to himself.

'I'll have a squizzy at the local talent but I *will* behave myself. I will not do anything that could attract attention, at least not on the first day.' He smirked as he headed off in the direction of the children's entertainment area.

Sun City was developed by the hotel magnate Sol Kerzner, as part of his Sun International group of properties. It was officially opened on 7 December 1979; at the time it was located in the Bantustan of Bophuthatswana. As Bophuthatswana had been declared an independent state by South Africa's apartheid government, it was allowed under the South African law at the time, to provide entertainment such as gambling and topless revue shows, which were banned in South Africa. These factors, as well as its relatively close location to Pretoria and Johannesburg, ensured that Sun City soon became a popular holiday and weekend destination.

On the third day of his stay, two things happened; a storm of religious proportions struck the resort and lingered the whole day convincing the guests to stay indoors and second, a family of four booked in; mother and father and their twin boys aged twelve.

Johnny's roaming eye zoned in on the two boys as a cheetah selects a specific Springbok to feast upon. He had behaved himself admirably to date; spending his days eyeing up little boys with evil intent, but managing to rein in his crushing, almost overwhelming impulses.

The twins were eating hamburgers at a fast-food joint; their parents were in the casino filling Kerzner's coffers. Johnny sat down at their table and greeted the young boys.

'Hello and what are your names?'

They stared at this strange little man for a moment and then replied in a practiced way, 'I'm Colin,' and 'I'm Charles.'

Walters' timing was out of kilt; the father entered the restaurant and stormed up to the table.

'Who are you' he asked angrily, 'and what are you doing at this table?'

'Ag sorry sir, I was just asking the boys if the burgers are good. I don't know what to order' he said.

The boys' father scrutinised the funny little man, creating a mental image and said sternly, 'okay, but in future leave them alone alright?'

'Yes sir, sorry sir, I didn't mean anything.' Johnny left the restaurant hastily. He could 'feel' angry, suspicious eyes surveying his departure.

'I must be more careful next time; you can't be too careful. They *are* sweet though, worth a gamble' he said and couldn't help a little chuckle.

Anderson personally questioned Andrew Holmes; the jogger who saw someone acting suspiciously early on the morning of the Cuban Hat homicide. 'I'm sorry to take up your time sir, but could you tell me what you saw that morning?'

'I'm sure I told your colleague everything, but no problem. At about five thirty, I was jogging along the beachfront, when a car approached me from the north and pulled to the side of the road about a hundred metres ahead. A young white man with blonde hair climbed out and ran to my side of the road. He fiddled in his pockets. I assume he was looking for change. Then he made a call from a phone box on the corner of Weldon Street. I noticed that the car he was driving was a red BMW M5; not a very common vehicle and I'm almost certain his shirt and pants were stained. I was perhaps another hundred metres further when the same man drove past me heading north.'

'Did you notice anything strange or outstanding about the driver Mr Holmes?'

'Now I think of it, I 'm sure his hair and shirt were wet.'

'Did you notice anything else?'

'Not that I can think of . . . . except he may not have been too steady; he was staggering slightly, maybe swaying more than staggering.'

'Did you manage to notice the car's registration number?'

'It's like I told that other fellow, Detective Sergeant whatever . . . I know it was an ND registration and I think the first two letters were 57.'

'Thank you very much Mr Holmes. You've been most helpful and have a good day.'

'I must ask my sister if she is able to draw up a rough psychological profile of the type of person capable of committing this type of brutal murder.' Anderson made a mental note to give her a call.

He got back to his office and rallied the troupes.

'How is that registration ID search coming along Sergeant?'

'Sir, good news; we think the owner of the BMW is a white male by the name of Dr Benjamin Mcpherson; last known address is 252a Kingsway, Amanzimtoti.

'Good work Sergeant. It's a long shot, but I think I should give the good doctor a visit.'

CHAPTER THIRTEEN

T he next morning the skies were clear and at eight-thirty the temperature was in the high twenties. Johnny was raring to go. He donned his bathing trunks and T shirt emblazoned with 'I Won Gold in the Olympic Heavy Petting Competition' and walked down to the breakfast room. He ate slightly more than a hungry hog can consume at two sittings. The pool water was an inviting 28° Celsius. The twins were cavorting with a couple of other kids. Walters lay back on a recliner digesting his enormous breakfast. He put on his sunglasses and proceeded to ogle the boys furtively.

'There's no law say's I can't look' he reckoned. 'I'll wear my dark glasses though, as one can't be too careful.'

After ten minutes of this, bored and frustrated, he decided to cool off in more ways than one; he removed his glasses and dived into the tepid water. The twins were unaware of his presence and continued frolicking with an ever-growing crowd of children. Someone had introduced a beach ball to the cavorting and Pieter found himself drawn into the game. He worked his way over to one of the boys and accidently rubbed up against him. He was recognised and the boy immediately summoned his twin. They climbed out of the pool and ran off inside.

'Oh well, there's plenty more fish in the sea' he giggled, eternally amazed at his quick wittedness.

The twins' parents were enjoying a late breakfast when Colin and Charles ran in. 'Daddy that man you said we should stay away from, well he was in the pool and he rubbed up against me.'

'He did what? Johan exploded.

'We were all playing with a big plastic ball and that man just joined in with us and then he moved next to me and sort of fell and rubbed his wee-wee on me.'

Taking out his wallet, he handed them each ten rand. 'If you want to swim, find another pool or go and play some games in the arcade and don't let that man bother you, I'll sort him out.' Johnny had incensed a retired Northern Transvaal rugby player.

Besides bothering a few kids in the games room, Johnny was able to stay out of trouble for the rest of the day. Earlier, he had bought a ticket to attend the Christmas Extravaganza in the Superdome. After the show, he took a stroll in the magnificent gardens at the back of the complex. Two men approached; he recognised the larger of the two, he was the father of the twin boys Walters found so irresistible.

'If I see you even glance in my boys' direction you will never be heard of again.' Johan threw a punch at Johnny. He staggered as a series of blows rained down on him. When he eventually fell to the ground, the two of them put the boot in.

Later, back in his room, Walters contemplated reporting the beating to hotel security then reconsidered; it would attract unwanted attention and even the SAP could get involved. He examined his face in the mirror, 'there's going to be a lot of bruising in the morning.' He lifted his shirt to reveal red and blue welts across his back and down the left extent of his body.

'Bastard can't even fight his own battles.' Johnny started to connive; 'he's fucked with the wrong guy, I'll show that gorilla, I'll shoot him in the ear *and* that cutie-pie bitch wife of his!' He ranted and raved, using ever more threatening and obscene language. He eventually calmed down when a waiter arrived with three double brandies.

The strongest environmental factors recognised as contributing to psychopathic personality disorder are; having a convicted father or mother, physical neglect of the child, low involvement of the father with the boy, low family income, and coming from a disrupted or dysfunctional family. Other significant factors include poor supervision, harsh discipline, a young mother, depressed mother, low social class, and sub-standard housing.

Walters' scorecard was ticked in every block; it was almost inevitable he would succumb to PPD. In addition, behavioural signs had been evident at a young age; he maltreated family pets—his mother eventually stopped taking in strays or buying pets of any kind as they all died under suspicious circumstances—he craved instant gratification, was unreliable, was narcissistic, untruthful and insincere and he lacked remorse and shame.

Walters stared at his bruised and swollen face as he shaved. 'There's no way I can go out in public looking like this. Maybe I should, I should let his wife take a look at that bastard's handiwork.' After ordering room service, Walters spent the rest of the day in his room eating, drinking, watching TV and every so often flying off the handle.

The first week into the New Year, I began setting up my practise, not in Umhlanga, but in Durban North; the leases were slightly too high in my preferred location and I was finding it difficult to acquire the appropriate office space. I hired an elderly lady who would double as my receptionist and general dog's body. Sue was a grey-haired handsome woman of sixty. Her husband had died two years prior after suffering a series of debilitating strokes. She needed the work; the medical expenses had put a significant dent in their nest egg and Sue was forced to supplement her meagre income just to make ends meet. She had submitted a very acceptable CV, and from the moment Joss and I had met her, we agreed Sue was destined to work for me. I offered her the going rate plus 33%. Do the maths.

Sue Hurley spoke with a Northern Irish inflection. She and Donald had shilly-shallied; South Africa or Australia? In 1968, the protestant-catholic troubles had speeded up their decision, as she later told me, they were both known protestant royalists. Christopher their twenty five year old son had been successfully courted by Sinn Fein having been subjected to romantic tales of heroism, brave Irish forefathers, the bastard murdering English and other such nationalist baloney. Their only child was won over as were similar young impressionable men through the ages; men who were prepared to give their lives for one cause or another.

In 1971, Sue received a letter from her sister Mary to inform her that Christopher had been killed in a skirmish with British troops in Derry. The fruits of fanatical causes are never consumed cheaply.

The office consisted of a small reception area, toilets, a storeroom and my therapy room furnished with a large mahogany desk donated by Rodney, two recliner-style chairs and a chaise-lounge. Sue immediately set about 'making a room worth visiting' by lightening my rapidly depleting bank balance on colossal ferns and other plants. I bought a few expensive prints for the bare walls and hey presto; we had turned it into a 'room worth visiting'. I hung a few impressive looking degrees and diplomas on the wall behind my desk and all that was lacking were lots of crazy patients with heavy purses or wallets. I'm not a sexist.

Sue busied herself, sorting out all the legal requirements plus telephones, buying stationary, letterheads, printing, etc. I visited doctors in the immediate vicinity and beyond in order to drum up business. I met with the medical and dental association and eventually received clearance to treat the mad, the crazy and the insane. Who was I to talk?

Much to Rodney's dismay and disappointment, I had rejected the Broederbond as being too old and too Afrikaans. I was Scots and felt I would be betraying the land of my birth by joining a nationalistic organisation such as this. If I were prone to nationalism, I should rather join a Scottish cause. Jocelyn was rather relieved by this turn of events. She hadn't been at all keen on the idea of her future husband being associated with 'right-wing bogeymen' as she called them.

She defined me as follows: 'Benjamin, you are fanatical about one thing and one thing only; you are fanatically middle-of-the-road.' I loved this paradox; this beautiful absurdity, which only Jocelyn could have thought up.

Rodney was adamant he would involve me in his political games. I summate the real purpose behind it all was simplistic, he had no male beneficiary and was determined to cast me in his image. From a psychologist's perspective, he bemoaned not having an heir to his throne, to the extent that I had become his intended target who still required much work. It was his intent to mould me into the great Rodney Borrister Esq.

He needed someone to pass the baton to. He was a good man in many ways however, was a closet-narcissist and a racist to boot. Had he been born to Attila the Hun and his no doubt loving frau, he would have snuggled up to this warlord and felt quite at home. Nevertheless, I still loved the old scoundrel. Next, the NIS came a wooing.

When I arrived at the Borristers in the late afternoon, I was suffering the stress caused by all the nonsensical red tape that goes along with the opening of a business. I walked in on a trio of anxious looking individuals.

Hello there, all you happy-looking people.' I greeted them with a broad smile and kissed Joss.

'Benjamin, we had a visit from the Durban CID today.' I waited for the patriarch to continue while glancing at Joss; her face was flinty.

'He wants to interview you regarding a car registration number or something of that nature. Why would a Detective Anderson, I think his name was, come from Durban to question you about a licence plate?'

It was time to lie, big time. Jocelyn's look had changed from one of stone to one of pleading, begging me to handle this with composure.

'Rodney' I stared him straight in his eyes, 'I have absolutely no idea' I said with a shrug and as much confidence I could rally.

'If there's something you need to tell us, anything . . . . we are here for you Ben, you know that.' 'No, there is nothing. Did he say when he wants to speak to me?'

'I gave him your business address and he said he'll see you tomorrow morning.'

We went to bed early; Joss and I lay discussing how I should play it or had the time come for me to pack it in? That night I made a strange request, last request of a condemned man? I asked if I could address her as Jos with one 'ess' instead of Joss. For a moment she looked at me as though I were demented. Then it dawned on her as she applied basic arithmetic on her fingers. Whether she is known as Jos Borrister or Jos Mcpherson, the sum of first and surname equalled twelve; whether I wrote her name or spoke it, I would refer to her as Jos with one 'ess'. She became Jos with three letters for the rest of her life. Whenever she wrote her name from that day onward, she used my preferred spelling of Jos.

I told Sue I was expecting a visit from a policeman, a Detective Anderson and would she send him straight through. I sat on tenterhooks until ten thirty when he at last graced me with his unwanted presence.

We went through the formalities until he asked, 'Doctor, I have a statement from someone who reported seeing you on the Golden Mile at five-thirty on Sunday 13th of November last year. Do you remember what you were doing at that time in the vicinity of the Cuban Hat Roadhouse?'

'Not offhand no, but until I went on a short vacation to the UK, I often went scuba diving on the weekends and would leave home early in the mornings.'

I wondered whether he noticed the sweat pouring down my face. Or was my mind merely playing tricks on me? I sat frozen in my chair, too self-conscious to even raise my hand to my face to wipe away the imaginary torrents of perspiration.

'The report stated that you were driving south toward West Street, U-turned, made a brief call from a phone booth and then drove off in the direction of Durban North.'

'Ah Detective I *do* remember that morning; I'd left my scuba mask at my girlfriend's place in Morningside and called her to bring it to the gate as I was running late for the dive. What is all of this about Detective?'

I had nearly made a grave mistake by neglecting to ask the nature of his enquiries. That could have been a *fatal* mistake.

'There was a particularly brutal murder committed near the Cuban Hat late on the Saturday night or early on Sunday morning. We have to follow-up on all leads Sir. And your girlfriend's name and contact details Doctor, do you have them?'

'My ex-girlfriend Detective; we are no longer together.'

I gave him Carol's home address and telephone number and fortunately I wasn't asked to supply him with her work number. He thanked me and left my office. I was pleased he hadn't said, 'Oh just one more thing Sir' with a one-eyed doff of the hat.' Maybe I watch too many cops and robbers shows. Now I had to act swiftly; contact Carol and pray she would be my alibi.

The house was in darkness, besides a low-wattage outside light spreading its feeble watery glow above the back door. He could hear a dog barking in the distance. Even at two-thirty in the morning, he felt dampness in his armpits and sweat forming tiny rivulets down his chest. Johnny wore a black tracksuit, and black running shoes finished off with a dark peaked baseball cap. He'd chosen this particular dwelling as the man of the house worked night shifts and would not be home until after six in the morning.

He was hungry, ravenous; he lusted after young forgiving flesh, he needed to appease this perverse wanting, which for the last long time had dominated his every waking moment. It was a primordial harking that drove him onwards, dangerous and without fear. This was the nature of the beast that resided within him. This was the living entity all mortals fear; nature gone mad, a creature lacking conscience and empathy.

He was very nearly without reason as he gently sliced the flimsy mosquito netting on a rear window. He stood and listened for any noise emanating from the pitch-black interior. He decided to linger for a few minutes; 'You can't be too careful.' He lifted his scrawny body to window level and soundlessly edged himself into the room below. His erection was stiff and warm in his tracksuit.

'I love you my friend.' he said under his breath. 'We're going to have some huge fun tonight' stifling a 'mad clown type' chuckle.

Helene slept soundlessly as Johnny slunk into her bedroom. He freed his penis and holding his tracksuit elastic down with his left thumb, stood masturbating above her. She stirred and he quickly returned himself to his pants. He picked up the heavy bronze bedside lamp and smashed it down on her cranium with demented force. She moaned softly and he struck her again and again. His head was filled with images of his mother as he pummelled her repeatedly until she lay silenced. He tweaked his buttocks to prevent himself from climaxing.

Walters had never experienced the pleasures of a female's inner thighs. As inquisitive as a horny young teenager, he pulled back the bloodied bedding and nightgown and examined her while stimulating his engorged organ. He 'came' and suddenly his rage and overriding sexual drive dissipated, as a pricked balloon at once loses its potential energy. In death, Helene had unwittingly saved her precious young offspring from buggery and strangulation.

He drove off into a rainbow of depressing shades of grey; the puny hues of pre-dawn. He experienced shame, confusion and disappointment; all of these emotions alien to him. 'This woman who made me experience ecstasy—nothing like I have ever known before—I want to hold her, I want her to hold me, to nurture me. I love her, I adore her. Why did I have to kill her? I should have taken her to my bed, to embrace and care for. I need someone to love me, to encourage me to suckle at her breast. I need someone I can love.' Johnny slowed his Anglia to the curb and wept without shame or requisite deception for the first time since his deprived and degenerate childhood.

✤

Captain van der Merwe was summoned to a meeting at John Vorster Square in Johannesburg. A summoning to JVS meant either citation or condemnation and he had done nothing lately worthy of reward. The progress on the Bethal butchering was pathetic to say the least. In fact there *was* no progress; it had almost become a cold-case file, at least in his opinion. He was to learn that a special task force was being considered by the heads of the CID. This team would serve the south-eastern Transvaal embracing the towns of Ermelo in the south to Devon in the north. Other towns under its jurisdiction would include Standerton, Evander and Secunda, Kinross, Leslie and Trichardt.

There was broad consensus among CID officers that the string of murders and rapes were by the hand of one man. This person had been nicknamed 'The Night Rider'. The modus operandi of all three crime scenes were similar; forced entry, murder by shooting, rape of young males, trussing of victims all seemingly taking place in the early morning hours. Except for the Kinross crime; the perpetrator had beaten the mother to death and ejaculated on her. Her son was unharmed and slept through the whole thing. Cappie was filled-in regarding the additional three crimes; one in Devon, another in Standerton and the most recent in Kinross.

This part of the south-eastern Transvaal is featureless and flat; for the main part void of waterways, mountains, lakes or other redeeming qualities. Underground however, is buried a king's ransom in gold and coal. Above ground are field upon field of maize commonly referred to as mielies. The Vaal River flows some thirty five miles south-west of Secunda through Standerton; another maize farming community. The winters are bitterly cold and the summers hot and windy. It is said that hunting is perilous, as a dark shape on the horizon may be the back of your head.

'This 'Night Rider' if it is one person, is a spook, the 'Invisible Man'. Colonel Naudé had a face the colour of boiled beetroot; his hair was flaxen with grey streaks around the ears and sideburns and his belly was large and heavy. He wore his trousers too high up giving him the appearance of Tweedle Dee or Tweedle Dum, almost challenging anyone to choose.

'Captain, I am appointing you head of this task team. You can second ten men of your choice and you will be based in Evander if you are okay with this. The reason I chose Evander is that it is centralised and there is office space available. Are you okay with this?'

Whenever the Colonel asked if you 'are okay with this', it was prudent to say 'Yes Colonel'. The Captain answered, 'Yes Colonel, that makes sense Sir' being careful not to sound condescending. Unbeknown to both Walters and the police, the CID Special Task Force was to be based approximately one kilometre from the 'Night Rider's' lair.

Cappie chose his team well, which included his rather slow but always willing Sergeant Botha and within twenty four hours they had assembled in their temporary offices in Evander and were raring to go.

Carol answered her work phone, 'Carol Moir speaking, how may I help you?' 'Hi Carol its Ben speaking, how are you?'

'Great Ben, how are you?' she sounded genuinely pleased to hear my voice.

'I'm in a bit of a pickle actually. That night I never made it home until God knows what hour of the morning, someone reported seeing my car near the scene of that beachfront murder.' Carol was silent. I was hoping against hope she hadn't seen the newspaper reports carrying the surfer's release. I told her about the detective, the dive meet, the forgotten scuba mask and then asked if she would be prepared to be my alibi.

My innards turned to ice when she said, 'But what about the mugging at the golf club and you being held for observation at Addington Ben? I told Louise and Susan that's what happened that night.'

'Shit Carol, I forgot all about that.'

Just as well I had; if I had given that story to Anderson, it would have been very easy for him to have confirmed my lie.

'Okay but would you please verify my story if they come knocking?'

She was silent again for what seemed like an eternity. 'Alright Benjamin, I'll do it, but this is the last; I'm not going to lie for you again. And you owe me dinner for this one Mr Mcpherson' she added portentously.

'Let's lay our cards on the table' Rodney said. 'I was wrong about the Broederbond, in fact I should have known better. Was it Jocelyn who changed your mind by the way?'

'I don't think it mattered what she would have said. My mind was made up from the outset Rod.'

'Ben, you are well aware that I do advisory work for the NIS' he said in a conniving voice.

'I'm well aware Rodney.' I couldn't hide the irritation in my voice. This wasn't the rock-solid, confident Rodney Borrister I was used to dealing with; there was a hidden agenda here. There was a subtle change to his persona. This schoolchild conspiracy attitude wasn't him at all. I sensed another pitch on its way.

'I'm sorry, I know you know. That was rather inane of me. Well for the last three years, the NIS has been on a staffing drive; we are desperately short of good men, men we can trust and men who are qualified to do what is required of them.'

The sycophantic, toady approach didn't rub it with me. What was going on? This was so out of character for him. Then it struck me; it *was* a conspiracy. He was in the process of enlisting me, but this was to remain between him and me; Jos was not to know a thing about it. My God I thought he could at least have waited until after our nuptials before he solicited his son-in-law into a cloak and dagger agency that does God knows what and must be kept undisclosed from my fiancée. This was no small fry; this was an organisation that had people killed in the 'line of duty', spooks and spies, James Bond, Simon Templar type stuff. Or was I romanticising it all?

'Why me Rodney, I am in the throes of establishing a psychology practise, which will require my full-time attention by the way. What makes you assume I'm qualified for the job whatever it entails?'

'Ben, you are one of the coolest, calm and collected men I have ever known. I have never seen you ruffled. You also happen to be highly intelligent and you possess the judgment of one much older than yourself.' There was still an air of condescension about him; he was blowing smoke up my backside.

'And yet you insist on your daughter being kept in the dark?'

'It's not just Jocelyn, but Jean and your family and friends too; in fact everyone who doesn't need to know. It just works better that way. I've been compromised and it could backfire on me.'

'Obviously I couldn't work as a full-time whatever, so what would be my role, a part-time spy?' I asked trying to lighten the mood.

Rodney laughed and said, 'That would be established after comprehensive training and profiling. It won't be full-time obviously and we would never put your life in danger. Are you willing to consider?' he asked.

✣

Jocelyn was running late for her meeting. She was dressed in an old pair of denims and a baggy corduroy shirt; the less attention she attracted the better. The rendezvous was a farmhouse 10 km outside of Pietermaritzburg. She was to meet with Vusi Mpondo and Carl Beyleveldt, both field agents of uMkhonto we Sizwe. She was to relate her side of the story with regard to the fiasco of the claymores and the strange disappearance of Red Rogers. There were some very discontented comrades who were of the opinion Jocelyn had been turned.

She had decided to stick to her guns; tell it like it happened, except for a few omissions; she would not tell of her father's involvement and she would not be able to explain the reasons for her life being spared. She had been abducted by SA agents and dumped on the French coast and had made her way back to South Africa thinking she could be implicated by the British police in Rogers disappearance. She deduced the mines and Rogers body were in all probability dumped at sea.

Her story was finally acknowledged with a certain amount of scepticism by both parties. Their concern was when and how Jocelyn would be reactivated. Vusi disappeared and returned after a short while. There was work to be done and someone higher up had given his telephonic go-ahead; to earn her 'redemption' she would be tasked to carry out their plans. 'You must never lose sight of the fact that you are indebted to us. Do you think the money we paid for you to obtain your doctorate grew on trees comrade?'

A small shopping complex in Umkomaas was the intended target. A bomb would be placed in a refuse bin outside a busy eatery and detonated remotely at two-thirty pm. The restaurant would be at its busiest on a Friday at that time and the damage would be devastating. An anonymous telephone call claiming responsibility would be made to the SABC shortly thereafter. Jocelyn was ordered to position and detonate it.

George King's ears pricked up. He was busy on his third cup of coffee and fourth cigarette in less than an hour. When in Johannesburg, he frequented the German coffee house in Hillbrow. It was on the second floor and it granted him a panoramic view of the perilous streets below. There were entities down there that required advanced warning.

'Talk to me, tell me that again very slowly' Georgie Porgie asked softly.

The man opposite, partly covering his mouth with his fingers said, 'the farmer's daughter is involved with an operation about to go down somewhere on the South Coast. I overheard a little birdie mention Margate or Umkomaas; one of the two. It sounded as if it's going to be a claymore and that's all I know.' Albert Vosloo had contacted King and told him he had information of interest. They arranged to meet at the normal Joburg rendezvous.

'That is very interesting' King thought. 'Borrie is under the impression he's turned his daughter.'

'Thanks, I really appreciate the info. Keep in touch.' He handed the informant an envelope containing two hundred rand, stubbed out his Camel and stood up to signal the end of the meeting. He strode away whistling 'Colonel Bogey' leaving the account for Vossie as per normal. 'God knows, I pay him enough.'

King resided in Krugersdorp on the West Rand. He lived a quiet life when not in the services of the NIS. The area features an abundance of private clubs, second-class hotels and a few other privately-owned watering holes. George patronised all of them. He carried a host of club membership cards granting entrance to places as far afield as Carletonville and Roodepoort, a radius of some 80 km. He occasionally sipped a single-malt at the various hotels in the vicinity. He wasn't a drinker; he was a gatherer, a collector of information. Georgie was also a hunter; a seeker of weak men who were prepared to sell out their fellow man for a few bucks, men such as Vosloo whom he had recruited in a drinking establishment in Randfontein.

King was an unknown quantity; if anyone were to be asked who he was, they would propound, 'I think he's a salesman or something.' And if you requested any additional information, those same people would answer, 'That's all I know about him.' He was a non-entity, a conservative dresser who kept his opinions to himself. Just as well no-one ever picked a fight with him as he was highly trained in Brazilian Jiu Jitsu, courtesy of the South African defence Force, which many agree is the most lethal form of all martial arts.

Once, in a pub in the southern suburbs, shortly after being recruited by the NIS, a group of young thugs had the misfortune of looking for trouble with him. They had allegorically and physically backed him into a corner. As the saying goes; they looked for trouble and they surely got it. All four woke up in the South Rand Hospital with serious injuries. No complaints were lodged however King received a warning from his supervisor and was ordered to visit his assailants. The story goes that upon recognising King, one of the wounded attempted to rise from his bed and make a dash for the exit, shattered knee and all. Georgie Porgie had subsequently learned to restrain himself and to walk away if at all possible. And when he did walk away, it was indubitably to the strains of Colonel Bogey.

CHAPTER FOURTEEN

What of Jos, what of the expected disloyalty to her? Why was I even considering being part of this clandestine organisation? Was it simply that I felt obliged to please my future father-in-law; to keep in his good books? How absurd, I was contemplating being disloyal to my fiancée to show allegiance to my future father-in-law! Even more ridiculous was the notion that I would be 'employed' by the NIS and Jocelyn was an ex MK member. Was I driven enough, South African enough to fight for a cause I wasn't wholly committed to?

Perhaps, if I joined and served my adopted country, I would acquire steadfastness, a devotion to *my* land. It had been good to me and asked nothing in return. I had never heard a word regarding national service duties, apparently as a result of my British nationality. I had strolled in its halls of learning, lived a more than comfortable life and loved the sunshine on my shoulders. Perhaps it was a privilege, an honour to be identified to serve. I would be performing my national service, albeit in a divergent fashion I rationalised.

March came and went and we celebrated Jocelyn's birthday with a balloon trip over the Drakensberg foothills followed by a champagne breakfast—I had sparkling wine—completed by an overnight stay at a beautiful hotel overlooking Giant's Castle. She had once again become reticent, reserved and wasn't the old cheerful Jos of Christmas past. I pondered long trying to rationalise her behaviour.

I was to commence special training, assessment and profiling in Pretoria in June but had requested it to be postponed until August due to my marriage and resultant honeymoon. Rodney was nonetheless chuffed; I had agreed to present myself for the initial psychological battery of tests and that seemed to be good enough for him.

During the third week of April, a bomb exploded outside a restaurant in Umkomaas, incredibly with zero fatalities and negligible injuries. The ANC's military wing had claimed responsibility for this latest terrorist attack. Rodney had disappeared a week prior to the blast and I wondered if there was a link; had the NIS been forewarned perhaps, as the timing seemed too coincidental. On his return, Rodney had acted oddly. He seemed apprehensive and incensed; he was snapping at Jean over trivial matters, he wasn't talking to his daughter or me. He acted as a bear with a toothache and throbbing piles and yet wasn't prepared to consult a dentist nor a proctologist.

'I'm very serious Mr Borrister, that's what my informant said. His exact words were 'the farmer's daughter'.'

'And who is this informant George?'

'A guy named Albert Vosloo; he's been on my books for about two years now. As far as I can ascertain, he's straight down the line Sir. I pay him well for reliable information.'

'Could he have been fed false info George, on purpose I mean to get back at us for the Folkestone Operation?

'There's always a possibility, but I'm afraid, in context, it sounded genuine. I'm very sorry Sir.'

'Here's what I want you to do' Borrister said. Damn it, where does she get all this crap from? She'd had a balanced childhood, a good upbringing; a *privileged* upbringing, if the truth be known. This is how she repays me; by joining the ranks of the enemy for God's sake! It was most unusual for Rodney Borrister to blaspheme, yet under the circumstances, he felt more than justified.

'How is it possible to break one's own heart?' Jos asked herself. 'I let conviction in and keep devotion at bay. You can do this you silly little bitch; one way or another you have to.' Her emotions yo-yoed back and forth. Feelings of guilt stabbed her in the gut and then feelings of dread overwhelmed her.

'I love Benjy to death; I love Mom and Dad. What are you doing, you silly bitch? You must stop being so self-derogative. To hell with everyone else, you are a stupid idiotic female.' Confused thoughts crammed her mind. 'I hate lying to him.' She'd informed Ben that she was going to visit Valerie, an old polo friend, who had contracted breast cancer. She felt it her duty to spend the night with her before Valerie's mastectomy. Her friend lived in Nottingham Road yet she would be home for dinner on Friday night she told him. Jocelyn had in fact booked into the Cutty Sark Hotel. Thursday night she would set up the mine and the Friday afternoon she would detonate it from a remote place.

Jocelyn took delivery of the suitcase at eleven on the Thursday morning. There is a viaduct that trickles underneath the N2 highway between Prospecton—a large industrial estate and home of the Toyota manufacturing plant—and Amanzimtoti. It is rarely used, except by municipal workers, armed with bush cutters paid to maintain the free flow of water, which occasionally surges from the west side of the highway to the east. The two vehicles met in the reeds and a hasty transfer of lethal merchandise was completed. Jocelyn Borrister was the disconsolate recipient of two pounds of deadly explosives. The device had been couriered from KwaMashu; a sprawling black township on the north coast of Natal. The driver was ignorant as to the nature of the cargo. He had been paid a handsome fee and had received instructions and directions to the drop point.

George King maintained a distance of a few hundred metres as she turned south on to the highway. He changed lanes and as he caught up, instructed his partner to keep low and indicated to her to pull over to the side of the road.

Her first instinct was to accelerate and make a run for it. She looked at the man who was slowly forcing her closer and closer to the verge and with relief thought, 'I know this man, I've met him before somewhere.' She *had* met him briefly; he had once visited her father's farm to attend a braai after his induction. Not too sure as to where and when they had met, she slowed and pulled over onto the burm thinking he is hopefully a family friend and I can't outrun his vehicle even if I tried. He stopped behind her, climbed out and approached the vehicle.

She wound down her window and said, 'hello, are you who I think you are?' for want of a better introduction.

'Hi Jocelyn, I'm here to show you how to position an incendiary device in such a way it couldn't hurt a fly.'

I'm sorry,' she said feigning puzzlement, 'I have no idea what you are talking about.' Her foot went to the accelerator pedal and in her haste; her left slipped off the clutch. George thrust his arm through the driver's window and ripped the keys from the ignition. The Toyota hopped kangaroo-style and the engine spluttered and died. He jumped to his right following the motion of the car and stood in the doorway preventing any possibility of flight.

'If you cause a scene or struggle in any way, I will punch you in your jaw so hard you'll eat through a straw for a month, is that clear my darling?' a merciless leer crossing his face.

'You may be my colleague's daughter, but you're still a snivelling cowardly terrorist.' Jocelyn had met a few hard men in her brief career as a fugitive, but the look in this man's eyes said it all; 'wild animal, do not touch, keep your hands away from the cage'.

'Now slide over to the passenger seat and put on your seat belt love.' He returned to his vehicle and instructed his partner to tail them, all the while keeping one eye on Ms Borrister. George King returned and climbed into the driver's side.

'Now let's go and make a big bang.' They drove in the direction of Umkomaas complemented by the sound of Georgie Porgie tirelessly whistling Colonel Bogey.

Detective Anderson called his sister. He called her the clever one. She had been awarded a doctorate in psychology and had her own consulting rooms in the city.

'Hi Sis, can I pop by sometime today? I have a favour to ask of you if it's okay.'

'That's no problem at all. I have a cancellation at two, if that suits you Dave'

Psychological profiling was a relatively new discipline in the early eighties. It had been developed by the FBI and had proven to be effective in narrowing down the field of suspects. It was by no way a perfect science, if a science at all. Dr Dianne Shields was one of five who had attended a five-day conference at the J. Edgar Hoover Building on Pennsylvania Avenue in Washington. The profiling convention was courtesy of Wits University, UNISA and the South African Police. She had never applied the tools acquired and when David asked her if she would be able to provide a profile for him, she jumped at the chance.

The current technique used by the FBI today is called Crime Scene Analysis. This methodology of criminal profiling can be credited to the work of two men, Howard Teten and Pat Mullany. They studied offenders regarding their backgrounds, crimes, crime scenes and victims. The two of them also spent much time focusing on court documents, police reports, and psychiatric and criminal records. From this research they created a model known as Crime Scene Analysis. This profiling process consists of six parts; profiling inputs, decision process models, crime assessment, criminal profile, investigation, and lastly apprehension. The CIA methodology of criminal profiling is nowadays used extensively by crime-fighting units throughout the world.

Between 1940 and 1956, a serial bomber terrorised New York City by planting bombs in public places including movie theatres, phone booths, Radio City Music Hall, Grand Central Terminal and Pennsylvania Station. In 1956, the frustrated police requested a profile from psychiatrist James A. Brussel, who was New York State's assistant commissioner of mental hygiene. Doctor Brussel studied photographs of the crime scenes and analysed the so-called 'mad bomber's' mail he had sent to the press. Soon he came up with a detailed description of the offender. In his profile, Doctor Brussel suggested that the unknown offender would be a heavy middle-aged man, unmarried, but perhaps living with a sibling. Moreover, the offender would be a skilled mechanic from Connecticut, who was a Catholic immigrant and, while having an obsessional love for his mother, would harbour a hatred for his father. Brussel noted that the offender had a personal vendetta against Consolidated Edison, the city's power company; the first bomb targeted its 67th Street headquarters. Doctor Brussel also mentioned to the police that, upon the offender's discovery, the chances are, he will be wearing a double-breasted suit buttoned up.

The profile helped police to track down George Metesky in Waterbury, Connecticut. He was arrested in January 1957 and confessed immediately. The police found Brussel's profile most accurate when they met the heavy, single, Catholic, and foreign-born Metesky. When they told him to get dressed, he went to his bedroom and returned wearing a double-breasted suit, fully buttoned, just as Doctor Brussel had predicted. He was previously employed by Consolidated Edison.

They began by sorting through all collected data from the three crimes attributed to the killer, including crime scene photographs and autopsy reports. They had hardly made a start when Dianne's receptionist brought through her three o' clock. They agreed to meet over the weekend and involve their spouses by having a braai; 'meat while we meet' David added.

On the Saturday following their initial conversation, David and Dianne put their heads together and grew a sketchy outline for what it was worth. It was Dianne's first attempt and she was unaware of the accuracy of her effort. The profile read as follows:

Age:	Early thirties.
Sex:	Male
Education:	Post-matric, possibly has degree or higher, creative, possibly a musician or artist
Race:	Caucasian
Occupation:	Unknown, possibly business owner
Marital Status:	Single
Mental State:	Sociopathic, depressive, anger issues, mood swings, (MPD?)
Sexual Preference:	Homosexual/bi-sexual; may be latent or perhaps subconsciously suppressed.
Physicality:	Well-built, well-dressed/presentable, appearance allows him to mingle easily under differing conditions, charismatic, articulate, probably English-speaking.

Had Benjamin read Alan's profile, he would have awarded Dianne Shields her dues; hers was a near-perfect scorecard. He would have concurred on all points except where she deduced the killer was a latent homosexual or possibly bi-sexual.

David was pleased with the overall outcome. It was uncanny how one suspect instantly sprang to mind. Conversely, Mcpherson didn't strike him as homosexual though. 'On the contrary, his ex-girlfriend is certainly all-female and his current girlfriend Jocelyn Borrister is an absolute stunner' he mused. He'd met her only once when he called upon her father to question Mcpherson. As a result of some good old-fashioned detective work, he had ascertained that Jocelyn Borrister and Ben Mcpherson had been involved for years. There was little doubt of Mcpherson's sexual preferences.

He further established that they were apart for roughly a year when she had relocated overseas. There was no official documentation as to her exact whereabouts or when she re-entered the country, all rather perplexing. 'I must find out if Ben Mcpherson has any mental issues' he thought as he and his wife Bonnie said their goodbyes and thanks to Dianne and her husband.

⚓

King drove past Umkomaas and turned into a side-street and entered a dilapidated property with no obvious signs of life. 'Is the device in the boot?' She nodded sullenly.

'Now listen to me young lady, if I didn't know your father, you would be sitting in an aeroplane right now on your way to Joburg. Do you have any idea what interrogation is like at John Vorster? Christ you'll squeal like a tomcat with its balls in a vice. A few unfortunate bastards have failed their flying licences, crash-landing into the very hard surface of Commissioner Street. Is that what you want Jocelyn? It's no skin off my nose; lots of skin off your entire body though. This is strike two. One more strike and you're out, do you hear me? Not even your father will be able to save your sorry arse.' Jocelyn nodded once again.

'If I didn't have so much respect for your father, *I would* throw you to the wolves.' he continued. 'How would be able to live with yourself if your folks or Ben had planned to eat at Millers today and you blew the place to smithereens?'

'Okay that's enough; you've made your point, whoever you are. Christ, why don't you put me over your lap and spank me?' she retorted. A man appeared at George's window and without a word passed two Cokes to him. 'Thanks Jannie, is the garage open?' 'Yes it is' Jannie replied. 'Come on missy, grab that thing out of the boot, it's getting late.'

King, with great precision and caution, split open the device insisting Jocelyn stand beside him as he worked. He removed the shrapnel and most of the explosive, effectively turning this most fatal weapon into a loud firework.

'Why are you doing this? I mean, why go to all this trouble to disarm the mine, why not just dispose of it?'

'Because your father said that it must look as if the operation went ahead as planned so as to get the MK off your back. He has stuck out his neck for you and it is high time you began to appreciate it young lady.'

They waited until after midnight and returned to the outskirts of Umkomaas. They skulked in the shadows until the security guard disappeared around the back of the complex. Jocelyn silently approached Millers and tossed the package into the 'Tilt a Bin' some ten feet from the entrance.

'You are not sleeping at any Cutty Sark Hotel tonight. You are staying at Jannie's house and we will complete this little escapade in the morning as planned.' Jocelyn was not about to argue. In fact, she was over the moon. She wanted to kiss this knight in shining armour; her saviour. If George King had only known her pouting was all pretence. She may get off scot-free if she were able convince her father and Ben that she had been coerced under fear of death. 'Two failed missions, I'm not much of a terrorist am I' Jocelyn smiled in the darkness. She nodded off while listening to the soothing white-sound of the Indian Ocean.

❦

Johnny Walters was a worried man; he had been informed by his foreman that all employees of SASOL and its contractual workers were to be fingerprinted. It was a requirement of the newly installed electronic payroll system. Late in 1983, a female working in the payroll office had been suspected of fraud. She was, it seemed, creating fictitious employees and pocketing 'their' wages. In order to prevent any embarrassment to the company and the fact she had been so ingenious in setting up her lucrative little scam—there was a dearth of concrete proof—management had dismissed her without involving the law.

The story had eventually spread, much to the chagrin of top management and in a short time she had become a bit of a heroine, a 'legend in her own crime'.

Johnny Walters' concern was genuine; the fingerprints he was being asked to surrender belonged to one Pieter Gouws.

'What should I do?' he pondered. 'I think I should consider moving, you can't be too careful nowadays. These new fan dangled electronics are a pain in the arse. What if the SAP gets their grubby little mitts on them? These computer contraptions can do anything nowadays.'

Pieter Gouws had been a free man for almost nine years and had developed a sense of invincibility. He tried to remind himself every so often that he was a criminal at large, but it was becoming increasingly difficult to do. He thought of himself as Jonathan Walters, Johnny for short. Pieter Gouws was someone from a past life, another time and place. Beside his 'bad habit' as he referred to his murderous raping ways, he had become a contributing, fully-fledged member of society. He paid his taxes, he was employed and he was nice to little old ladies; 'Little old ladies, as a rule, don't have twelve year old sons' he cackled.

'And now the bastards want my fingerprints.' Johnny was rapidly building up a head of steam. 'Why can't they just let me be? I feel like poking some prick in the eye with a screwdriver. Then I'll make him watch me do his precious little angel with the good eye. Stuff them all, they can take my fingerprints and shove them up their arses. They'll never catch me.' He poured another strong brandy and planned the night's proceedings.

The Boy Scouts hall was situated scarcely two hundred metres away from Walters' furnished quarters. He had eyed the place out ever since his move to Evander and had stuck to his maxim, 'don't take a dump on your own doorstep'. Nevertheless, he was inebriated, aroused and his rage was making him reckless. He came to a decision; 'I'll walk over to the trees opposite and take a closer peep at the boys when they finish for the night. I'll just watch, hands in pockets' he promised himself.

At ten to eight he took up his position behind the trees awarding him a safe outlook. They started to trickle out, some youngsters running to cars waiting in the parking lot adjoining the hall.

He removed himself from his zipper and began stimulating his growing penis, his earlier promise shattered. He ogled the lads exiting the hall with growing feelings of unworried brazenness. He moved away from the tree, exposing his genitals to the world. He was unmindful of a curtain opening in a house across the way. Then he did something he had always been unable to do; he stopped and took stock of his behaviour, returned himself to his trousers and sauntered to his quarters, a mystified, crest-fallen man.

CHAPTER FIFTEEN

Rodney Borrister was on the verge of flying into a rage. I had heard of but never witnessed this level of fury in him before. It was patently obvious from whom Jos had inherited her wrath. It was true what du Plessis had told her on the train; don't cross him. He had convened an emergency meeting on the Saturday subsequent to the failed terrorist attack in Umkomaas. Jocelyn had returned to the farm on the Friday afternoon. I had worked late into the evening seeing patients until seven and compiling summations until nine. I had arrived home just before ten, eaten some leftover supper and gone to bed to find Jos sound asleep.

In attendance were Rodney and Jocelyn and a man by the name of George King whom I had met at breakfast. We were gathered around a small circular table in Rod's office. Jean was nowhere to be seen. She was becoming increasingly introverted.

I was rather annoyed by the summoning, as Jocelyn and I had planned to go shopping for additional furniture for our newly purchased house in Adelaide Drive, Glen Ashley. Jos had said very little at breakfast and I was taken aback when Rod strode into the dining room and called the meeting.

'You are so close to being handed over my girl. I don't have the words to describe my absolute disappointment in you.' I looked over at Jocelyn; she sat head bowed like an admonished schoolgirl. 'Do you realise that even being associated with the ANC liberation movement is seen as terrorism, let alone the MK?'

John Vorster Square is a police station in downtown Johannesburg, a notorious site of interrogation, torture and abuse by the South African security police of apartheid resistance fighters. It was named after J.B. Vorster, the fourth prime minister of South Africa. John Vorster Square was also used as a detention centre mostly for political activists. People who were detained there were not allowed to have any contact with family members, lawyers or any outside help. They were effectively cut off from the outside world. Detention could last for a few hours to a few months, depending on the police.

More than seventy political activists apparently 'lost their lives' in John Vorster Square. There is understandable doubt regarding some of the official reasons put forward for these deaths. Many were explained away as victims of hunger strikes, falling out of the tenth storey window, falling down the stairs, suicide by hanging and the bizarre slipping on a bar of soap. John Vorster Square was an extremely hazardous place according to the safety record.

'Now please explain yourself young lady. You are living in my home and while this is so, you will behave yourself with restraint and decorum.'

'If you will let me speak, I will explain my actions Daddy.'

'Well explain yourself please, we're all ears' Rodney said with exasperation.

'I was summoned to a meeting in Northdale two weeks ago Dad'

'Yes we know' he replied brusquely. Unbeknown to her, she had been under constant surveillance since her return from England.

'I thought you might, after what happened on Thursday' she replied. 'I need you to believe what I'm about to tell you because it's the truth, I swear to God above Daddy. Ben, I have never lied to you in the past. I lied out of necessity the other night.' She stared at me waiting for accord.

I nodded bemusedly and she continued, 'about two weeks after I was brought back from England, I was approached by an MK comrade.'

'Don't use that term; you're not in Russia now!' Rodney barked at her. 'Christ I thought you were over all this commie crap.'

'I'm sorry, force of habit. As I was saying, I was contacted by a member of the uMkhonto we Sizwe. His name is Vusi Mpondo and he told me I had been summoned to a meeting in Northdale as I told you.'

'This is all history Jocelyn; we know all about Mpondo *and* Beyleveldt' King interjected. 'What we want to know is what in God's name possessed you to accept the job?'

'When they explained the nature of the operation to me, I declined immediately, telling them in no uncertain terms that I'm no murderer. I was not and never will be interested in killing innocents for whatever cause. It deteriorated into a political bun fight until finally I told them I'm leaving. That's when the threats began; they would put the word out that I was a double-agent, you had turned me Daddy, I wouldn't last a week they promised, they would organise a hit on Ben and you and Mom.'

Rodney turned to King, 'when are we picking up Mpondo and Beyleveldt George?' 'We'll be arresting them in the morning Mr Borrister.'

'Daddy I was totally ecstatic when I realised what this man was going to do. Removing the shrapnel and allowing a controlled explosion to take place was brilliant.'

'By the way Miss Borrister, that was your Dad's idea. The MK is off your back, a few cuts and bruises here and there, *and* your handlers will soon be safely behind bars.'

His expression softened, 'Jocelyn, I must ask for your forgiveness regarding the way I spoke to you. I didn't know who or what I was dealing with at the time, I'm sorry, you could have been carrying a gun for all I knew' King said. Jocelyn nodded and smiled at this strange man who in a way had possibly saved her life.

'My love I feel what I'm about to say is redundant but I'm going to say it regardless. I believe everything you've said and I trust this is the last of your political activism. I suspected you had been threatened into action. The next time you want to blow up anything, tell me and I'll buy a packet of party balloons.'

He rose from his chair, hugged Jocelyn and turned to George, 'come on George, let's get a fire on the go, I'm starving. I'm sure my daughter and soon to be son-in-law need some time alone.' He threw me a look which I interpreted as 'You *will* marry my daughter won't you'. They exited to the sound of King whistling what I thought were the opening bars of 'Colonel Bogey' the military march from Bridge on the River Kwai.

There was a loud rapping on his door. He instinctively crouched and as if imitating a rhesus monkey, dashed to the window, carefully drew the curtain aside and peeped out. His legs turned to jelly. There were two uniformed policemen on his doorstep.

'Oh shit, what do I do now?' he thought. 'Don't panic, stay calm.' He looked around his lounge. Walters had a disorganised and filthy mind and he kept a disorganised and filthy home; a result of years of training and programming by his mother. The knocking came again. He opened the door and looked surprised.

'Oh hello Officers, how may I help you?' he said in his best neutral accent.

'Good evening Mr Walters, would you mind if we came in and asked you a few questions?'

'Not at all gentlemen, please come in and take a seat. Excuse the mess, my au pair hasn't been in for a few days' he laughed. Johnny's heartbeat was a steady 65 BPM and his blood pressure remained at 125 over 80.

'No problem sir' the older policeman said, completely missing Walters attempt at humour, 'I'll get straight to the point. We received a complaint from a neighbour that you exposed yourself in public on Wednesday night. This person alleges you, excuse the expression, masturbated in the open sir, across the road there.'

'Good heavens officer, this person is very mistaken. What time was this supposed to have happened . . . this . . . incident?'

'Apparently just after eight Sir.'

'As far as I recall, I was down at the pub at that time gentlemen. I think I was playing darts with some of my friends.'

'And what pub would that be Mr Walters?' the younger officer enquired.

'The Evander Club, the pub downstairs, the one at the bottom of the stairs.' 'Okay Sir, since as it's her word against yours, there's nothing more to be done. It is very dark over there between the trees and probably difficult to see anything clearly at night. But I do advise you to be very careful in future Mr Walters. If there are any more complaints of a similar nature, I will be obliged to open up a formal case and take it further. However, consider this visit a warning Sir'

'I'm sorry I couldn't have been of more help, we can't be too careful nowadays. There're some very sick people out there. I'm sure you agree Officer.'

Johnny showed them out and congratulated himself on his nonchalant demeanour with a treble brandy, two blocks of ice and a dash of coke. 'It's time to hit the road' he decided.

Dad's brush with cancer had apparently abated; he was in remission. He had stopped smoking, gained ten pounds and looked the picture of health. He was on retirement and had taken up painting to while away his time and he wasn't half bad. I once mentioned to him that Andy Warhol better look out to which he replied, 'who the hell is Andy Warhol when he's at home?' Mom had become something of a local celebrity; she had played the lead role in numerous amateur dramatics productions. And being histrionic by nature, she had crucified all wannabe female leads. Margaret was . . . well Margaret. She and Danie were analogous to rabbits; she had punched out another two additions in three years, Danie continued to find all things hilarious and aspired to become the second Frank Lloyd Wright. Stephen discovered a flair for writing song lyrics— one of his compositions got to number fifteen on the American Billboard Top Hundred performed by some southern rock band—and Louise was content lecturing ichthyology part-time at Natal University and being a mother to her son Charles the rest of the time. The Mcphersons and the Schoemans were doing just fine.

This Mcpherson on the other hand, was juggling a few hot potatoes. I had a wedding rushing up on me, a practise consuming virtually every waking moment, Alan, who was threatening to make a grave reappearance and Carol. Carol called me at least twice a week. 'When are you taking me to dinner?' 'Can you get away for the weekend?' 'Can we meet for drinks tonight?' I told Jos and she shrugged it off saying, 'you know my philosophy on affairs Ben, it's always the male's decision, never the female.'

I had begun prescribing my own medication. Dr Shields had agreed to this arrangement as long as I consulted her quarterly. Most psychologists, who are concerned about their own mental health, visit a 'shrink' on a regular basis. I had had a few 'funny turns' and Jos was keeping a close watch over me. One night I 'arrived back' to find myself in the middle of the back garden, in my pyjamas with an unopened bottle of wine in my hand. The sickly-sweet after effects haunted me; how had he escaped, or should I say attempted to escape? Another time I 'disappeared' for an entire weekend; I came back with the remnants of a new name in my mind. The latest personality's handle was Keegan. There was no sugary taste on my return plus Jocelyn said he was basically me 'but nicer' and insisted on cooking and he made love gently and considerately. He had stipulated that he be addressed as Ben but told Jos his real name was Keegan. Anyone but Jocelyn would have run a mile.

This outlandish brain of mine was becoming a smidgen over-crowded. I informed Jos that seeing as she had slept with a stranger, I may just accept Carol's offer, to looks of fake outrage. On the Monday morning, I called Shields to make an appointment.

As I have said, Alan is a cunning and conniving son of a bitch. 'The storage of all alcohol is banned henceforth.' I told Jos. If we had guests, at the end of the night, the leftover drink was to be returned or poured down the drain. We couldn't very well say to our visitors, 'before you go, here's half a bottle of Glenfiddich' or 'help yourself at the wine-rack'.

Walters didn't believe in banks. Every cent he had saved as a fisherman and at his current job was stashed under his mattress. He had close on six thousand rand. He could flee and lay low for at least six months if necessary. He was then again, limited to within the boundaries of South Africa; 'buying' a false ID book was one thing while a passport was tricky and didn't come cheap. He was chancing his arm by over-staying his welcome and was not prepared to take the risk of having his fingerprints taken. 'There was already a set in some police file somewhere and that should suffice' he reckoned.

He entered the foreman's office; 'boss my Mom's terminally ill. She has no-one to care for her.'

'I'll be sorry to see you go but there'll always be a job waiting as long as I'm in charge' his foreman had said truthfully. He signed off at personnel, picked up his outstanding wages, said his goodbyes and by twelve o' clock was unemployed, footloose and fancy free. He spent the afternoon drinking large brandies at the club, spinning the same yarn of his failing mother in Barberton. He had no idea where his mother lived or if she was in fact alive or had shuffled off this mortal coil. He didn't much care either way.

That night Johnny had one important decision to make, 'where to from here?' The fickle finger of fate pointed a bony tentacle in the general direction of Natal. 'Go south young man and make your destiny' he hammed it up. 'And why not, after all, it is my birthplace? Let's go and see the sea.'

The following morning Walters packed his meagre possessions, handed his key to the building supervisor and with a feeling of disquiet, motored down the N3 highway to Durban.

During the eight hour drive, he deliberated on his life. Since the night he gazed upon the dead woman's body, fundamentally, he had changed. The anger had subsided significantly and his sexual drive had withered. 'Maybe there's hope for me yet' he laughed. 'Maybe I'm not as bad as people say I am.' By the time he stopped for a bite to eat at The Green Lantern Hotel on top of van Reenen's Pass, he had promised himself to seek help and the feeling of foreboding had fizzled out. Perhaps it was the fresh mountain air, perhaps the missing piece of the jigsaw puzzle had slotted into place in his less than perfect cerebrum. Who knew? Perhaps the beating at Sun City had knocked something into its proper place.

Pieter Gouws had become exhausted from the interminable running and deception. 'There must be more to life.' Gouws was developing a conscience, albeit not as imposing as his fellow man but a set of principles nonetheless.

'I could visit a psychiatrist, incognito of course, and maybe he would give me a prescription for the same stuff they used to feed me in Pretoria Central.'

The Green Lantern Inn has catered for weary travellers for many a year. Walters stopped for lunch as did his step-father and mother every time they traversed the borders of Natal and the Orange Free State. It was melancholic, sitting down to a meal of calf's liver and onions with thick slices of brown bread, brought back sweet memories of years long ago swept away, destroyed as a result of poverty and sexual deviance he and his sister were fated to suffer. This only augmented his wanting to improve his lot, to be a normal person, 'if such an animal exists' he questioned cynically.

He left the hotel positive and resolute. 'This is the first day of my brand-new life; the reinvented, reborn Johnny Walters. 'I have to get a new identity too, I'm sick of Walters; he's a loser.'

He arrived in Durban just after five in the afternoon and booked into the sea-facing Blue Waters Hotel adjacent to the military fort. The Sun had disappeared westwards and the cold June waters were indistinct as regards to their alluring qualities.

The next morning he put the word out he was in the market for a new ID book. On his third day in Durban, while enjoying a buffet lunch of curried seafood he was approached by an Indian waiter.

'There's no problem, five hundred bucks Sir. Give me a preferred name and age, and photos and it will be sorted in five days.'

'How can I trust you?' Johnny asked guardedly.

'I've worked here for twelve years Sir, I'm not going anywhere' Raj Sharma replied.

Walters feeling slightly more assured said, 'oh and one more thing, it must contain a valid driver's licence, code ten, okay?'

'Another fifty and it's a done deal Sir.'

Captain van der Merwe was standing at the cold-water dispenser when he overheard a young constable discussing a person who in his opinion, had got away with a masturbation incident near the Evander Scout Hall.

'When was this Constable?' Cappie asked.

'Some woman reported seeing this guy playing with himself last Wednesday night Captain, round about eight.'

'Damn it, why wasn't I told? I need the docket on my desk immediately' he said irately.

'There isn't a docket Captain. The Sergeant just gave Walters a verbal warning due to a lack of proof. It was basically her word against his sir. The lady involved, agreed not to lay a formal complaint.'

'Did this Walters person have an alibi for the alleged time Constable?'

'He did Sir; he said he was playing darts at the mine club Captain.'

'And you didn't bother checking it did you?' 'No we didn't Sir, because she didn't . . . . ,'

'Lay a formal complaint' Cappie butted in. 'I want you to check out his alibi right now and get back to me ASAP. Damn it Constable, what were you thinking?'

At two-thirty the Constable entered Cappie's office. 'He definitely wasn't playing darts Captain. There was a tournament on Wednesday and the Barman distinctly remembers Walters being conspicuous in his absence.'

'Right let's go' he said walking in to the open-plan office. 'Botha, Theunissen, let's go ladies. Let's visit a certain Mr Walters.'

'He told me his mother is terminally ill and he had to resign to look after her' the Personnel Officer said. 'Did he say where?' Botha intervened.

'Actually he did, he said Barberton, and I have a time share between Barberton and Nelspruit that's why I remember so easily.'

The previous evening, the single-quarters' supervisor had informed the Captain that Walters had checked out almost a week before.

'Damn it to hell, the first real suspect we have and he's buggered off to who knows where?' he vented to his team. 'Okay, he drives a black Anglia with a TBJ registration number and according to him he was heading for Barberton. I wouldn't be surprised if this man has something to hide gentlemen. I don't like coincidences and this one has whopper written all over it. Men, I don't have to tell you what needs doing, let's get on with it ladies.' The Operations room became a hive of activity.

CHAPTER SIXTEEN

In KwaMashu, Vusi Mpondo was woken by the sound of agitated dogs barking. 'They just don't sound right, they're over-excited' he concluded. He looked at his clock radio next to his bed; three-forty. Vusi turned to Nandi his wife lying next to him and whispered, 'Get up Umfazi, quickly, put on your clothes. I think the umlungu are here.' The words were barely out of his mouth when there was an angry knocking on his front door.

KwaMashu is a sprawling township twenty miles north of Durban with very high levels of poverty and crime. The name is in honour of Sir Marshall Campbell and means Place of Marshall. Sir Marshall Campbell (1848-1917) was a Natal pioneer of the sugar industry and parliamentarian ironically concerned with Bantu affairs as they were referred to at the time.

'Open up Mpondo or we'll blast our way in! We know you're in there.'

'Alright, I'll open up. Just give me two seconds to put on my clothes.'

Two seconds later, the wooden door split in two from the force of a battering ram swung by two burly security policemen. Mpondo threw his arms into the air, realising any form of struggle was futile. The yielding gesture was not enough to deter one of the storm troopers from swinging his baton and splitting open Vusi's jaw. He fell to the ground bleeding profusely. Nandi and his two daughters watched silently, in the beam of the police Maglites, as they swept him up and dragged him to the waiting security vehicle.

Beyleveldt had been arrested at three-thirty in the morning. This is roughly the time favoured by police and security forces to carry out surprise arrests; human fortitude is generally at its lowest point and consequently resistance is minimal. The hammering had jolted him awake and his wits scattered by sleep quickly gathered themselves together. He tried to evade his worst nightmare by climbing out of a toilet window, clad only in his sleeping shorts. To no avail; he received a blow to the top of his head which sent him straight back to the land of the fairies.

A black man entered the cold bare cell, aimed a hosepipe at Mpondo and turned the valve once again. Mpondo had been sleep-deprived for forty-eight hours. His initial obstinacy was fading rapidly. A stream of icy-cold water struck him in the small of his back and he let out an involuntary whimper. Vusi was ignorant of the fact that this particular torment was the first in a series of atrocities intended to break the most tenacious pig-headed dissenter. The excruciating torrent ceased and an attractive blond-haired young man entered.

'Are you ready to give up the names of your unit yet Vusi? Come on, we don't like doing this to you. Give me a few names and I'll take you out of here and I guarantee you a big breakfast and your clothes back. What do you say my man?'

The friendly tone of the man touched him. He found himself wanting to forgive them and render names; just one or two to please this kind angel. But he knew deep down in his heart, he could not betray his comrades. He must fight on in spite of these bizarre emotions he was experiencing. He snapped back to reality, his resolve returning, 'I don't know any names' Mpondo said steadfastly.

He was hauled into an adjoining dry cell by a different man, assisted by the black water-tormentor. His fair-haired 'angel' had disappeared. The cell contained a small oblong table and a few plastic chairs. On top of the table was an electrical contraption with two thin cables hanging loosely. A more substantial chair, positioned next to the apparatus, had a hole through the seat and a plastic tray placed underneath. It had straps attached to the arms and legs and was bolted solidly to the concrete floor.

Beyleveldt lay on his bare cot attempting to shut out the blood-curdling screams intended for his ears. When they came for him later, he was geared up to sell out Jesus and any other saviour if need be.

Before 'sentence' was passed, he had been grilled on reasons for his treachery Beyleveldt amused them by spewing out a prepared speech. 'The Europeans, who colonised this fertile tip of Africa, did so at their masters bidding out of pure greed and power lust, blah, blah . . . . The indigenous tribes of Southern Africa lacked the coordination and arsenal to fight off the invading 'ghosts' from across the waters. Nationalism and religious fanaticism has forever been the scourge of mankind and blah, blah, blah . . . . ' Beyleveldt continued on with his well-rehearsed homily for fifteen minutes. There were some ums and ahs and a few shakes of the head.

The men he addressed were neither ignorant nor uneducated however they took exception to him stating that religious fanaticism is a scourge of mankind. These were dyed in the wool Calvinists, a branch of Christianity not too far removed from extremism and they took it as a personal affront.

'It's one thing to beat the living daylights out of someone or kill them when necessary but don't call religion a scourge' they effectively had agreed. Their hypocrisy soared over their heads without disturbing a single hair.

Beyleveldt was under the false notion he would be sentenced to some hard time if he came clean and accordingly had offered up names and addresses. His parents never heard of or from him again. Carl Beyleveldt became just one more casualty of a most cruel and unnecessary war of attrition.

The wedding took place on the 22nd of June on the Borristers' farm outside Amanzimtoti. Four hundred people were invited; obviously very few from my side of the family. There were many well-known people in attendance. I was reminded just how popular Rodney was and how far-afield his influence stretched.

An embarrassment of workers toiled for two days, prior to the big day, pitching a Billy Smart Circus size marquee, fetching and positioning tables and chairs, constructing a bandstand and running temporary cables in all directions for power and lighting. The caterers spent the Friday loading off their paraphernalia. Watching, I thought, 'Rod really needs this wedding.' I had the distinct impression it wasn't about Jos and me at all.

Jos and I had wanted to holiday in the homeland for some time. We had drawn up a list of places we would like to see which included the spa town of Bath, Stonehenge, the Lake District, the Scottish Highlands and much more. It wasn't an ideal time to fulfil our dream as my patients would have to be handed off to colleagues, the serious cases anyway and the rest would be expected to pocket their maladies until my return. The trip was to cost a king's ransom as it was summer in the UK and flights and hotel prices were at a premium. Nevertheless, we booked and flew out as Mr Mcpherson and Miss Borrister on the Sunday evening; we had booked the tickets some weeks earlier.

Although it was supposed to be *our wedding*, in my humble opinion, a wedding is a wedding is a wedding. Not to be mistaken, it was a great day; the food was well-chosen and scrumptious, the guests behaved themselves, the band was first class and being June, the weather was both dry and cool. I think the last family affair had put me off weddings for life. I noticed Carol parading her partner around like the owner of the winning horse at The Durban July. I walked passed her and she snubbed me with a childish flick of her hair which made me realise how fortunate I had been terminating our relationship. The audacity of attending a wedding and then cold-shouldering the groom was way beyond me.

A couple approached Jos and me. Momentarily, I didn't recognise either of them. 'Congratulations Mr and Mrs Mcpherson' George King said with a softening grin using his face. He shook my hand with a vice-like grip then hugged and kissed Jos. Jocelyn held on to him slightly longer than is the norm. She grinned widely and I knew it was her way of showing her gratitude to this man for saving her skin and I suppose making this wedding a reality. It was ironic how a former agent of uMkhonto we Sizwe and a security agent of the National Intelligence Service could behave as if they were dear old friends. 'There's still hope for all of us' I deduced.

'Oh I apologise' George said his face reddening a touch, 'let me introduce you to Emily Badenhorst, my good friend who came all the way from Krugersdorp to be at your wedding.'

'Thank you both for the pleasure of your company' I replied happily. I knew what he did for a living, yet there was just something about the man, I couldn't help but like.

Out of pure frustration, Anderson decided he was going to bend the rules; not break the law exactly, but he was about to behave unethically at the very least. He parked his police car opposite the closest pharmacy to Mcpherson's office. He asked for the owner and was pointed in the direction of a tall red-headed woman behind the far counter.

'Afternoon Madam' he started, 'official police business' he continued showing her his badge. 'I need to know if you fill a prescription for a Dr Mcpherson.'

'I fill a lot of prescriptions for Dr Mcpherson Officer' she said patronisingly, as if addressing an imbecile. 'He practises around the corner from here. I fill at least ten per week.'

'You misunderstand me Madam. Does he submit a prescription for himself, medication he requires for his own use? Or does another doctor make out a script for him perhaps?'

'What is this all about Officer? I can't divulge that sort of information, it's privileged.'

'Madam, I'll be back with the authorisation required to demand you give it to me. All I need to know is does he receive medication on an on-going basis for some sort of condition?' He had failed. The office would never give him the authorisation he needed. He tried to bluff his way, 'if you want to be charged with defeating the ends of justice, that's fine' hoping she would renege and cooperate.

'You can charge me with Bambi's murder if you want' she fired back at him defiantly. 'You're not getting anything from me without a court order.'

The moment he turned his back to leave, she picked up the phone and called Dr Mcpherson. 'I'm sorry Jenny, the doctor is still overseas, but he'll be back on Monday though' Sue replied. 'Do you want me to give him a message?'

'No don't worry Sue I'll call him when he gets back.' She hesitated briefly and then added, 'no better still, ask him to phone me the minute he gets in please Sue.'

We saw all the sights we had planned and then some including The Cavern in Liverpool; the home of The Beatles and a bus tour which included a quick stop at the famous Strawberry Fields. After showing

Jos all the sights London has to offer, we spent a day on The Downs outside of Cheltenham, two days hiking across the Yorkshire Moors and the Yorkshire Dales. In Scotland, we visited long-lost family members in Stirling and Dundee, drove to Loch Ness, visited Edinburgh Castle and stopped for lunch at Robbie Burns' watering hole in Ayr. Wherever we went we were smothered in hospitality; so much for the legend of the stingy Scot. On our way back to Heathrow, I made a quick detour to Abbey Road and asked a complete stranger to take a photo of Jos and me walking across the famous zebra-crossing featured on the front cover of The Beatles album of the same name.

Jos was so enthralled by her tourist visit to the UK and once again was totally taken aback by the lack of racial segregation. She asked me on our last night if I would ever consider living there. Her words reminded me of the night on the Beach Hotel veranda while considering the whims of naive holiday makers. I admit I was and remained for some time tempted to do just that.

We arrived back sated, filled with great memories and a suitcase stuffed with gifts and memorabilia. I had a business to attend to and a home to make with my new bride and best-friend. Two challenges were to be overcome in the immediate future; dominance over Alan and how to approach Jos concerning the NIS, if at all. Two challenges and a weighty problem; Anderson was once again on my tail.

I had called Dianne on my return to the office and feigned ignorance. I was not surprised to hear he was still hounding me months after the killing. I was the perpetrator after all and he was merely doing his job with a devotion I begrudgingly admired. I had become rather nonchalant regarding the whole ghastly affair. I was of a mind that there couldn't be any solid evidence or I would already be imprisoned awaiting the hangman's noose. Unquestionably, I had been a preferred saint in a previous life. Providence walked hand in hand with me.

Jean had called and informed me that they were moving off the farm into their Toti residence. The farmhouse was to be converted into two separate dwellings; one of which would be the newly-appointed foreman's residence and the other to be rented out. They didn't know what to do with the grand piano. Had we perhaps room for it? I had it collected and delivered on Saturday morning after Jos had gone up to Nottingham Road for a polo tournament with her folks. The lounge was *made* for a Steinway. It looked stately positioned off to the one side. I wished Jos would start playing again; she hadn't touched the keys since before the blow-up in front of Rodney's friends. Having it in the house may induce her to play I hoped. I polished, restrung and placed my cello to the left, hit a few notes on the piano, did some perfect-fifth tuning and hoped the two of us could make musical magic once again.

In Ladysmith, central Natal, Nandi Mpondo was being beckoned by her ancestors.

'Nandi Ndlovukazi kaBhebe eLangeni, Queen Mother of the Zulus, use the spear of the nation; smite down the ghost from afar, afore he has his ghostly ways with the sons of Shaka and the lands of his sons and the sons of his sons.'

She awoke, clear of mind, with an undertaking foremost in her mind; a work to be completed, in the name of her forefathers. The 'how' and the 'who' and the 'where' had not been communicated to her as yet, but Nandi was quite confident these trivialities would be made clear to her at her ancestors discretion.

Her daughters awoke next to her at four-thirty and began their daily routine of fetching water from the single tap, supposedly adequate to satisfy the entire needs of five hundred residents squatting in a one square kilometre locale. They then rekindled the communal fire on the doorstep of their mud hut, ate a bowl of porridge and finally washed and prepared themselves for school, a four km walk to the north. Nandi was adamant her daughters would receive an adequate education. She had 'completed' her education aged nine to assist with domestic chores and learn the art of beadwork as her sisters before.

Since witnessing her husband's disappearance from their home in KwaMashu, she and little Nandi and Bongi, her two daughters had returned to the place of her husband's birth. There was no work to be found and food was scarce. However, the extended family of her absent husband threw scraps their way and she had added to this by using the skills of her childhood, standing for hours in the scorching Sun and peddling her wares to rich white travellers on their way to who knows where. The main arterial road running north to south no longer passed the township and vehicles were scarce hence making competition fierce.

Nandi had grown up in a kraal twenty km from Newcastle in northern Natal, to a mother of seven children and a father who spent three weeks a year at home. He had been employed on the gold mines, one of a handful of Zulus who made up the massive numbers of migrant workers employed by the deep-mining companies on the Rand. He passed away when Nandi was seven years old, lying in his sick bed, coughing up blood-speckled pieces of his diseased lungs—a result of pneumoconiosis brought about by the constant inhalation of dust particles leading to fibrosis—as he struggled to take his dying breath. Her mother's name was Nandi. She had claimed royal lineage passed down from her mother and her mother before her. Long gone to join her ancestors, she had possessed the features of nobility; a chiselled nose, a strong square jaw anchoring perfect teeth, high cheek bones and eyes that shone with a worldly wisdom and knowledge of the way things were destined to be. She would throw the bones, much to the children's amusement and the tribe would gather from afar to take heed of this widely-respected oracle.

On the eve of her first menstruation, Gogo Nandi or Grandma Nandi had 'seen' the lengthy suppression of a wise man of the fists, his ensuing liberation empowering him to walk proudly in the midst of adoring men and in the presence of royalty from abroad.

Nandi retired the girls to bed earlier than normal that night. She yearned for the sleep of the dead; the state of being necessary for her royal ancestors to enter her regal body and counsel her as to the path forward. 'Vulandhela, Vulandhlela' she whispered as the mists of sleep engulfed her. 'Open the road.'

❧

Johnny Walters was dead and Andrew van Breda of Durban was very pleased. Durban or eThekwini in Zulu, from itheku meaning bay or lagoon, is the largest city in Natal. It is also the second most important manufacturing hub in South Africa after Johannesburg. Durban is famous for being the busiest port in Africa. It is also seen as one of the major centres of tourism because of the city's warm subtropical climate and extensive beaches. Many 'gentlemen of the road' are drawn to Durban in the winter months as a result of the mild temperatures.

Archaeological evidence from the Drakensberg Mountains, suggests that the Durban area has been inhabited by communities of hunter-gatherers since 100,000 BC. These people lived throughout the area of present day Natal until the expansion of Bantu farmers and pastoralists from the north saw their gradual displacement, incorporation or extermination.

Little is known of the history of the first residents, as there is no written history of the area until it was sighted by Portuguese explorer Vasco da Gama, who sailed parallel to the Natal coast at Christmastide in 1497, while searching for a route from Europe to India. He named the area 'Natal', or Christmas in Portuguese.

'How do you do, my name is Andrew van Breda' he said to the image in the mirror. 'It sounds rather high-class, rather posh, van Breda, van Breda, Andrew van Breda.' He repeated his newly-acquired name over and over again in order to familiarise himself. 'You can't be too careful now, can you Andrew van Breda.'

Andrew's good spirits had not waned, in fact, since being handed his new identity his positive outlook on life had already reaped benefits. He went to buy a car and ended up being offered employment. After shooting the breeze, the Branch Manager had spoken of work telling him, 'I need salesmen who are articulate and confident. How would you like a job with us Mr van Breda? 'I'm not looking for fancy CVs and the like. I need someone capable of moving units. What do you say, Andrew is it?' Barely half an hour later, Andrew proudly flashed his brand-new ID book and signed on the dotted line. He traded-in his antique Anglia in lieu of the required deposit and drove off in a brand-new Ford Cortina. In effect, he had 'moved' his first unit. He would start work the following Wednesday; needing time to find permanent digs and a doctor who could refer him to a psychiatrist.

On his arrival at his hotel a week prior, he had taken a stroll along the beachfront to check his resolve and to shake loose the muscle fatigue brought on by the long drive from up country. He strolled after sunset, the street lights illuminating the pavements below sufficiently for Walters to discern faces and gender of after-dinner amblers. This was the litmus test; Johnny had wanted to ascertain the measure of his newly-discovered resurgence, his renaissance. He had planned to rate himself on his level of excitement when he observed any good-looking young boy pass by. He was flabbergasted to discover his new-born interest in females, not particularly of a sexual nature, more one of awe and admiration. This epiphany gave Johnny a euphoric feeling. He was overcome with joy. God had looked down from above and blessed him with ordinariness.

Before returning to his room, he had joined other guests in the hotel bar. He struck up a conversation with a plain-looking woman sitting unaccompanied close to him. Within the hour the two of them were laughing and joking like bosom-buddies of yesteryear. The disparities between his first homecoming ten years ago and the present were astounding. He had been overwhelmed with anger and frustration, his sexual preferences had tilted and he was becoming a sociable and somewhat likeable fellow. He prayed to God that night for His divine intervention and asked for His forgiveness for all of the atrocities he had committed over the years. Time would say that God had been on vacation that night.

Hell hath no fury like a woman scorned or words to that effect. We had a name for William Shakespeare at school: Billy Wobblestick we'd called him. Roddy had become a keen scuba diver; Carol and I had introduced him to the sport which he had taken to like a fish to water if you'll excuse the pun. He phoned one night to ask me if I would like to join him and a bunch of others on a dive on the Sunday. I readily accepted as Jos had won through to the semi-finals of a polo competition and would be away in Notties for the weekend and due to return on the Monday. The event was named The Annual Winter Polo Pony Breeders Cup. Where on earth did they find a trophy large enough on which to have that moniker engraved?

My Saturday was planned; I had been coerced into a round of self-flagellation on the Umbogintwini Golf Course, followed by dinner at Steve and Louise's with a couple of their friends. Once again, the golf trounced me. I paid over the ante willingly as I had thoroughly enjoyed the outing. I jokingly challenged the four-ball to a cello-playing competition on the following Saturday.

Sitting in the nineteenth, Sydney, one of our regular four-ballers told us a cracker of a joke. 'A man is eating breakfast along with his wife of

88

some twenty years' he started. 'All he can talk about is Natal rugby; Up Natal', Natal is the greatest! Up Natal'. 'Eventually the wife says, 'you know Koos I think you love Natal more than you love me' to which he replies indignantly, 'that's just not true, I love Northerns more than I love you.' It's the way you tell them.

The meal with Steve and friends as always was a delight. I had been ordered to bring my guitar along and we ended the night singing all the old favourites in a cacophony of false harmonies and mislaid lead vocals. My body ached the next morning, the result of swinging violently at a little white ball more than a hundred times and playing guitar for the first time in living memory; the tips of my fingers were blistered and sore through to the bone and beyond. Besides my aching body and permanently damaged hands, I was the picture of health as I set out to the dive site at five o' clock; a little behind schedule.

I arrived at the prearranged site. There were approximately six divers in all, standing around on the beach busy checking their bottles and other gear. I parked, unloaded my equipment and joined them apologising for my tardiness. A woman in the middle of the group greeted me acerbically, 'Good *afternoon* Doctor, I'm so glad you could join us.' I recognised Carol's voice and turning to her I replied graciously, 'Good morning Carol, it's nice to see you again.' If Roddy had mentioned she was to be part of the group, I doubt I would have accepted his invitation. The way she had treated me at our wedding was unforgiveable.

We slithered into our wetsuits and carrying our bottles waded into the shallows. The Indian Ocean waters were a temperate 23^0 Celsius. The rubber dingy was hauled off the sands and we clambered aboard. The dingy revved, spun around and headed out to an underwater reef approximately five hundred metres from shore.

I was classified as a novice diver, whereas Carol had been diving most of her life recreationally and as part of her line of work as a marine biologist. She had worked on exploratory dives as far afield as The Comoros, The Arctic Ocean and The Great Barrier Reef to name but a few. She recommended I accompany her on the dive as we were descending to depths of twenty metres plus. I initially viewed her newly-found concern for my wellbeing with caution. However, there would be at least four of us in the water at any given time and she was surely not going to do anything silly.

In Ladysmith, central Natal, Nandi Mpondo had again been beckoned by her ancestors.

'Nandi Ndlovukazi kaBhebe eLangeni, use the spear of the nation; smite down the ghostly ntombi who rides like the wind, the one who placed a great distance between the Queen Mother of the Zulus and her princely ndota, afore she has her ghostly ways with the sons of Shaka and the lands of his sons and the sons of his sons.'

Nandi awoke with a purity of purpose and clarity of mind as if the answers she had sought had been etched upon the very surface of her consciousness. Her husband had often spoken of a fair-haired ntombi who had joined The Spear of the Nation; the rebellious daughter of a rich and powerful leader of the umlungu, who would, given half a chance, slit each and every one of our mnyama or black throats.

Her ancestors had spelled it out; 'I must avenge my sweet and loving husband's death, for he is dead as sure as the Sun sets when the birds settle in the trees. And the target of my vengeance is the treacherous pale-skinned ntombi from afar.'

Polo is a team sport played on horseback in which the objective is to score goals against an opposing team. Players score by driving a small white plastic or wooden ball, roughly the same size as a cricket ball, into the opposing team's goal using a long-handled mallet. The traditional sport of polo is played at speed on a large grass field up to 300 yards long by 160 yards wide, and each polo team consists of four riders and their mounts. Field polo is played with a solid plastic ball, which has replaced the wooden ball in much of the sport. The modern game lasts roughly two hours and is divided into periods called chukkas. Polo is played professionally in 16 countries.

It is not uncommon for the best player on the team to play number two so long as another strong player is available to play three. Number two was Jocelyn's chosen position at which she excelled. Fotheringham, the soon to be stauncher of blood, the life-saver, played at number three.

Jos' team were ahead at the end of the second chukka. During play she had experienced an eerie sensation of someone 'examining' her, watching her closely. She dismounted and took note of a tall stately looking black woman adorned in traditional Zulu attire standing quite still on the side of the field. From a distance she appeared tall for a black female and yet very attractive. No, this woman was remarkable, not attractive as such; she had about her an air of menace, a wolf in sheep's clothing and fascinating to gaze upon. Jos summed up all of this in a matter of seconds. She walked over to the contest organiser and asked, 'Excuse me Mr Marshall,' pointing to the far side line, 'do you know who that black woman is standing over there?' He turned and looked to where Jos had indicated. 'What woman would that be Jocelyn?' Jocelyn stared confused, the woman had vanished; there one second and gone the next. 'Oh she must have left' she said.

Jocelyn was confounded; 'My God I saw her, I didn't imagine her, she wasn't some sort of Castle in Spain.'

Her team went on to lose the game and on Sunday would compete in the playoffs for third place. After the game, the team captain had commented on Jocelyn's lack of concentration. 'What's up old girl?' he enquired in his uppity British accent.

'I don't know Fothers, I'm really not feeling quite myself ever since last week's eliminating rounds in Shongweni' she replied honestly. 'By the way, did you notice a black female standing on the side-lines during the second chukka?' she asked with anticipation.

'Not that I recall Jossie' he replied somewhat bemused. 'Is there something wrong old girl?'

'No nothing really, I thought she was someone I knew' she lied.

Jocelyn tried calling home, hankering after some comforting and reassuring words from Ben. It rang for some time and then remembered he would be at Steve and Louise's home. She dialled their number and eventually he came on the line. She told him of her earlier experience and he sympathised and advised her to have an early night and she would be fine in the morning. 'It was probably a stress thing or the shadows playing games with you' he said condescendingly as many doctors are inclined to do. She was slightly miffed; 'take two aspirin and call me in the morning.' Seeing the lighter side of it, she turned off the bedside lamp and briefly considered her lack of menstruation and fell asleep.

The next morning, she met her parents for breakfast in the hotel dining room. She had awoken feeling nauseous nonetheless, refreshed and looking forward to participating in the playoffs. The strange occurrence of yesterday was already receding rapidly to the back of her mind. 'It must have been a trick of the light or anxiety as Ben said' she convinced herself.

The Borristers had patronised the Nottingham Road Hotel since Jocelyn was a babe in arms constantly treating the staff with the utmost respect and it had been reciprocated in spades. Rodney had received many invitations to stay over at friends' homes during polo matches but had always declined, preferring the freedom of being a paying guest as opposed to being a pain guest.

The bedroom maid came up to their table interrupting Jocelyn's train of thought. She held out a package.

'Your laundry Missie, should I put it in your room?'

'Thank you Elsie, yes please take it to my room. They're my jodhpurs, I forgot to bring an extra pair' she explained, looking across at her mother. Something caught her eye outside the window directly behind her father's back; the face of an alluring yet threatening black woman stared at her. The woman's stare penetrated the very core of Jocelyn's soul allowing her to fleetingly witness her own demise. She glimpsed the steely loathing of the beast and felt sick.

'Oh my God, it's her!' she exclaimed. Her father dropped his fork and leapt to his feet. 'What's wrong Jos?'

'Look, look over there' she commanded. Her parents both swung around but the fleeting figure had gone.

Jocelyn was as white as a sheet, almost ghostly. She tried to stand up. 'I must confront this thing.' Her legs buckled and her father grabbed her before she would collapse to the floor. The head waiter came scuttling across the room.

'Miss Jossie, Miss Jossie, what is wrong?' What is wrong Miss Jossie?' Her father lowered her back to her chair and said to the waiter, 'Amos, bring Miss Jossie a cup of sweet tea please.'

Amos scampered away as Jocelyn put her head on the table for a few moments. He returned almost immediately. 'What is it my darling, what just happened?' her father said handing her the teacup. She took it with trembling hands and in a wavering voice conveyed the events of yesterday.

The dining room had returned to a state of calm and most of the patrons had gone back to their rooms to finish packing and check out before the ten o' clock deadline.

'Well I just don't know what to say my love. Are you sure you saw this apparition, this . . . thing?'

'I saw her Daddy, as sure as the nose on my face, I saw her.'

'I would like to suggest we head on home and give the playoffs a miss. What do you think Jos, Jean?'

'I don't know Daddy; I let the team down yesterday. Mommy what do you think?'

Amos had done a round of the building and returned to tell them he had seen nothing or no-one out of the ordinary.

'If someone tries to hurt my Miss Jossie, eish I will kill them dead Baas Borrister, I will kill them dead, I promise you, eish!'

They mutually decided to stay for the rest of the tournament and return home on the Monday as originally planned.

I followed Carol down to a beautiful reef some twenty five metres below the choppy surface.

Scuba diving is a form of underwater diving, in our case for recreational pleasure in which we used a self—contained underwater breathing apparatus or scuba for short to breathe underwater.

Unlike other modes of diving, which rely either on holding ones breath or breath-hold or on air pumped from the surface, we carried our own source of breathing gas—compressed air—allowing us greater freedom of movement than with an airline or diver's umbilical. We moved around underwater by using fins attached to our feet.

It was the closest I have ever been to paradise. The world was hushed and the Sun's rays were filtered and feeble. The only sound I could hear was the hiss of my breathing apparatus. The marine life surviving on this length of reef seemed to me to be both tumultuous and perfectly ordered. The fish swarmed and broke in chaotic fashion then reformed in a silvery flash only to split again. The larger species swam about with abandon, ignoring their more highly evolved descendants invading their environment. Carol gesticulated to me to come closer while pointing out different features and characteristics of the reef. I was completely engrossed and enjoying this knowledgeable woman's company. How had I suspected her of plotting anything devious? Sarcasm and snubbing do not equate to murderous intent. On the contrary, later on, in the boat, eating hard-boiled eggs and sandwiches for breakfast, Carol was very charming and acting unexceptionally.

'When are you expecting Jocelyn home Ben?' Carol asked in an un-tailored manner.

'In the morning' I replied, 'probably around lunch time. Her team lost the semis, but she's playing for third place this afternoon otherwise she would have come home today.'

'I was just thinking, why don't I make us something for lunch and we can catch up on the latest news?'

On my way to Morningside, I suffered twinges of guilt. Was this the right thing to do? What would Jos think? I concluded that she trusted me and I was doing nothing untoward; I was joining a friend for lunch which was an innocent act as far as I was concerned.

The spread was sumptuous, however Jocelyn ate sparingly as the game was due to begin within the half hour; she felt queasy, also she never enjoyed playing on a full stomach. She had butterflies playing havoc with her insides. She was undecided whether they were a result of pre-game nerves or the remnants of the unwanted attention affianced her by the black apparition.

Her steed had been immaculately groomed. Jocelyn stood admiring 'Blazing Saddles' from outside of a paddock where her private stable-hand was in the process of warming him up; trotting and then breaking into the occasional short sprint enough to raise a slight sheen to his coat. To purchase, train and stable a quality polo pony is a costly endeavour. Rod Borrister owned four of the most magnificent specimens' money could buy; bought and trained in Argentina.

Blazing Saddles shied and bucked, tossing his mount to the ground at the precise moment Jocelyn felt the blade of a short stabbing spear penetrate her abdomen. The blade was withdrawn and thrust once again into her side with redundant vigour. Jocelyn collapsed to the dusty earth dying. The last thing she remembered before sliding into unconsciousness was the image of a tall semi-clad Zulu maiden straddling her, ululating wildly, her large drooping bosoms aquiver and the blood of menstruation leaking down her thighs.

CHAPTER SEVENTEEN

T hrough old-fashioned investigative techniques and many worn-down soles and souls, Cappie's team had concluded that Johnny Walters was their man. Times and places fitted perfectly and the mass of fingerprints lifted and tested, identified him as one Pieter Johannes Gouws, an escaped convict sentenced to life imprisonment in 1965 for the brutal rape of two young boys. He had served ten years of his sentence before absconding from Pretoria Central under suspicious circumstances.

'We must assume he's changed his identity again.' Cappie had gathered his team together for a review of the case.

'So far we have established the following; our suspect was born in Durban, he is a certified psychopath, he drives or drove a black Ford Anglia with the old-style registration number, TBJ3786, his mother and father are both deceased, he has a sister living in Pietermaritzburg and a step-father serving time in the Fort in Joburg for sex crimes. He is forty-five years old, a trained reporter, welds like a master artisan according to his last employer and likes little boys. Do you have any questions so far manne?'

'I have a question Cappie.' 'Go ahead Sergeant Botha' Cappie said resignedly.

'What is a psychopath Sir?' There were a few stifled chuckles around the room. 'No, I mean really Sir, what does a psychopath look like?'

Captain van der Merwe gave his team members a stern look in turn and then answered patiently, 'tonight I want you to visit the local movie outlet and rent a film by the name of 'Psycho' and that's an order Sergeant.'

'Yes Sir, I will do Sir' Botha answered sheepishly.

'Our friends in Barberton informed us that if Gouws had headed in their direction, they would have known. So where does that leave us gentlemen and lady? I'll tell you where it leaves us; it leaves us in the crapper. I want progress, I want you to get out there and explore every avenue. Talk to your contacts and informants; beat the hell out of them if necessary. I don't care how you do it but I want results and I would preferably like them on my desk by last week Tuesday. Now let's get to it ladies.' There was no laughter from the team; they knew when to hold their peace.

I left Carol's at five-thirty and walked into my house to the sound of the phone ringing off the hook. It was Rodney. He said I should drive immediately to Addington Hospital. Jos was to be air-lifted there; something about an attack, a stabbing. I couldn't quite make out what he was trying to tell me through his hysteria. Then the line went dead.

I had heard Jos, attack and Addington Hospital. That was enough for me. The roads are relatively quiet on Sunday afternoons and I arrived at the hospital in less than ten minutes even in the rain. As I drove up to the entrance, I heard the sound of a helicopter hovering above. I screeched to a halt and ran to the admissions desk.

'Jocelyn Mcpherson, has she been admitted?'

'They are due to land any minute now Sir.' The chopper was just another indicator of Rodney's influence.

Jocelyn was rushed into surgery while her parents and I waited outside wringing our hands in despair, waiting for any news from the surgical trauma team. Rodney, who by this time had managed to gather his wits about him, told me what happened. Apparently Jocelyn had been stabbed by a delusional black woman who maintained she was the Queen of the Zulu nation. She had been instructed by her ancestors to avenge the death of her husband. Rodney, being fluent in IsiZulu had listened to her explanation while waiting for the medevac chopper to arrive from

Durban. Jean continued, 'Rodney was dragged off that bitch by a couple of club members. They should have left him to strangle the cow!'

Howard Fotheringham, the team captain, had staunched the bleeding having had first-aid training during his national service. Howard was a strapping young man who had all his life idolised Jocelyn from afar. He had learned, as his brother before him, the finer nuances of horsemanship on his father's stud farm and resultantly became an exceptional polo player. He however preferred rearing race horses on his own farm outside Eshowe.

We squatted by the operating theatre for what seemed like an eternity. A green angel of mercy eventually emerged and approached us. 'I'm not going to beat about the bush; Mrs Mcpherson is critical and her chances of survival are slim to say the least. There is massive internal trauma and she will be in surgery for a while yet' he brusquely informed us. 'I suggest you speak to Matron and see if she has a bed for you Mr Mcpherson.'

He further informed us that Jos had lost a child; she had been about two months pregnant. She had phoned me on the Saturday night expressing her concerns. God damn it, why hadn't I insisted she return on the Saturday? Jean sobbed inconsolably. They finally left, leaving strict instructions about informing them of any further developments. They would be back in the morning.

I awoke with a start and looked around at the white walls confused and then realised I was in the recovery room next to surgery. I jumped off the bed, looking for a sister or a nurse.

Thoughts of revenge inhabited the edges of my mind. The truth had been suppressed by Rodney and his cronies but he had filled in the gaps for me. There were times, if Nandi Mpondo had been within reach, I would have gladly finished the job Rodney had so sorely wanted to accomplish. However, in a way, I understood Nandi's actions; she was driven by an insane thirsting for reprisal, a balancing of the scales. It was Old Testament justice in its most unsophisticated form; an eye for an eye, a wife for a husband. Yes, Jos had betrayed Nandi's husband if the truth be known, but his cover had already been blown. Mpondo had been destined to come face-to-face with his adversaries. I had quizzed Rodney regarding his fate; he informed me that he had confessed to numerous acts of terrorism and been sentenced to death.

Vusi spent his last night on earth coming to terms with his lot. The justification behind the bombings and the slayings was still clear in his mind. He was about to give up his life, as he had sworn to, for the struggle. He had no gripe with whites per se. 'It was never a black and white issue.' he rationalised. Basically, all he had strived for was his place in the Sun; he wanted use of all the facilities his brothers and sisters had sweated over, working for a slave's wage. He did not want to be constantly reminded his skin colour disqualified him entering certain places, or should not waste his time applying for certain jobs. Most of all, he believed in the age-old, clichéd maxim of 'one man one vote' which was so rare throughout Africa, yet still worth fighting for. The muti he had often paid the sangoma or witch doctor handsomely for, had not granted him the invisibility he had requested.

The warden scratched his keys across the bars of Vusi's death cell. He had been transferred from 'The Pot' the day before. The Pot is the unofficial name for the section that housed condemned prisoners in Pretoria Central. At one time, the prison gallows could hang up to 7 people at a time.

'Come my friend, it's time to take a little walk.' Earlier, he had been offered a breakfast of his choice, he had declined, requesting instead a meagre cup of weak sweet tea. The thought of never seeing his cherished Nandi and daughters again triggered a channel of silent tears to spill over his cheeks down onto his khaki overalls. He cried for his daughters and his wife; not for himself. He was resolute on meeting his end with dignity befitting a comrade of uMkhonto we Sizwe.

This was his thirty fifth year and he had fought and loved well throughout his short life. He had produced four strong and healthy children. His beautiful and regal Nandi had born him two daughters and his girlfriend—or second wife—in Ulundi, had provided him with two sons. Vusi had no regrets, except that he would never be able to teach his boys the way of the Zulu spear and shield. His thoughts lingered as he silently prayed to Unkulunkulu, the greatest God, to show kindness to all of his children and bless them and allow them to be raised in the ways of their ancestors.

His stomach strained to empty itself as he climbed the wooden staircase leading up to the gallows. 'The Spear of the Nation lives on in my sons' he said quietly to himself—four steps to go, 'my wives and my daughters, I will watch over you' Three steps to go, 'the Spear will protect you.' Two steps to go, 'in the name of my ancestors, let the killing cease.'

He climbed the last step and stumbled to the floor. The wardens helped him to his feet and walked him the last few yards to the platform. The black hood was quickly pulled over his head and the noose positioned round his neck with the knot carefully sited underneath Vusi's right ear. 'God forgive me.' His heartbeat escalated to over one hundred and sixty, his breathing shallow and rapid and then the floor fell away.

'God damn it to hell, damn you to hell Alan' I shouted, as I looked around, trying to make sense of my surroundings. It was dark and I was in a strange room, standing peering down at water, that all too familiar taste of honey and sugar choking me. I became suddenly overcome by nausea. My body was drenched in sweat and I was trembling uncontrollably. I felt, as a heroin addict must feel when in dire need of a fix. I was exhausted, totally burnt out. I flopped down on a chair next to me and waited for the nausea to subside before deciding on my next move.

I was obviously alone in this . . . what, hotel room? As I improved and my head cleared, a familiar smell filled my nostrils. I struggled to my feet and groped for a light switch in the corner of the room. I turned on an overhead lamp and immediately wished I hadn't. It *was* a hotel room, a hotel room awash in blood from the ceiling to the carpet. In the middle of the double bed lay the naked and dead body of a young man, his throat slashed and minus his genitals. I looked down at my clothes; my shirt and trousers bore witness of my evident involvement in this butchery. The blood was still wet, indicating to me the killing had just occurred. The smell was one of a copper and iron alloy, spiced with a pinch of salt. I checked that the door was bolted, removed my clothing and returned to my chair to think. 'You've really done it this time Alan' I said to no-one there.

If I could have only called Jocelyn, things would have been simple; she would have been here in a jiffy with a set of clean clothes and to help me collect myself. Who was I fooling? If I had been able to phone Joss at that ungodly hour, I would have left a trail as piquant as a bitch on heat.

The same restriction applied to Stephen, Roddy and everyone I knew except for one man.

I decided to sit it out until morning and reconsider my options in the common sensical light of day. I recovered two spare blankets from the wardrobe; I threw one over the poor young man and covered my nakedness with the second.

I heard the sound of the Beatles 'Eleanor Rigby' on the cello. 'My most loving and adorable brother tells everyone who will listen that I gifted him with the love of music, perhaps there is truth in this. He will also proclaim I am his most avid fan, this is the truth. Benjamin is the most talented cellist I have ever known. He also happens to be the only cellist I have ever known.' He paused until the laughter subsided. 'Perhaps some of you are wondering why I speak of my brother as I deliver a eulogy for my late sister Jocelyn. I will remind you; When I talk of Benjamin, I talk of Jocelyn too as they were one. Jocelyn will forever live on in the soul of my brother. I believe in the heart of my heart that Benjamin will too reside in Jocelyn's soul in perpetuity. She spread joy wherever she went; she was a gentle and caring being, adored by everyone who crossed her path. One Christmas I remember her bringing our fishing convoy to a shuddering halt on our way to Mozambique. She had spotted a lonely duckling wandering in the middle of approaching traffic and she jumped out of the Jeep bringing two lanes of traffic to a screeching standstill. Jocelyn returned the ugly duckling to its nonchalant mother. She acted as though this was her sole purpose in life. In fact it was; for she understood the meaning of life; she believed in the sanctity and inviolability of all living things. I recall, with absolute clarity, something she once said to me, she said: 'If you don't have the courage to love everyone for whom and what they are, don't ever think you can love yourself.' God bless her and may God reside in both of you forever and the horse she rode in on. I bless her in the name of her father and her mother and someone else, I can't quite remember who . . . .'

The grey light of dawn stretched itself into my chamber of horrors. I had dreamed my wife's eulogy mixed in with parts of Steve's best man speech; how bizarre, it was uncannily realistic to boot, except that last bit; 'What was that all about?' I wondered. I removed the hotel menu and information brochure from the bedside table. The Riverside Hotel was impressed on the front of its binder. I examined the key hanging in the keyhole; Room 303. 'Alright,' I said out loud, 'I'm in room 303 of the Riverside Hotel on the north bank of the Umgeni River. The time is now six-ten and I'm in the dwang, the crapper, I'm up the creek so to speak. The room number is in my favour at least' I realised.

'Rodney, It's Ben here, I know it's early and I'm about to ask you to do something for me which nobody should ask of anyone, but I have no choice.' Less than an hour later, there was a gentle knocking on the door. I had hung the 'Do Not Disturb' sign on the outside of the door hoping it would deter any over-eager chambermaid. 'Ben? It's me.' I recognised Rod's voice and let him in. I stood facing him in my blood-stained clothes which I had pulled on after showering. He took one look at me and blew a drawn-out whistle of disbelief.

He handed me a pair of khaki pants, a golf shirt with a small crocodile logo on the front, underwear and socks. His very first question was, 'where is your car parked?'

'I'm not sure, but I know it'll be close by' I told him from experience. 'I have my keys though' I added.

'We'll talk later' he said lifting the blanket off the badly spoiled deceased.

His face deadpan, he turned to me and said, 'get back to Addington and make yourself visible. You've been there all night, do you understand? And not one word of this to anybody.'

He accompanied me as far as the front desk and told me to carry on walking. I turned to watch him approach the young lady behind reception and show her something. I assumed it was some type of NIS identification card or badge or whatever spooks use nowadays. I found my BMW parked one block away from the hotel.

I entered the hospital through the emergency entrance, ruffled my hair to create the appearance of sleeping rough and made my way up to intensive care. Jocelyn was on the critical list and had been for the last two days. Monday it had been touch and go As far as I knew, I was by her side at eleven o' clock the previous night. Where had I vanished to? Where had Alan met the unfortunate young man lying in room 303? She seemed to be sleeping peacefully, the machines attached to her beeping and bleeping away softly, yet reassuringly.

Nandi Mpondo, Vusi's most venerable wife, was incarcerated in the non-white section of Kroonstad Prison for Women in the Orange Free State. In 1985, apartheid in the prison system had not as yet been formally abolished. The repeal of the section requiring black and white prisoners to be housed separately occurred in 1990. The Prisons Service was separated from the Department of Justice and renamed the Department of Correctional Services; the Prisons Act was renamed the Correctional Services Act in 1991. A new sentence of 'correctional supervision' was also introduced, allowing the possibility of a reduction in the prison population and acknowledging the limited usefulness of custodial sentences. Further legislation drastically reduced the circumstances in which the death penalty might be imposed, all existing death sentences were reviewed and many commuted to life, and a moratorium on hangings was introduced. This had come about too late for her husband. She learned of Vusi's execution only weeks into her twelve year sentence for attempted murder.

CHAPTER EIGHTEEN

We sat in a Chinese restaurant two blocks from the Hospital. Rodney had arrived back at intensive-care at eleven thirty and beckoned to me from the door. He had chosen a table at the back of the room away from the throng of lunch-time diners. My practise was once again closed indefinitely and I had to consider closing it or selling it off as a going concern. The one person I would sorely miss would be Sue; the second love of my life. If it hadn't been for her, my business would have closed before it even had a fighting chance of success. She was excellent; rescheduling appointments, organising stand-in psychologists, paying the bills and if the truth be known, generally running the practise.

I hadn't thought it necessary to install any sort of security system on the front entrance to the office. During normal hours, anyone and everyone had free access to the reception area; delivering the local newspaper, collecting for charities, asking for directions *and* the occasional patient. A few weeks before the attack on Jocelyn, two men had wandered in. The smaller of the two was brandishing a gun which he pointed at Sue while demanding the keys to the safe. Had I been missing something? Do psychologists keep wads of cash locked away in safes? These two were either total idiots or I was doing something terribly wrong. Sue, possibly as a result of her years in Belfast, remained calm and collected and ever so politely escorted the pair to the storeroom where the 'safe' was kept. I asked her what she had been planning to do once inside. 'I have no idea' she replied.

On closer inspection, she noticed that the gun was in fact a plastic replica, courtesy of Hong Kong. She dragged her heel down the idiot's shin with such a force that he dropped the toy and howled in agony clutching at his leg. The second idiot made a run for it and collided with the door, breaking his nose in the process. I, by this time, had come through from my office to see what all the commotion was about. Sue shouted, 'grab him Doctor, grab him.' I pulled the telephone cord out of the socket and managed to wrap it around idiot number two's ankles. We man-handled the pair of would-be robbers into the storeroom and locked the door. My eleven o' clock stood at the entrance to my consulting room gazing in awe at the debacle playing out. She told me later that it was the best therapy session she had ever attended.

We ordered and Rodney said, 'talk to me Benjamin, I want to hear everything, I want to know all about the dark side of my daughter's husband.' I started from the top, leaving nothing out. I told him of the multiple personalities, the pharmacological treatment and the prior killings. I spoke of my childhood rape and the battering I had endured, the affect alcohol and stress had on me, my utter love for his daughter and her absolute safety and welfare when under my care. I even mentioned Detective Anderson and his tenacious ways. I imparted this to a man whom I feared and yet respected deeply. I had come to love him over the years and trusted completely. He was the sort of man every boy would want as a father; worldly wise, fearless and yet kind and caring. I spilt the beans and held nothing back. He was silent as I spoke for a good hour and a half. He watched with ardent eyes, wordlessly with an unlocked mind.

'We can't allow the antichrist to run amok' he said passionately. 'I know the word is probably not used in a psychologist's lexis Ben, but what I saw this morning was the work of the devil.'

'What you saw this morning was the work of Alan, That's what I've been trying to tell you for the last ninety minutes for God's sake; he *is* the devil Rod,' I *am* the devil personified for Christ's sake! I should be kept under lock and key until the end of days.' The reason I'm walking around a free man is because Jocelyn believes in me and allows it Rodney. She allowed me life; she gave me life at the expense of the poor dead bastards out there.

'No Ben, she allowed you your freedom to kill in spite of her abhorrence. She and you decided these freaks of nature weren't worth the time of day. You murdered discriminately and you both allowed it to continue as long as they were, in your opinions, a sub-species not worth giving a damn about.'

'And this comes from a man who is set to kill in the name of nationalism?' I questioned. 'And I must add Rodney I don't view homosexuals as freaks of nature.'

'You are so mistaken my young son in both instances; I have never killed in the name of jingoism or patriotism. I have killed and will kill again in the name of survival, survival and to protect my loved ones my naive friend. It's the law of the jungle out there Ben. But man should never kill indiscriminately or without reason.' And I *do* view sexual deviancy as freakish behaviour and I make no apologies.'

'But Dad, you have to realise it's not me doing the killing' I stated pleadingly.

Oh but it is Ben. Whether you like it or not, the people who died at Alan's hand, were in fact murdered by Benjamin Mcpherson. It was your hand that took the knife to that young man, was it not? Would you put it to me that six million Jews died at the hands of one thousand individuals or conceivably ten thousand, a million? I think not my son. Responsibility is never a collective affair; the buck always stops somewhere and at someone's door.'

'You have to realise that Alan does the killing Rod. I know it is ultimately me who carries out the act, but I'm not in control when he decides to carry out his brutal work.'

'That is just too easy to profess. We have a brilliant doctor who works for us and you *are* going to see her. Ben, you are my daughter's husband, and that makes you my son. We will make some sense out of all of this. The deceased is history; the thing that didn't happen last night didn't happen, okay? What a bad bastard I must have been in my previous life to deserve the two of you. Let's get back to Jocelyn and see her through this my boy.'

Nothing appeared in the local or national press. As far as the public was concerned, nobody was mutilated in room thirty something at the River whatever Hotel. Two months later an unclaimed cadaver was interred in a pauper's grave in Stellawood Cemetery. Nobody came to the funeral and nobody was mourned; the miserable cost of anonymity.

After hearing my confession, 'Father Rodney' said that everything would go away and I needn't fear retribution in any guise. He made me make a promise to him I knew I wouldn't honour. Unbeknown to me, shortly thereafter he had made contact with two of his most trusted associates, who were formerly involved with affairs of the family. He requested a favour and filled them in with the details. He chose wisely as they would willingly have offered up their lives for the farmer from Natal.

George King was a very happy man; he woke to the sound of Emily showering in the on-suite bathroom and the smell of bacon wafting through from the kitchen. 'What more can I ask for?' he asked rhetorically. His work had always come first. George's schedule had made it difficult to form any lasting relationships. His frenetic lifestyle and the secret nature of his work complicated things. He had started to wonder whether he would end up a grumpy old man, forevermore accepting his right hand as his one and only true companion in life.

He returned from supervising a pick-up or 'snatch' in Zambia. They flew into Lanseria to the north-west of Johannesburg, a lesser airport than Jan Smuts, used widely by smaller and privately-owned aircraft, situated near his home town of Krugersdorp. The pilot taxied toward the terminal in the Beechcraft Premier 1 as King discussed security arrangements with ground staff. Unbeknown to the general populations of both Zambia and the Republic, there was an existing agreement, at ministerial level, allowing for the 'recovery' of political dissidents from the north. Zambia condemned South Africa and its apartheid regime vociferously and openly as did countries around the globe nevertheless, under a veil of secrecy, it received economic and strategic commodities assistance and as there is always a price to pay, certain arrangements were underhandedly agreed to.

The grab had gone down in a public marketplace on the dusty outskirts of Kitwe, a small mining town situated in the heart of the copper belt. The Zambian police were instructed beforehand to turn a blind eye to anything unusual going down regarding a white four-wheel drive vehicle. A Toyota Land Cruiser came to a dusty halt, two men jumped out and bundled a small black man—chatting to a woman wearing a Che Guevara T-shirt—into the rear of the vehicle. As the Toyota sped away, he struggled for a short while and then sank back in his seat as the intravenously administered midazolam took effect.

King sat patiently in the co-pilot's seat, on the apron of a rarely used airstrip, engines idling in anticipation of the arrival of the Toyota and its human cargo. He whistled Colonel Bogey obliviously. The woman wearing the iconic shirt had done her job and would be well-paid for an hour or two's work. A sleeper agent of the SA government, Mavis had been instructed to befriend Zilane and make sure he would be in a pre-arranged spot at a given time; pish-posh for the highly-trained foreign officer. She also happened to be happily married to a white South African. She and her husband resided in Lusaka in the lap of luxury brought about by executing shady diamond deals on behalf of a National Party Minister who shall forever remain anonymous.

David Zilane lay drowsily in the second row of the plane, handcuffed to the base of his seat, listening to the co-pilot discussing his arrival at the terminal with the female head of security. None of what he overheard made sense to his tangled brain. He was guided through the terminal; any form of passport control arrogantly overlooked by the two NIS agents accompanying him. The three men climbed into a Volkswagen Golf in the airport parking lot. Zilane would be handed over to his 'host' on a secluded and covert farm some ten km from Lanseria where the interrogation process would begin.

After the successful completion of yet another operation, King sipped on a cold Castle Lager and took a deep drag on his third Camel plain while chatting to Emily Badenhorst, the recently appointed head of Lanseria Airport security. Within the hour, he had asked her, rather awkwardly, if he could see her socially, to which she readily agreed. Emily lived two km from George King in the rapidly expanding up-market suburb of Noordheuwel. Over the months they became almost inseparable, to the extent she spent every free weekend at his house and week nights when she could. He had told her of his dedication to King and country. She giggled at his play on words. Emily loved the notion that their work and political beliefs were of an identical nature. He had smiled benevolently at the thought of any similarity between their jobs. Dodging bullets in an unfriendly country and the disparity of checking the credentials of an incoming minor bureaucrat from Botswana could never be offset. Although he never mentioned the obvious differences, he respected her for what she did for a living and over a very short time, the whistler came to love her dearly.

He had recently turned thirty five and was well aware it was still early days in their relationship, but over a breakfast of bacon, eggs and black pudding—which Emily had recently sampled and loved—George tested the waters.

'So what are you planning for the next fifty years Emily?' She scrutinised him as if making one of the biggest decisions in her entire life.

'I plan to spend them with a gorgeous man who lives down the road from me.' She reached across the table and took his hands in hers. Georgie Porgie didn't kiss this girl and make her cry on the contrary, he had swept her into a state of bliss.

Emily Badenhorst, nee Harding, had married at twenty to a wild-child by the name of Eric, a biker who had effectively committed suicide while racing his 1100 Yamaha motorbike on the Krugersdorp—Pretoria highway. His mean machine had developed a speed wobble while travelling in excess of two hundred kilometres per hour. He was flung like a rag doll twenty metres to the opposite side of the road, into the path of an oncoming eighteen-wheeler. One of the ambulance crew had said that of all the road accidents he had attended, he had never set eyes on anything so grisly. She had sworn at the time to avoid serious relationships like the plague.

Emily was an attractive brunette with brown doe-like eyes, a large mouth and big bones inherited from her father an orthodontist, who was six foot six tall. She had matriculated out of Krugersdorp High School, a popular vice head-girl who had excelled at tennis and target-shooting. She had developed a mild drug problem leading to the act of defiance that was Eric. She was two inches shorter than George who stood just north of six foot. Her previous oath forgotten, she decided, if he proposed, she would consent in the blink of an eye. Emily was going on thirty and wanted to bear little princes and princesses, with lots of input from King.

Two weeks lapsed before Jocelyn was removed from the critical list. She had lost partial use of her left leg and would never bear children. After another month of intensive physiotherapy, she was allowed to vacate her sickbed and be released into the custody of her parent's. Jean was suffering with the early stages of Alzheimer's and hence not capable of fully caring for her daughter. It dawned on me that this appalling disease was the reason she had been increasingly withdrawing from every-day life. Rodney juggled his time looking after Jocelyn and keeping an eye on his mentally-deteriorating wife. I was battling to keep my practise afloat while more and more GP's were referring their impaired patients to alternative therapists.

Following the fiasco in room 303, Rod had me referred to a psychotherapist on the payroll of the NIS. She dealt primarily with cases of post-traumatic stress endured by agents who had witnessed things never meant for human consumption. Her name was Dr Maxilla de Harnes, whom from my first consultation, scared me shitless. She had a way about her that made honesty and openness compulsory. She was Belgian, but I was of the impression she was born the most cruel and eldest daughter of Dr Goebbels. She was nonetheless excellent and within a month, had me admitting to stealing a slab of chocolate from the kitchen dresser at the age of seven. She had clearly been prepped by Dr Shields and immediately got down to brass tacks. I had never been subjected to such intense analysis. I began to wonder whether this is what had been de rigueur all these years.

Alan, Keegan, Alex and a host of personalities introduced themselves to her. She finally empowered me to take cognisance of seven dissimilar persona residing inside my clearly acquiescent and all-welcoming psyche. There were five males; Alan, Alex, Keegan and twins John and James and females Anne and Fiona.

Multiple personality disorder, also known as dissociative identity disorder, is an extremely rare mental condition characterized by at least two distinct and relatively enduring identities or dissociated personality states that alternately control a person's behaviour. It is accompanied by memory impairment for important information not explained by ordinary forgetfulness. These symptoms are not accounted for by substance abuse, seizures other medical conditions nor by imaginative play in children.

Diagnosis is often difficult as there is considerable comorbidity with other mental disorders. Malingering should be considered, if there is possible financial or forensic gain, as well as factitious disorder if help-seeking behaviour is prominent. MPD is one of the most controversial psychiatric disorders with no clear consensus regarding its diagnosis or treatment. Research on treatment effectiveness still focuses mainly on clinical approaches and case studies. Dissociative symptoms range from common lapses in attention becoming distracted by something else and daydreaming, to pathological dissociative disorders. No systematic, empirically-supported definition of 'dissociation' exists.

People diagnosed with MPD often report that they have experienced severe physical and sexual abuse, especially during early to mid-childhood and others report an early loss, serious medical illness or other traumatic event. They also report more historical psychological trauma than those diagnosed with any other mental illness. Severe sexual, physical, or psychological trauma in childhood has been proposed as an explanation for its development. Awareness, memories and emotions of harmful actions or events caused by the trauma are removed from consciousness and alternate personalities or sub-personalities form with differing memories, emotions and behaviour. MPD is attributed to extremes of stress or disorders of attachment.

What may be expressed as post-traumatic stress disorder in adults may become MPD when occurring in children. Possibly due to developmental changes and a more coherent sense of self, past the age of six, the experience of extreme trauma may result in different, though also complex, dissociative symptoms and identity disturbances. A specific relationship between childhood abuse, disorganized attachment and lack of social support are thought to be necessary components of MPD. Other suggested explanations include insufficient childhood nurturing combined with the innate ability of children in general to dissociate memories or experiences from consciousness.

I listened to Dr de Harnes, fascinated to learn of the multitude of explanations, reasons, components and symptoms of my disorder. Some I recognised, others I discarded as quickly as a smouldering cinder handled in error. I believed with all my heart my parents had nurtured me with great expertise and attention to detail. I had never been subjected to physical abuse in my formative years. I was eleven when I was sexually abused, which da Harnes deemed as an unprocessed post-traumatic stress disorder.

In 1974 the highly influential book Sybil was published, and later made into a movie in 1976. It presented a detailed discussion of the problems of treatment of 'Sybil', a pseudonym for Shirley Ardell Mason who purportedly had, if my memory serves me correctly, sixteen to eighteen alternate personalities. Though the book and subsequent film helped popularize the diagnosis, later analysis of the case suggested different interpretations, ranging from Mason's problems being iatrogenically induced through the therapeutic methods used by her psychiatrist or an inadvertent hoax due in part to the lucrative publishing rights of the book.

I remember the Emmy Award-winning film starring Sally Field in the role of Sybil and Joanne Woodward as her psychiatrist, Dr Cornelia Wilbur. I mentioned to de Harnes I should write my memoirs and retire a wealthy man. I was severely reprimanded regarding the seriousness of my mental condition. I am led to believe the Belgians are not over-endowed with a sense of humour.

The analysis was thorough and at times painfully revealing. I learned things about myself that shocked me to the core and I challenged the doctor to prove these disturbing character traits, her raison d'être, to which she replied, 'All in good time doctor. Have a little patience my friend.' She had to be the most patronising hard-arsed bitch ever. I mentioned this once to Rodney, he smiled and said, 'that 'hard-arsed bitch' you talk of has rescued lost souls Benjamin; she has saved people whom there was no possibility of salvaging. There are many in the mental-health community who wish for more hard-arsed bitches like her.' The longer I knew Rodney, the easier it became to empathise with Jocelyn's rebelliousness. Shit, at times Rod's smug self-righteousness made me want to strangle him! All he could have said to me in reply was 'She strikes me in the same way Ben.' But no, that would have been too easy for *my* Rodney.

The therapy continued for two years and even today I occasionally consult Dr de Harnes as a patient and in my professional capacity (I reopened a small practise in the nineties). She spends time abroad presenting papers and every so often she is invited to lecture at the prestigious Northwestern University in Chicago. The varsity's motto is: 'Quaecumque Sunt Vera' or 'Whatsoever Things Are True'. I think this dictum is appropriate to me and my rag-tag team of leeches. However unbelievable my alternate personalities appear to be, they *are* authentic and 'live' inside me, needing very little motivation to enjoy a day's outing. I still work extremely hard at containing them. One last thing on the subject, I would eventually become very fond of Doctor Maxilla de Harnes; do the maths.

There was a loud urgent knocking on his front door. It was Saturday and Detective Anderson's wife Bonnie had gone out to do the week's grocery shopping. He was sitting at the dining room table attempting to catch up with the mountain of paperwork; a policeman's lot. He removed his glasses as the banging continued. 'I'm coming, hold your horses, Jees' he shouted. He was frustrated beyond measure; Benjamin Mcpherson remained a free man and Anderson was convinced, beyond a shadow of a doubt, he was guilty of at least the beachfront slaying and possibly two other cold-cases. It was mostly based on his cop's intuition, a gut feel. Dave knew from experience to ignore his sixth sense at his peril.

He had dug deep over the last few months discovering that Mcpherson had been the unfortunate victim of a particularly sadistic attack when he was eleven. In addition Anderson had bullied a male pharmacist in the Berea into imparting some enlightening information about Mcpherson's medication. 'Fair enough, the prescription is from five or six years' ago' he admitted. Nonetheless, his sister Dianne had confirmed his suspicions; the medication was prescribed to patients suffering from paranoia, schizophrenia, MPD and other similar personality disorders. 'This is one slippery character' Dave concluded.

He opened the door to a pair of burly mean-looking individuals. The short back and sides, non-descript well-tailored suits and black-boned shoes screamed 'official government business' and by their overall appearance, were 'definitely not here to do a tax audit' Anderson concluded.

'Good morning Detective Anderson, my name is King and my colleague's name is du Plessis. We're here on official business of the National Intelligence Service' he lied; there was *nothing* official about this visit. They shook hands and George said, 'may we come in Detective?' 'Certainly' Anderson replied flummoxed.

He made coffee and joined them in the sitting room. 'What's this in connection with Mr King?' correctly assuming King was the superior officer.

'I'm afraid it's a very touchy subject and I must insist not a word of this is ever mentioned again, not to your colleagues, to any family member nor to friends. I hope you understand what I'm saying to you Detective. This meeting here today, never happened and what I'm about to tell you, I'm imparting in total secrecy. Do you understand?'

Anderson had heard rumours of citizens being 'visited' in the early hours of the morning by messengers of the state. He had further heard of ordinary law-abiding citizens going missing in perpetuity for not heeding whatever advice they had been given. Anderson recognised that this was quickly deteriorating into one of those situations.

'We were informed that for some time now, you've been heading up an investigation into the murder of a queer beach bum near the Cuban Hat Roadhouse, is this correct detective?'

'Among other homicides, yes I'm leading the investigation into the murder of a white male in the proximity of that roadhouse.'

'Okay Anderson, I am not here to listen to police mumbo jumbo or so much political correctness. According to our information, the guy was a male prostitute or something of that nature, in other words a low-life fag, a queer, a fudge-packer.'

'If that's your take on it Sir, that's your business. I am not particularly concerned about his sexual preferences. I *am* however interested in apprehending the person who committed this crime. That's my job Mr King; to put perpetrators behind bars.'

It was time for pressure to be applied; 'Detective, we have further been informed that your number one suspect is a doctor by the name of Benjamin Mcpherson. Is this true?'

'I am not at liberty to divulge that kind of information.' Anderson was knocked off his box. 'How could they possibly be privy to that?' Just who the hell are these two and from where or more likely from whom do they get their facts?' he wondered, at a complete loss for words.

'I have been sent to inform you that starting as of now Detective Anderson, Doctor Mcpherson's name will be removed from the case docket and any further investigations into Mcpherson or his immediate family will be frowned upon by people in high places. All I can add is that the Doctor is involved with top secret work for the government and if this work were to be in any way interfered with or compromised, the repercussions would be grave. If you want to confirm who we say we are, feel free to call the NIS' King said in conclusion giving Anderson a contact number and flashing a security card of sorts.

'Oh, by the way, thanks for the coffee.'

They departed leaving behind a worried and befuddled homicide detective. Sitting in the Avis rental car, they gave one another a look of amusement and in chorus doubled over in fits of laughter. 'Jesus George that bit about top secret government work was a bit over the top wasn't it?' 'I know, but did you see that poor bastards face? It was a treat. I was so close to collapsing then and there, I had to imagine some horrible thoughts to control myself.' This brought on another round of raucous laughter.

'You don't thing Rodney's son is involved in any of this do you George?'

'Who, Benjamin . . . . no way, a more balanced, level-headed man I have yet to meet. It's an obvious case of mistaken identity.'

'And what if he calls HO?'

'I don't think he'll chance it, he wouldn't want to compromise state security.'

George gave Andre a glance while raising both eyebrows in a questioning manner causing them to break into more convulsive laughter. They headed towards Louis Botha Airport for a pub lunch and a short flight back to Johannesburg.

A month later Detective Anderson received notification that he was to be transferred to Pietermaritzburg Central Police station as head of the Criminal Investigation Department. The NIS, if approached for comment, would say, 'who the hell is Detective Anderson?'

Sergeant Botha had hit the jackpot. He made a conscious effort not to break into a run on his way to the boss's office. 'Cappie is going to love this.' Botha involuntary gave his best Cheshire cat impression as he knocked and entered.

Captain van der Merwe had spent the previous day at John Vorster Square attempting to justify his team's lack of progress. The killings had ceased from the time they had let Gouws slip through their net, affirming the squad's mutual conviction. Colonel Naudé had ranted and raved; how disappointed he was in Andries, he was considering disbanding the team at the end of the month and the Captain's excellent reputation was in the process of being eroded away.

The rest of the day, van der Merwe attended a briefing on burgeoning crime scene investigation techniques and his mood lightened when Naudé hinted at deploying a few permanent CSI teams in major cities as recommended by a visiting team of FBI CSI boffins. He would need to redeem himself and quickly, to be considered for an opening.

'Captain, good news Sir, we received a telex from Durban Central this morning' Botha said out of breath.

'That is splendid news Sergeant, you've made my day' he replied.

'But Sir I haven't even told . . . . ag Sir, that's a good one' Botha grinned. 'No Sir, the telex is a list of Ford trade-ins in the Durban area from June until yesterday.' The Captain's ears pricked up. 'There was a Ford Anglia traded in at the beginning of July and get this Cappie, it had a TBJ registration number.'

'Now that *is* splendid news Sergeant. Is there a name we can attach to this transaction?'

'Yes Sir, the man's name is Andrew van Breda. The address he gave was The Blue Waters Hotel, North Beach. The best part is his ID number; it belongs to a deceased woman who died in a car accident two years ago.'

'I could kiss you on your premature bald spot Botha.' The sergeant blushed and giggled like a little girl.

'I need you to contact the hotel and check . . . '

'I have already Sir' he interrupted, 'the receptionist said no-one by that name has stayed or is staying there presently.'

'You are on the ball Sergeant Botha; I must remember to increase your Smartie ration. This is our Pieter Gouws; I can feel it in my waters.

Gather the ladies together in the briefing room my good man, we have work to do.'

My parents had planned a family get-together for the first weekend in October. Jocelyn had returned to our home mid-September and was recovering well. She walked with a noticeable limp, caused by composite nerve damage. In addition, she suffered occasional bouts of intense abdominal pain for which she was taking large amounts of Syndol; a highly-addictive pain killer. The general prognosis was fortunately optimistic; the painful episodes were becoming less frequent and due to daily physiotherapy, her gait was improving by the week. The scarring caused by the spear, plus the surgeon's needlework was extensive and in Jos' eyes hideous, 'preferable to the alternative' I pointed out to her.

The day at the folks was as always great fun. Jocelyn was treated as a celebrity and although she thought her battle wounds 'hideous' showed them to all interested parties. Mom had a funny turn when she viewed the disfigurement and needed a double G and T with a twist; 'for purely medicinal purposes' she informed everyone. The entire clan was in attendance. Dad had set up tables and chairs on the patio and treated us to one of his special barbeques or braais as they are locally known.

The swarm of kids spent the entire day screaming and splashing in and around the pool. Louise asked my opinion regarding a tiny growth on her shoulder which was red and inflamed. I advised her to consult a doctor on Monday morning, Steve said, 'you see Louise' turning to me he continued, 'I've been telling her for weeks to see a doctor. She never listens to me.' Roddy and his girlfriend Melissa joined us for lunch and he entertained all of us with his never-ending supply of hilarious shaggy dog stories and gag after gag.

I noticed Dad was restless, fidgety and he kept glancing at his watch. The old man was up to something. The front-door bell rang and he was out of his chair like a jack-in-the-box. He returned with a couple I didn't recognise however, the man looked vaguely familiar. My Dad introduced them to everybody, 'everyone, let me introduce you to Douglas and Belinda Green.' I did a classic double-take and the penny dropped; it was my masked gung-ho stuntman from my youth, the hero of our 'Great Show'.

Apparently Mom had never stopped communicating with Dougie's mother throughout the years and on hearing of his up and coming holiday in South Africa, Dad had insisted they spend a night or two with them. Doug and his wife had arrived in Joburg that morning and caught an inter-connecting flight to Louis Botha and voila, here they were. What a day, what a reunion. We spent the afternoon reminiscing, and I told the tale of the masked rider much to my mother's astonishment. 'If I had known things like that were going on behind my back, I would never have left home.' 'What *did* you tell your folks the day you nearly snuffed it Doug?

'As far as I can remember, I told them I was a victim of a hit and run of some sort' Dougie replied. 'My Dad went charging off in a rage to find a car with fitting scrapes or bumps and you know what Ben, believe it or not, he never found it.'

We said our farewells and arranged to meet Major Douglas Green and his rather gorgeous wife for lunch the following day at a local hotel. On the Sunday, after lunch we said our final goodbyes with promises of visiting them in the UK in a year or two. Such assurances made with so much sincerity at the time, sadly rarely materialise.

CHAPTER NINETEEN

Andrew van Breda's life had become tedious; one long robotic routine. He arose, ate breakfast and the rest of his day sold cars to people who either couldn't afford or didn't need one. In the afternoons, he returned home to his small rented apartment in Mayville, cooked and went to bed, read a paragraph or two only to start the entire process over the following morning. Ever since he had started taking the prescribed medication, his sexual urges had dwindled away and he found it difficult to *really* feel something about anything; to experience *real* anger or any emotion for that matter. At least his old self had lived on the cusp; on a permanent high. His resolve had so far held out, yet he yearned for a release from this dreariness, this monotony. 'I am in a theatre watching a boring stage production and I'm playing the leading role.' He had feelings of detachment, a state of being previously unknown, a lack of involvement and his indifference to all things around him should be of concern but were not. However, somewhere in the thick fog, he paradoxically fretted about his lack of concern.

He had recently attempted to read Dante's Inferno and was fascinated by a passage toward the end of the first epic poem which he summarised as follows:

'Before entering Hell completely, Dante and his guide see the 'Uncommitted', **souls of people who in life did nothing, neither for**

***good nor evil**. These souls are neither in Hell nor out of it, but reside on the shores of the Acheron, their punishment to eternally pursue a banner (or conscience?) while pursued wasps and hornets that continually sting them, as maggots and other such insects drink their blood and tears.'

What he had gleaned from this was that the world needed both good and evil to maintain a cosmic balance. 'My behaviour is therefore an integral part of and necessary to the nature of all things. I bring a balance to the world' he concluded with a twinge of self-satisfaction. Philosophy was never his strong suit. Andrew flushed the pills down the lavatory.

Within days his cynicism returned and he wondered what in the name of Beelzebub had brought about his fleeting stint batting for the other side, his lustful cravings for the female form? Andrew's erections returned and were welcomed with a firm shake of the hand.

'Maybe I should chance my arm again; it's been roughly five days longer than infinity.' He smiled and thought out loud, 'Look out boys, Pieter's back.' He took a slow cruise to the ice rink for 'a well-deserved and long overdue squizzy. 'I must be ultra-chary, you can't be too careful *Andrew*, not Pieter remember.' He had watched on the news that Rock Hudson died as a result of AIDS on October 2. 'I must keep one or two French letters on me at all times; you never know your luck or lack of it.' He spent an hour in the change-room checking out the local talent but found 'nothing' to his taste.

❁

'I want you to listen very carefully Ben before you make an uninformed decision. Over the last two months Limpet mines damaged the basement of OK Bazaars in Smith Street, Game Stores and Checkers, all supermarkets in central Durban as you know, and a limpet mine was fortunately defused in the Spar Supermarket.'

'I do watch the news Rodney' I replied. It was going to be another 'listen to *me*' episode.

Rodney continued undeterred, 'the so called 'Trojan Horse Massacre' was broadcast across the world my son. What was our security force to do, stand back and allow the situation to deteriorate into anarchy before taking any action?'

'The shooting and killing of three young men should never be condoned Rodney and you know it' I said defiantly.

'Then what about the incident at Grosvenor Girls School on the Bluff, how many innocent young girls could have been slaughtered if the Limpet mine hadn't detonated prematurely? In August a bomb exploded in a night club at a hotel in Zululand injuring 30 children. Must I carry on?'

'I just can't imagine how I can make a difference. What would be my contribution?'

'It would be infinitesimal Benjamin, in the bigger picture that is. The point I'm trying to get across is, your input would not be one of quantity; I want you to add quality to the battle, we lack men with brains, with intellect. Also, I have witnessed you function under extreme stress while showing scant emotion. National intelligence is not a game for sissies Ben. We need men with cool heads capable of making difficult decisions under pressure.'

'We've spoken of these things many times Rod. The crux of it all is I would require Jocelyn's consent and you have implied each time I've brought this up, it's proscribed. I would be disloyal if I were to be a representative of everything she is against. And she is Rodney, after her scrape with death she has become pacifistic. She would rather roll over than fight. All our lives everyone has said Jos and I are 'one' and I want to maintain the status quo. I refuse to castigate her for her anti-violence values. She's my wife for God's sake Rod and might I remind you, she's your daughter. I will not do anything behind her back, end of story. I know you made me promise to avail myself as your protégé in turn for your help, but I can't do it Rodney; not to the detriment of Jocelyn and my relationship. Surely you can appreciate that.'

'Damn it Benjamin, discuss it with her then, test the water if you must. I'll soon be retiring my services and the family will need a shield at a level that can provide protection from the ghouls and phantoms, invisibly circling like vultures. You have yet to realise that within eight to ten years, the black man will be in control; this land of ours will be governed by bastards who don't have the expertise to manage the corner cafe. It's probably not their fault, but true nonetheless.' He continued dejectedly, 'also, I will always help you without asking for anything in return, and you know that Ben.'

'Yes I know that, I'm sorry Rodney' I said, 'but at least the corner cafe will be in the hands of the right bastards.' He had no answer and refused to be drawn into an unguarded corner.

'Take your cheap shots my boy. Within five years our government—probably headed up by that de Klerk—will capitulate and we will be on the slippery slope to perdition and you can count on that my noninterventionist friend' he said with buckets full of credence. 'He *will* be our next President, mark my words' he said like a man in the know.

For van Breda to 'score' in relative safety, he would have to head out to one of the satellite towns bordering the city. He disliked the idea of Amanzimtoti. Twenty years had passed since he 'lucked-out' there but still considered it a bad place to go on the hunt. Perhaps he should take a drive in-land. 'What of Pietermaritzburg?' he questioned. 'Or even further afield, such as Nottingham Road or Mooi River or even Ladysmith?' he queried. His undertaking, made with so much alacrity at the summit of van Reenen, had for reasons beyond his comprehension, but to his liking, had dissolved.

He drove down the main road leading into Howick. It was Sunday morning and he was in his element; brass in pocket and ecstatic at the idea of performing his first recce in months. Andrew found himself in the area of Harvard Street and Braemar Crescent and to his delight 'discovered' a primary school in the vicinity. 'It's such a pity it's a weekend' he mused dreamily. The reconnaissance served two main purposes; to get to know the area comprehensively and second to choose the target. The scouting could be a time-consuming procedure as the preferred mark needed to live in an area conducive to his technique; isolated and dimly lit. Then there was the question of the parents; single mothers preferably or a father who worked at night. All of these were critical factors that needed to be substantiated. His motto always came into play: 'I can't be too careful now can I. I mean it's worked for me for the last ten years. Why should I change a winning formula?'

He would ask for two day's compassionate leave on Wednesday inventing a death in the family and return to scrupulously complete the first phase of his assignment. In addition, he would work incognito, and from a safe distance, make the school his starting point. He had once parked adjacent to a primary school and opened up the bonnet to appear as if his car had broken down, only to be approached by one or two good Samaritans offering assistance, and consequently had had to move on. Plus they got a good look at him, forcing cancellation of that particular plot, to the benefit of one enormously fortunate child. 'This is going to be something special; the maestro's greatest opus yet' he gleamed. Andrew van Breda held himself in very high esteem.

There was one issue his fastidiousness had not taken into account and that was the dogged relentless nature of Captain van der Merwe. When choosing a new identity, van Breda would have fared much better by opting for a more common surname; a Botha, Smith or Pretorius being the more prudent choice. They lie third, fifth and sixth respectively on the list of the thousand most common surnames in South Africa. It made Cappie's task a lot easier to trace one Andrew van Breda as opposed to an individual called John Smith or Johan Botha. The thoughtlessness of vanity and the consequences thereof can be damning.

'Captain, I've just got off the phone with Detective Jooste from Durban Central Sir.'

'Oh the humanity!' the Captain said, raising his hands to his head in a dramatic pose, 'And what did he have to say Sergeant?'

Andries was exceptionally fond of Botha; he especially admired his willingness and his dedication to the force. Cappie had once witnessed the Sergeant do a sixty hour shift with the occasional twenty-minute catnap. He admired his tenacious spirit and interminable optimism. Botha had the knack of cheering up the most pessimistic of colleagues with his ever-present smile and considerate manner; asking after everyone's wellbeing including their spouses and children and chickens and goats.

'Gouws works as a salesman for a Ford dealership in Russell Street Sir or should I call him van Breda Captain? I mean, when we arrest him what should we call him Sir?'

'Sergeant you can call him Mickey Mouse if you like.' We leave tomorrow morning for Durban. Ask Marie to make the necessary arrangements. Oh and thanks for the good work *and* great news.'

It never ceased to amuse van der Merwe; an hour and a half trip from Evander to the airport, a distance of approximately seventy five miles, followed by a flight to Durban, a distance of three hundred and fifty miles, in less than an hour. Rather ironic he thought. The plane landed in Durban and they disembarked into a hot and sticky Louis Botha Airport. Detective Jooste was waiting and whisked them off to Durban Central into the comfort of an air-conditioned meeting room.

'How do you want to play this Captain?' Jooste asked. 'I think he should be taken down before he enters his place of work. We deploy two unmarked cars, one either side of the dealership from seven in the morning. You and I' he said looking at Jooste, 'in one vehicle and Sarge and one of your men in the other, stationed at the back of the building. I would prefer to make an arrest before he enters the showroom for obvious reasons. If we are spotted and he tries to flee, shoot for his legs gentlemen; he is not to escape, I repeat he is *not* to get away. Are there any questions manne? One more thing Detective, I would like one of you to be in plain clothes.'

Russell Street was relatively quiet at six-fifty in the morning but by seven-thirty would become like any other trunk road as rush hour sets in. The skies were dark and gloomy and a slight drizzle was falling. Nevertheless, Cappie's shirt was showing signs of the rising humidity and the apprehension of the hunt. Seven-thirty came and went and the silence was broken by the pop and hiss of the police-band radio. It was Botha, 'Is there anything happening Captain? It's all quiet here Sir.'

'If anything happens, I promise that you will be the first to know Sergeant. Please maintain radio silence, you could be spotted talking into your mike.'

Yes Sir sorry Sir, I didn't think about that. I'm just a bit nervous'

'Oh my Lord' he said under his breath, 'That's enough Sarge!' he said forcefully.

By eight-thirty the Captain decided he had to put plan B into action. He radioed the other car and explained what he required done. Detective Jan Klaasen, Piet Jooste's sidekick, entered the showroom and asked for Andrew van Breda. His brother-in-law had recommended him as he was in the market for a new Ford Cortina and he'd been advised to do the deal through him.

'I'm sorry Mr . . . . ?' the sales manager prompted. 'Smit, Johan Smit' Klaasen said. 'Andrew will not be in for a few days, he's had a death in the family. He should be back on Friday, could *I* perhaps help you Mr Smit?'

'Ag not to worry hey, I'll come back then. Do you have his telephone number perhaps?'

'I'll give you his business card if you like.' the manager obliged.

I arrived home from work just after seven in the evening and entering the back door, I was met by the haunting sounds of Anatoly Alexandrov's Andante Pathetico for cello and piano opus 17. Jos sat at the piano playing like a maestro. She looked up at me and smiled and continued to play note-perfect. I took a seat, picked up my cello and started to accompany her, mostly improvisation, as I knew the piece but unlike Jocelyn, required the sheet music for this particular composition. We made music for an hour or so and then she petered out and turned and faced me wearing one of her 'famous' smiles.

'Can we adopt? Can we adopt a child Benjy?' I nearly fell off my stool. I was well aware that as we had got older, when Jos addressed me as Benjy and wearing her special smile, it meant she wanted something; buttering me up.

'Jesus Jos, what brought this on? I'm sorry that didn't come out right.'

'I've been thinking about it ever since I came out of hospital. What do you think Ben? Please say yes, or at least consider it please, please.'

'My darling if it makes you happy you can adopt Godzilla if you like.' I paused, 'Of course I agree. Where's the closest adoption store and what time do they close?'

She laughed in a way I hadn't heard her laugh for far too long. She had been cruelly stripped of her womanhood and we were jointly suffering the loss of a child, however little the embryo had been. I understood her privation and her want to reinstate the normal balance of nature; the mother and child reunion if you like.

The following week we met with a pleasant enough yet very bureaucratic lady from the adoption agency. She subjected both of us to the third degree; what, who, where, why and how and did your grandmother ever pee in the soup? We completed a dozen different forms in triplicate and were entered onto a computer listing. She concluded by telling us there would be an inspection of our home and a thorough investigation into our past. Judging by her level of diligence, Jos and I had great fun imagining the type of questions she would pose to our family and friends; had I ever been a member of Hitler's 'Sturmabteilung'? Had either of us ever been associated with Johnny 'The Chin' Giotti? Three weeks later the lady from the Spanish Inquisition called to inform us we had been accepted.

Jocelyn requested in addition to the 'first big question' whether we could afford a new car for her and the imminent family addition. I consented as my, albeit rather neglected business, was faring surprisingly well. Jos wanted a station wagon as 'there is more than ample space' for a carrier cot and a pram, a car seat and the kitchen sink. We settled on the latest model Ford Grenada Estate.

Emily looked stunning. George had returned from Botswana on the Thursday and booked dinner for the following night at an up-market restaurant on Hans Strijdom Drive west of Johannesburg.

Botswana was a 'hostile neighbouring country. Despite its location between neighbours ruled by white minority regimes; South Africa and Rhodesia, which acted as a buffer for South Africa against a rising tide of Black Nationalism, Botswana became a preferred point of departure for African National Congress and uMkhonto we Sizwe cadres heading to Europe and into exile.

In 1985 South African troupes raided Gaborone the capital, in an operation against the ANC and twelve people were killed. The United Nations condemned the action outright. The government of South Africa disputed compensation claims from the government of Botswana for damages caused by the July raid. The disagreement came after talks between the Minister of Foreign Affairs Pik Botha and his Botswana counterpart Gaositwe Chiepe had broken down. The government of Botswana demanded that South Africa cover the cost of reconstructing destroyed buildings and pay compensation for the loss of life. George King was a member of Pik Botha's security team.

He proposed in the traditional manner; down on one knee holding out the ring for Emily's inspection. 'Will you marry me Emily Badenhorst?' Everyone in the restaurant, as if it had been rehearsed, stood and applauded as she accepted his proposal with a resounding 'YES'.

The Champagne flowed and complemented the caviar starter and lobster mayonnaise entre.

Later he said, 'What would you say if I resigned and opened up a security company of my own . . . or should I say *our* own?' 'I would say yippee!' she cried. 'As long as you call it King Security, that's my only condition.' 'So be it and now to the next phase, when would it suit you to get married?' 'As soon as possible' she replied.

Jooste and van der Merwe had assembled a small task team who were battling to determine Gouws' address without approaching his employer; they were not sure of their relationship and if his boss would tip him off. The Captain was adamant; Gouws would not go free again. He would personally escort him back to the Transvaal to face the judge's wrath. They had built a watertight case against him and Cappie believed Gouws should hang, *twice* if possible. By mid-morning on Thursday, the team had established Pieter's address; a smallish semi-detached in Rowland Street in Mayville.

As they did a drive-by, it was apparent to him and Piet Jooste that no-one was home. 'If he has had a death in the family he could be anywhere. But that would imply he's in cahoots with relatives and I don't buy it.' The Captain continued, 'my gut feel is that he's up to no good and the death in the family is a scam. What do you think Piet?'

'I'm with you on that one Captain. My gut is telling me the same thing. I would like to suggest we deploy a twenty-four hour surveillance team Sir. He has to make an appearance sooner or later.' 'I agree with you Detective.' Within the hour a team was positioned across the street, manned by two junior constables with flasks of strong coffee and enough snack-type food to see them through the night and until the relief team was due to arrive at eight.

At the same time that the surveillance team were parking their nondescript vehicle outside his house, Andrew van Breda was his own one-man surveillance 'team' across from the prep school in Howick. Wednesday had been a literal washout; it had rained in religious proportions all day. He had sat expectantly for an hour but what with the rain and the misted-up windscreen had admitted defeat. He spent the rest of the day sitting at the rear of a poorly-lit bar close to the Howick Falls, quaffing back large Red Heart Rums and Coke. Pieter had become reckless and driven quite drunk to a cheap hotel some thirty km up the N3 highway. Today was a different kettle of fish; the skies were cloudless and the temperature was conducive to sitting in a car with no air-conditioning. The result of his drinking bout of the previous day had left him with a waning headache, a raging thirst and a horniness which he was finding problematic as it interfered with his thoughts.

'Oh yes, theeere he is.' He spotted a tall good-looking youngster with his satchel slung over his shoulder. He struck Gouws as being slightly effeminate; too pretty for a young boy. The lad strolled across the street to a waiting Mercedes saloon. An affluent looking female climbed out and greeted her son and opened the boot for his school bag. Gouws followed from a discreet distance until the Mercedes turned into a driveway about three km from the school. He drove on past, taking note of the street name and house number.

'I'll go and have some lunch, a few hairs of the dog and start my watch.' The excitement and expectation were mounting and the unnatural level of sexual arousal, caused by the rum overdose, rose a few points.

He returned to the house and took up a favourable viewing position. He learned little from his stakeout. There were no comings and goings the whole day and night.

'I can't let this one through my net. Fuck the work; I have to be here at the crack of dawn. I need more information. Tomorrow night is the night my man. I must be patient *and* careful.'

His diseased mind was made up. Ever since renouncing the medication his mind had deteriorated at an alarming rate, he had become detached, disconnected from the world. His reality revolved around himself and his all-consuming perverted sexual needs.

<hr />

Jean passed away in her sleep, coiled up in a foetal position. Jos and Rodney were hit hard but had expected it making it slightly easier to come to terms with. Nevertheless, Jocelyn's father asked me to assist with the funeral arrangements as he was 'just not up to it'. Jos and I comforted him as this larger-than-life character wept openly. We cried with him and it was then when I realised how much I adored this big bear of a man, along with his multitude of warts. He had prevented me from going to the gallows and he had saved his daughter from a lengthy prison term at the very least.

This not so gentle man had put his career on the line for those dear to him and was now destined to spend his golden years in solitude. This tragic family loss was not about the deceased, it was about the living. The night prior to the funeral, Jocelyn and I discussed her father's future. In my experience the most intimidating and heart-rending discussions take place under the cover of night or on windy days. That Tuesday night the rain poured down accompanied by a howling gale. We soon came to a palpable conclusion; he was to spend his remaining years with us under our roof, if he was in agreement naturally.

Rodney requested a small funeral. The church could not handle the throng who turned up to pay their respects, many standing outside throughout the entire service. Fortunately I had over-estimated the head count for the after-service gathering. There were two members of parliament in attendance, the head of SATV, numerous dignitaries and four Argentineans, a well-known actress and a few dignitaries and their wives from the Progressive Party. Also, there were three sugar barons, a few captains of industry and a group of hard looking men positioned on the perimeters I assumed were NIS personnel.

Jocelyn approached her father after everyone had left regarding our proposal of the previous night. It took some cajoling but we eventually persuaded the old man to accept our offer. He had one condition and he put it to us as follows, 'I graciously accept your offer with one condition; you accept an equal share of my entire estate, forty five per cent for each of you, leaving me with more than enough to enjoy the rest of my life comfortably. Who else could I possibly want to bequeath? You'll have to decide whether you want to continue farming or sell the lot and let the money work for you. It's your decision my two most loved people in the world.' His words started a fresh river of tears and runny noses.

A week later we took guardianship of a six-week old bundle called Amelia, a gorgeous product of a destitute single mother who had grudgingly put her lovely little girl up for adoption, or so we were informed by Hitler with tits. Jocelyn had fashioned a nursery equipped with every gadget, machine and luxury item imaginable. I realised it was time to expedite the purchase of the Ford Estate. Money was no longer a concern. I could have bought Jocelyn ten new Range Rovers if she so wished, but she insisted on the Grenada.

Born and nurtured surrounded by money, had the effect of making her immune to the allure of the root of all evil. We were as fortunate and privileged as any couple could wish for; no financial problems, we were devoted to one another; we owned our own home and were the proud parents of a beautiful little girl. Things were going along too smoothly.

Gouws cum Walters cum van Breda was still lacking vital information which would allow him to safely breach the stronghold of his desire. He reluctantly agreed with the last vestige of sanity rattling around inside his burnt-out head. 'Can't be *too* careless now can I? Is that right?' he questioned himself. 'Or should I be *careful?*' His brain had turned wet and the synapses in the deep cloak and dagger depth of his limbic system were short-circuiting, sending out muddled data.

He shook his head from side to side in an attempt to rid himself of the crushing desire to close his eyes. He had no idea that this was his third day devoid of sleep. He hadn't bathed since Wednesday. The natural body odours of his simian ancestors were competing with the new car smell of his Cortina and were winning the battle. He was hallucinating, his vision filled with vague memories of some pretty young thing.

'Oh my God,' he shouted out loud, 'I've killed them! Why am I still sitting here? I can smell death. I must get away.'

A police van stopped and a constable approached his car from behind. He snapped back into survival mode, wound down his window.

'Hello Sir, how can I be of assistance?' The constable studied Gouws for a few seconds before saying, 'It's time to move along please Sir.'

'I was just leaving Constable. I've been waiting for someone.' The policeman noticed Gouws' grimy shirt collar and unkempt hair.

'Can I ask you what your name is Sir?' For a brief moment he couldn't for the life of him remember his name.

'Umm . . . van Breda' he said finally, 'Andrew van Breda.' He went to retrieve his ID book from the cubbyhole but remembering what it contained, he froze.

'Okay Mr van Breda, you can move along now Sir.' He drove off and watched the policeman in his rear view mirror writing something in a little notebook.

Pieter Gouws had become thoroughly obsessed with his prey; he drove around the block and returned to the original spot. Luckily for him, the police van had disappeared. His state of mind had deteriorated to one of reckless neglect for his safety; his fixation, his complete fascination with the boy, pushing him forward regardless. In the distance he saw the police van crossing over Braemar Crescent. He started his car and with a screech of tyres departed Howick. He returned to the hotel where he had stayed on Wednesday.

The receptionist reluctantly allowed him to sign the register after he paid money up front and produced his ID book. Van Breda felt like stabbing the clerk in the eye with the ballpoint pen but managed to retain control by reflecting on his awaiting lover. His target was with his mother and school friends at a holiday resort in the Drakensberg. They had left their home on Friday lunchtime, when nature had prevailed forcing Gouws to visit the closest public toilets. Pieter showered, put on a clean set of clothes and within three hours was back at his sentry post surveying an empty house. He neglected to stock up with food or water.

It was nothing but a pleasure having Rodney live with us. He quickly fell into a daily routine of walking to the corner supermarket completing the crosswords at the breakfast table and pottering about in the garden for an hour or two. He would lend a hand with cooking and cleaning—Jos refused to hire a maid, 'They scare me Ben' she told me more than once—and whenever Jos needed to go shopping or on other errands, he would happily babysit, changing nappies and bottle-feeding Amy. He and my father had become close buddies and drove to a different pub once a week for lunch and a few pints, which Jos and I agreed was good for both of them.

The auditors supplied a breakdown of his vast estate, and Rodney was pleased as punch to inform us that Jos and I would share an amount of roughly twenty-two million. His fortune was valued at just less than twenty-five million Rand! We agreed to retain the sugar cane farms and Rodney assisted us in employing a general manager and an assistant manager for each farm. Rodney was in agreement with our decision to buy the Ford Granada Estate or station wagon as the estate is referred to in this country and he and I had arranged to see the dealer on the Monday.

There are three types of skin cancer; basal cell, squamous cell and malignant melanoma. Of the three, malignant melanoma is the most serious; it is predominately found in adults with fair skin and between seventy and eighty per cent of those diagnosed with this type of cancer succumb to it. Louise was diagnosed with malignant cell melanoma. Stephen had finally persuaded her to consult a doctor who immediately referred her to an oncologist. Stephen was inconsolable and asked questions of his Maker which were answered with stony silence. With Louise and Steve's blessing, I arranged a gathering of the clan at their home in Pinetown. Jos arranged kiddies' movies for Margaret and Danie's rugby side and toddler Charles overseen by thirteen-year old Anne. Louise was not feeling too well as a result of being subjected to radiation therapy the previous day.

Her oncologist had mentioned that a Swiss team was in the trial stages of a radical new treatment for this aggressive form of cancer with encouraging results. The following week, Louise and Stephen flew to Lausanne. The chances were slim of her being accepted as a trial patient but if it meant a significant donation to the research programme, Jos and I were more than willing to oblige. The entrance to the trials cost the equivalent of two-hundred and fifty thousand Rand in Swiss Franc donations but we would have donated every cent we owned if necessary. Everyone has a price.

CHAPTER TWENTY

C aptain van der Merwe was concerned that Gouws had been tipped off and done a runner. Colonel Naudé was constantly on the blower.

'What's going on Andries? I thought you'd gone to Durban to fetch him. How long is this going to take?' And so on and so forth.

'I would say we'll have him back in Evander on Monday Sir' he replied with more conviction than he felt.

'Don't just say it Captain, do it, you hear me!'

On the Friday 'Johan Smit' entered the showroom once again and approached the sales manager.

'Good morning, I'm back to see Andrew. Is he available?'

'I'm afraid not, he was supposed to have been at work today. I'm sorry but I don't know where he is' his manager answered apologetically.

'Ag it's no problem, I work around the corner so I'll pop in again on Monday, there's no rush hey?' Klaasen had returned to establish whether Gouws had called his boss regarding his absence.

'Can you afford to keep the house surveillance team in place Detective?'

'We'll make a plan Captain. He's got to show up soon. There's no way he could have cottoned on to us.'

'We'll grab him for sure Sir' Botha chipped in, in an attempt to cheer up the Captain, who was not himself of late. And *he* was suffering the brunt of his gloomy disposition.

'I propose we set up the team as before on Monday morning and let's hope it is a case of third time lucky. Are there any questions or comments ladies?' There were a few confused chuckles around the operations room.

❋

Gouws had been vigilant the entire Saturday and Sunday, continually on the lookout for patrolling police vans. The frequent sightings of a cruising van on Sunday night had forced him to occasionally move his vehicle around. At three in the morning, he parked two blocks west and kitted himself out in his work paraphernalia. He made his way back to his intended target, stealing from one shadow to the next. Gouws was high on a toxic blend of adrenaline and testosterone overloads.

'If this is Monday, then what happened to Thursday and Friday?' He had vague recollections of Saturday and Sunday. 'Fok it, I've been here since whenever. This little shit better be worth it.'

He quietly inched up the surrounding wall. His intense thirst and hunger pangs ignored as he dropped to the garden and began to skulk his way around the perimeter of the house, pausing to peer into each window. His penis became distended. The night was pitching black as was the inside of the house.

Something grabbed at his trouser cuff; he almost lost the contents of his bowels while involuntarily letting out a muffled whimper. He kicked out and a cat dashed away emitting the sounds of a screaming infant. He froze as he composed himself and became aware of a warm liquid trickling down the inside of his chinos; he realised in revulsion he had wet himself.

He discovered a partially open window at the back of the house and locked the pliers onto one of the burglar bars. After bending the strut back and forth some twenty times, it snapped from the resulting metal fatigue. The hole he created was big enough for Gouws to wiggle through. He wriggled his body to the floor and paused listening for any noises coming from the interior of the house. His eyes adjusted to the lack of light. His vision aided by a clock-radio flashing on a side-table next to an empty bed, he began to leopard crawl across the carpet and came into a passage with doors leading off it. He continued his army manoeuvre and discovered two empty bedrooms, one containing a king-sized bed and female paraphernalia on the dresser. The third was furnished with a large desk and comfortable-looking leather chairs. Expensive looking wall-to-wall bookshelves surrounded the entire room. The shelves were packed to the rafters with hardcovers and leather-bound books.

'There's no-one home for fuck's sake!' he realised seething at the futility of the last 'how long had it been, four or five days?'

He flicked on the torch and pointed it at the closest bookshelf. He laughed uncontrollably on reading the subject of the first volume he spotted; 'Psychopathic Behaviour and Treatments' and the second 'How to Recognise a Psychopath'. The book topics ranged from psychiatry and psychology to the diagnosis and treatment of various mental conditions and disorders. 'Ha, I've broken into a shrink's house, how ironic' he thought laughing loudly.

In his frustration, Gouws began methodically trashing the contents of the doctor's home. After discovering a set of golf clubs in the closet, he placed a two iron through a large TV screen and four wall-mounted Bang and Olufsen speakers. He played a quick game of golf on the stereo system and continued his destruction by tipping out the contents of the fridge and freezer onto the kitchen floor. He opened closets and emptied the contents all over the place. Pieter recognised the boy's room by means of the clothing in the closets; empty, all empty!! Thoughts stirred of the woman he had examined. He proceeded to the lady of the house's bedroom and pleasured himself while rubbing a pair of her lacy panties over his face.

He filched a bottle of Chateau Libertas from the wine rack for the road, before delighting in tossing the rest of the wine collection against the walls. He flushed his surgical gloves down the toilet and leaving the front door wide open, drove off to Durban.

'I suppose I could pop in at the office and explain my absence.' his rage and sexual frustration sated. It was a quarter to four on Monday morning.

David Zilane got wind of King's up-and-coming marriage and had put word out that he wanted revenge. He had managed to form a line of communication with a gardener employed on the Tweefontein Farm. After listening to idle chat between two of his tormentors regarding the up and coming nuptials, he had schemed and passed over information to his willing horticulturist.

The torture he had endured at the hands of his captors was atrocious; he would carry the mental and physical scars for the rest of his life. There was one particular session which had seen him on the very edge of capitulation. They had come for him in the middle of the night and dragged him off to a corrugated building away from the main compound. He was strapped to a work bench and crocodile clips were attached to his testicles. The act of affixing the clips was painful enough however, compared to what ensued was a breeze. Each time his oppressor wiggled the handle, a DC current would surge through Zilane's gonads. As his agonising screams died down to a whimper, the handle would be jiggled once again. This most pitiless of tortures had continued throughout the night.

He wanted retribution and King was an opportune choice. Plus, in his estimation, there would surely be more of his sort in attendance; an added bonus. The message was conveyed to the right people and the plotting had begun. David Zilane had been transferred to a long-term facility for political prisoners nevertheless, he was certain the news of any success would filter through to him.

The hotel chosen for the reception had negligible security and it was a piece of cake for the comrade to slip into the function room and strap a few kilos of Semtex to the bottom of the stage.

'Unite' had been employed as a temporary waiter for the day of the wedding and it would be a straightforward matter for him to leave the room briefly and detonate the deadly explosive.

The wedding party arrived at the hotel between four and five. They wandered in and out and enjoyed a drink at the bar while the bride and groom and their immediate family posed for the official photos in the hotel gardens. Ben and Jos had declined the invitation as Rodney was moving in that weekend and all arrangements had been confirmed. They had however asked George and Emily if it would be possible to visit them in the new-year.

The wedding table situated next to the stage was to be shifted to the side of the room as the band became louder and the effusive guests opened up the dance floor. Someone tapped a fork on a champagne glass and the best-man stood up.

'Emily, you are a very brave girl and an extremely beautiful bride may I add. For George or should I say Colonel Bogey, to have chosen you to be his wife, just goes to show that . . . . ' Not one person there would ever learn what 'just goes to show.'

A few minutes after six, the room exploded in an ear-shattering burst of rubble and acrid smoke. The five-piece band was obliterated in a nano-second, the force of the blast flinging them and their instruments twenty metres in the air. George King and his new wife, the couple's parents and his best-man Richard Crawley—his actual name—and wife were spread about the walls of the function room like so much hamburger patty.

The lead story on SABC's Channel One on the Sunday evening reported that twenty one people had lost their lives in a terrorist attack at a wedding reception in the Magaliesberg Mountains. They neglected to report at the time that five of the deceased were children and those who survived, seven would never walk again and three were rendered permanently deaf.

As I have stated previously, the Devil has a knack of coercing us into making decisions for his benefit. Who had started the ball rolling which led to the deaths of seventeen people? It may have been initiated through an innocent conversation between two individuals casually shooting the breeze. I firmly believe it was instigated by Satan for a bit of a laugh as he was having a tedious day or two. We don't have much say on the direction our lives will take and the roads we are called upon to travel.

I remember my father once telling me paradoxically 'the road to heaven is paved with mistakes.' I realised only much later in life what he had tried to impart to me. Although I had met George but twice and very succinctly, I could only hope his and his family's final road pointed skyward. God bless King and his royal family.

There was one quirk of fate regarding the death of those people; Rodney informed me that Unite Tshabalala accidently blew himself to smithereens—which I classify as divine intervention and just punishment—while attempting to set an explosive charge in the basement of a high school in Port Elizabeth in the Eastern Cape. There is a God after all, however unmerited. I would like to think that at the moment of his death George was happy, madly in love and at peace with the world and probably whistling his favourite piece of music of all time.

Captain van der Merwe received a phone call at his hotel on the Sunday afternoon. It was Colonel Naudé to say he was rooting for Andries and apologised for his behaviour on the Friday. He added that he was eager to see the back of this case and knew it would be resolved shortly.

'What the hell' Cappie thought replacing the handset. 'I wonder how many brandies he's had.' He posted his team at six-thirty and cursed the poor visibility caused by the rain and mist.

He had briefed them at five in the morning reemphasising the importance of an arrest 'at all costs.'

'We are dealing with one slippery customer who's managed to avoid arrest for ten years gentlemen. Think about that, ten whole years. I can't stress the point enough; Gouws has been on the run for a decade. And not just lying low; he's raped and murdered children and adults alike. This bastard has made the police force and my team in particular look like idiots; ineffectual, useless idiots! Go to it ladies.'

Gouws stopped at an all-night petrol station, ate a toasted sandwich washed down with strong sweet coffee and a lug of wine. He filled up his tank and had forty winks. He awoke had another cup of coffee and sat working out what excuse he could give his manager.

'Oh shit, who cares? I'll make up something before I get there.' It was seven o' clock. He was approximately an hour from work.

Rodney was up and about at sparrow's fart. He made breakfast while I showered and Jos busied herself with Amy. My first appointment was at ten so we had two hours from when the dealership opened to close the deal and get back to Durban North. We left at quarter to eight as it normally would take no more than fifteen minutes to the Russell Street dealership. It was literally bucketing down and my old enemy was blowing so hard it rocked my car from side to side. I had a touch of the blues which I put down to fretting over Stephen and Louise on the other side of the world. I saw flashing blue lights ahead and slowed down and then noticed a police barricade and orange cones across the road. Damn it! There'd been a collision and a long line of traffic had stacked up on both sides of the freeway. Just what the doctor ordered!

'Number two are you there?' 'We're here Captain and all's quiet.' The teams were using walkie-talkies. Okay, listen up guys we have a difficult task ahead of us made worse by this weather. Keep your eyes peeled and maintain radio silence, oh and good luck.'

It was five-to-eight and the Monday morning traffic was heavy but slow as a result of the rain which was tumbling down in torrents limiting visibility to some ten metres. Gouws turned into the open stand next to the dealership and stopped at the back of the lot. A slight drizzle had been falling as he passed the Westville turnoff. Now he was regretting his decision. The parking area was flooded and he would have to manoeuvre his way around lakes of rainwater.

'I'll phone him from home.' Gouws engaged gear and began reversing and had to pull up as a red BMW wanting to park blocked his path. Gouws hooted impatiently and the BMW moved over to the left of the lot creating a gap just big enough for the Cortina to squeeze through.

'This is one irritated prick. Hoot back at him Ben' he said indignantly.

The Captain had spotted him as Gouws slowed to turn. He spoke calmly into the handset.

'We see him. I repeat we have spotted him. He should be exiting the open space next the showroom imminently. Botha, Klaasen do you read?'

'Yes Sir, we're on our way.'

'Are you ready Jan?' Van der Merwe and Pelser jumped out of their vehicle, drew their 9mm pistols and broke into a sprint.

Gouws continued reversing between the Beemer and the line of parked cars to his right. He crawled along as the space available was tight and difficult to judge in the rain continuing to pelt down. He noticed two shapes as they appeared out of the mist running towards him from across the street dodging the on-coming cars and busses. As they neared to within five metres he realised this couple was not running to get out of the downpour; these two were clutching weapons of some sort. He slammed his foot down on the accelerator and threw his car into the traffic forcing the two policemen to dive to the side. Two vehicles slammed into the rear of his car throwing Gouws against the windscreen causing a large gash to his forehead.

He sat dazed for a second or two as the engine spluttered and died. He reached over and retrieved his pistol from the cubby and rolled out of the door onto the sodden tarmac. The traffic around him had screeched to a halt awarding him some cover. He crouched and sneaked a glance over the top of the bonnet bleeding profusely. He recognised the insignia of a police sergeant hunkered down, gun in hand, against the side of a stationary bus. He fired wildly in the cop's direction. Botha swung round and Gouws felt a slug whizz over the top of his head, missing him by inches.

At the sound of gunfire Rodney and I jumped out of the car. We were met by two policemen at the entrance to the parking lot.

'Stay back; go back to your vehicles' the larger of the two shouted. Rodney produced a police ID.

'What's going on Captain, can I help?'

'Oh sorry Colonel, I didn't realise' he said turning his attention back to the traffic. I listened, shocked, Rodney held the rank of Colonel? How much more had I to learn about this total enigma of a man?

'We have an armed fugitive on the other side of the road Sir. He's been on the run for ten years and he's probably ready to fight it out to the death.'

'Sorry my son, he said turning to me, 'stay here and keep your head down. Should we go and have a look what's happening Captain?' I could almost sense him bristling in anticipation of an old-fashioned gunfight as he drew a small arm from an ankle holster. 'Someone has to protect the family son' he said with a broad smile.

Another gunshot rattled around the buildings as Gouws made a run for the nearest entrance. Klaasen fired again and Gouws felt a fierce burning in his upper thigh. He ran through the pain and entered a book store. Two early customers and the shop assistant, who had been crouching behind the cashier's counter since the chaos began, made a dash for the door. Sergeant Botha screamed, 'get down get down!' The bookworms dove for cover as Botha and Klaasen charged through the entrance. Gouws had taken shelter behind a high bookshelf at the rear of the premises and was all set to fight to the death.

'There is absolutely no fucking way I'm ever going back to jail, no sir not me.'

The pain in his leg was almost unbearable and the gash in his head flowed freely. He had lost a lot of blood and was becoming lightheaded. He calculated there were five bullets left in his pistol.

'I'm sure I shot only once at that cop. Six minus one is five . . . I think or is it six minus five?' He listened to a voice in his head saying over and over, 'you can't be too careful Pieter, you can't be too careful.' The cavalry arrived, directed by the inevitable crowd who always seem to gather at crime scenes and car accidents.

Gouws heard another voice and he battled to determine whether it was real or another annoying interference emanating from within.

'Gouws give it up, throw your weapon down and come on out.'

'Are you crazy copper? You want to take *me* on?' He felt invincible as he jumped out from behind the shelf.

He managed to squeeze off three rounds before the first of the return fire penetrated his abdomen. The second round went through the bridge of his nose and exited the back of his head in a burst of crimson. A stray .22 round blew off a finger on Botha's left hand and another nicked Klaasen's side.

I had ignored my father-in-law and joined the large crowd gathered outside. He came out and walked over to me.

'It's all over, we got the bastard.' He seemed pleased and rather chuffed.

'Who was he Rod, do you know?'

'That's the best part Ben, his name *is* or *was* Pieter Gouws, take your pick!'

CHAPTER TWENTY ONE

Two weeks later, I received a call from Switzerland. A clearly elated Stephen informed me that Louise was reacting positively to the treatment. She was however, not out of the woods, but her blood count had improved considerably and the professor told him the prognosis was good, not excellent, but good. There was much jubilation that night and I chanced a glass or two of red wine without any adverse effects. Dr de Harnes had advised me if I drank in moderation, I should be able to maintain control; 'Kip zose ckicky leetle impersonators unda raps ja?'

Rodney, or the Colonel as I called him when feeling brave enough to poke fun at the lovable old fart, returned from a visit with his ex-boss, the Director, or some other scary title. He was pleased to inform me that the Captain on the Gouws case had taken early retirement from the Force and had become a maize farmer. He didn't neglect to add that he was a thirty-seventy business partner with the shooter of his son-in-law's rapist. It became apparent Rodney can't retire. Making money comes naturally to him; it's part of his make-up.

Another person 'perished' along with Gouws that day; Alan disappeared hopefully never to make resurgence. Pieter Gouws' death left me stone-cold. I realised I was free of the years of mental anguish I suffered as a result of that monstrosity. How many young boys' lives were ruined by his malevolence? As for me, I will have to live out the rest of my days with the blood of those poor young men, forever soiling my hands. I know some time or other, I will be asked to pay the ferryman. I believe Keegan comes to visit occasionally; just pops in to say hello. Jocelyn says he's welcome to stay as long as he likes.

The following winter, emphysema got the better of my mother. She was a truly saintly woman who cherished and nurtured us all her life, without a single complaint or hiccup along the way. Her one weakness was her propensity to bouts of severe depression. Since her mid-teens she had smoked at least two twenty packs a day. Her untimely and painful death persuaded both me and Jos to quit. However, I'm still not in the running for Vatican high office as I regularly enjoy a good whisky or red wine. Or is that not a requirement?

Rodney formed a second partnership. He noticed a gap in the market and convinced Dad to become a partner in a construction company. BorMac Pty LTD is planning on building a string of retirement villages up and down the South Coast; Rodney was never one for doing things in half measures. He has turned our house in Glen Ashley into office space for the construction company.

Margaret and Danie finally followed through with their plan to leave for lands afar. They live in Perth on the west coast of Australia. My sister teaches at a primary school and Danie is a partner in a small architectural company across the Swan River in Freemantle. Next year we plan on holding a family reunion in Australia. All things being equal, the trip will include Steve, Louise and their son, moreover Dad *and* Rodney, if we can convince the old spook that all Australians aren't as 'wicked and corrupt' as their national rugby players.

I sold off the practise to a couple of young and eager practitioners with two conditions attached; Sue remains in their employ until she feels it is time to retire and she be given a ten per cent partnership in the business. They agreed and I included the provisos in the contract. I hope she remains ignorant of the fact that I reduced the selling price of the business accordingly. Jos and I often pop in to see her and often treat Sue and Rod to a slap-up dinner at the restaurant of their choice. I recently heard a rumour that things are getting serious between the two of them.

Danie drafted the plans and BorMac constructed an old-fashioned farmhouse overlooking the waterfall where Jos and I had bequeathed our souls to one another all those years ago. We spend our days growing sugar cane, nurturing our daughter—without the influence of any badly mistaken quack out to make a quick buck—making music and every so often, swimming naked together in a natural pool, underneath a waterfall at the bottom of our garden.

Oh . . . one last thing; if anyone is wondering why I became a professional psychologist as opposed to a professional musician, well, do the maths.